ALSO BY ISAAC R HOWARD

<u>Fantasy Novel</u>

Village of the Night Forest

<u>Short Stories</u>

Squire for the Rose

VILLAGE OF THE NIGHT FOREST

ISAAC R HOWARD

inGingerous
Publishing

Published by inGingerous Publishing

Cover Design © by inGingerous Publishing

Interior Book Design © by inGingerous Publishing

ISBNs:

eBook: 978-1-970701-01-2

PaperBack: 978-1-970701-02-9

HardBack: 978-1-970701-03-6

 Formatted with Vellum

*For Andrea and her ability to put up
with all my shenanigans.*

VILLAGE OF THE NIGHT FOREST

CHAPTER 1

The blue light of the mage flame illuminated the area. The rich wood was darker now in the magical light than it was just an hour ago, when the sun had shone through the spacious windows of the Great Library of the Mystics. The dry smell of leather and the perfumed scents of dozens of different inks nearly overwhelmed Ossian. The table he currently occupied was a lighter brown than most of the library tables. Better for divination, he could already hear the old Mage Golon saying.

A book of divination was open in front of him. While he had read many words from it, not a single one stuck in his mind. Today was the day of assignment. Today was a day where a scribe would find him and present him with papers that would tell him where he would be assigned to work as a mage, potentially for the rest of his life. Ossian couldn't focus and had spent the entire day dreading where he would end up.

When he woke up this morning, he had tried to be honest with himself. He would not be assigned one of the nicer roles in research here with the Academy mages. Being a lowly farmer's son, he would be assigned to one of the outskirt villages. Something small, out of the way and left to his studies with only the resources he could scrounge up.

Which was exactly what Ossian wanted, if he could be honest with himself. An out of the way place where he could focus his studies on magic for farmers and laborers. Helping people like his father and mother, who labored day in and day out for the simplest of livings.

Looking at his own hands, Ossian remembered all too well the power of the first spell he had cast. The criss-crossing scars on his hands stood out like the bold warning they were. Even thinking about them now, they itched as the power coursed through his arms and hands. Focusing his mind bringing the shapes and symbols forefront into the concentration rings, his bare feet touching the stone and pushes the energy in the scars out through his feet into the stone.

Glancing into the mage flame, he had been waiting all day. So long, it felt even the sun had forsaken his assignment. He was beginning to wonder if assignment day was another of the cruel jokes the noble sons played on the low-born mages. His mentor, Mage Mahler, had assured him many times it was a normal practice of the Academy, no pomp and circumstance, just assignments out to councils, libraries, Academy mages assistants and lastly, the villages and outskirts.

Mage Mahler had assured him that village mages were just as necessary as council mages. Telling Ossian of Mage Mahlers' own original assignment to a war front during the Count Rohan incident.

Ossian had questioned Mage Mahler at that point. "So what does a village mage do, though?" He knew he would be assigned to a village. Even here and now, during his studies at the Academy, it wasn't uncommon for Mage Mahler to find him out talking with the farmers about some aspect of the seasons, crops or weather.

"One studies what one wants. I wanted to study the Night Forest, but when the war came, I was prepared to defend our lands. I got lucky in front of the King."

"Do you regret the appointment to the King's council?"

"It allowed me certain eccentricities, it's very few who the King allows to spend weeks in the catacombs researching what one wants. Knowledge and power comes with sacrifice though, as you well know. I was never allowed to even visit the Village of the Night Forest. No matter where you end up, you can learn from it. Now go away before someone thinks you've already been assigned."

After that, he'd relocated to the library, his sanctuary, a place where initially he had been behind all of his peers in the Academy. His farm background had hurt him dearly. Unable to read, he'd been relegated to Mage Mahler for bringing him up to speed with his peers. Mage Mahler was different, though. He'd taken one look at Ossian and knew that focusing purely on mental preparation would not be enough.

"Too many of our kind think that only knowledge matters. Look at half the mages, wizened fat things. Barely able to leave their desks."

Ossian had spent half-days with Mage Mahler learning how to read and the basics of magic. Followed by half days with the soldiers, endless marches followed by weapons training. Till he'd fall asleep dead to the world. Then the next morning when he was awoken all too early and it would start all over again. That's when his farm life had helped him, the incredibly long days of farm life were replaced with focused hours of learning, reading, writing, languages and magic followed up with even more hours of physically demanding marching, drilling, spears, swords and tactics. The only real perk was the food was of a much higher quality.

CHAPTER 2

The rough sound of someone clearing their throat woke Ossian up.

Ossian's face was sore. He'd fallen asleep on his quill. The long feather pressed into his face and still clung there as he looked up to see an apprentice with an official summons in his hand.

The apprentice smiled and bowed as he held out of the wax seal. "The Magus requests your presence."

Peeling the feather quill off his face, he placed it back on the table. "Of course. Let me put this stuff away."

"I can do that for you, Mage Ossian. I shall return your stuff to your room. The Magus does not like to wait."

Ossian stared at the squire. He'd called him Mage Ossian. Ossian had graduated.

The long days, the endless lectures by the resident mages. The tests they had taken. He'd never endured such a grueling limit to his knowledge. It had felt like the Academy Board had pushed him to the upper reaches of what he knew about magic. A limit they had taught him, so they knew where to push. Ossian was a Mage of the Academy of Fine Mystics and Magical Arts.

Slowly, his hand reached out and took the summons. Standing up, his feet moved of their own accord, making their way to the Magus' office. Before he knew it, he was in front of the singular metal door. The door was solid brass, covered in engravings all over its surface from the Time of Tribulations.

Raising his hand, he tapped out three short staccato raps on the door. Knowing he was about to face his future, he debated running. Could he be a rogue mage? Would he even make it back to his childhood home before the King's men found him?

Swinging open of its own accord, the door revealed Magus Senoraske, Mage Mahler and an apprentice judging by his robes.

Stepping through the threshold, Ossian was still in shock at having actually graduated. He knew he was one of the best mages in his class, but he was just a lowly farmers son. His tireless work ethic had made sure he caught up with the others. In fact, he was pretty confident he had surpassed most of them last year.

An awkward silence lingered in the air.

Finally, with an air of annoyance, the Head Magus Senoraske spoke, "Do you have questions about your..." his words were cut short as he stared at the seal in Ossian's hands. Waving his short fingers towards it, "Well... open it, Mage Ossian. How can you have questions when you don't know the assignment?"

Ossian stared blankly at the Magus for a bit. He'd called him mage as well. He'd never heard the Magus' voice be so calm before. His words had always been full volume screaming at him or another student to get a formula right, or change their posture or prepare an ingredient. These words were as a peer, soft and gentle, treating him like he deserved to be here. Ossian didn't like it. It made the hairs on the back of his neck stand up.

His mind finally snapped to attention and he glanced down at the wax seal in his hands. Ossian carefully put his fingers on opposite sides of the small green wax seal and snapped it in half.

The green seal dissolved quickly into a cloud of green glittery dust, swirling upwards and forming an image of the Head Magus.

While his lips moved, there was a very slight delay with the sound as the tiny cloud of green sparkles spoke to him.

"Congratulations on your graduation from the Academy of Fine Mystics and Magical Arts. It is an honor and a privilege to add you to our ranks of learned mages. You have joined a rare group that places above all else the eternal gathering of knowledge. Welcome to the order, Mage Ossian..."

The little green man coughed briefly and was about to continue to speak.

However, the real Head Magus had returned to his normal self. He was spitting furious, "I did not cough into a message seal, and why is the sound off? That upstart apprentice of mine is going—" which is when the Head Magus realized he was screaming out loud, and had shouted over Ossian's assignment message.

Somehow, the Head Magus composed himself. "Ossian, my apologies. I can't believe your graduation seal was so...well obviously the formula was less than perfect. I will have a word, or a backhand with my apprentice. This continued behavior of his is totally unacceptable..."

He'd graduated. The Head Magus was still speaking, but the only thing Ossian could think about was that his whole life, all he'd known, was the farm. Then he had been stripped from the farm, dumped here at the Academy and life finally seemed to fit. Now he was done with the Academy and he did not know where he was going next. Yet, still it would be as Mage Ossian, Wielder of Magic. Inside his head the words sounded big...no immense. Definitely out of proportion to his mental image of himself.

"Do you have questions, Mage Ossian?" The Head Magus stared at him, his face a mixture of apology and outrage.

And it finally clicked. His apprentice was standing in the room, yet he hadn't flinched or apologized or anything when the Head Magus had got vexed about his preparation of the message seal.

Come to think of it, he didn't recognize the apprentice either.

Looking over at the apprentice, he was definitely some high-born noble son. Well groomed, his shoes were some of the finest leather Ossian had ever seen, smooth grained green leather. Ossian couldn't even see the stitching from here. He suspected it was so fine it would be hard to notice if he was down at boot level, definitely out of place on most apprentices.

Mage Mahler finally spoke up, "Do you have questions, Mage Ossian?"

Snapping back to attention, "So, my assignment?"

"Yes, yes, my apologies for yelling over the top of your assignment. We're sending you to Mage Mahler's old dream. The Village of the Night Forest. There, hopefully you can study the Night Forest. Questions?"

"Well, yes. Dozens. However, none about the assignment or my graduation." Ossian said, straightening up his shoulders. Glancing over at the apprentice again, "I'm sorry, I don't recognize your apprentice. What's his name?"

Surprisingly, the Head Magus spoke, "Yes, yes. A mage must be curious. As well, you know. I am available to you if you have questions. As well, Mage Mahler." He bowed at that point, pointing a hand towards Mahler, "I wish you luck and I will deal with the apprentice and that seal."

A smile formed on the apprentice's face. "The Magus here was not wrong in suggesting you for the role." Turning to face the Head Magus he continued, "He is very observant."

"Yes, my Lord, he is," Senoraske said.

Ossian's jaw dropped. His mind was racing. He lowered himself to his knee. He'd never been in the presence of the King before.

The King's face quickly soured. "Don't do that. What would be the point of all this subterfuge and disguise if you bow before me and someone saw it?"

Ossian made to stand back up. Glancing between King Bacler and Mage Mahler. He wasn't sure how to respond. Most of the mages that taught him were not kind souls. Yelling, hitting and punishments were their default modes of education. Mage Mahler was different.

He was the singular mage who treated his students with respect. Even the Head Magus was more like the rest of the faculty than Mahler.

Finally, deciding he didn't like the silence, Ossian said, "I do like those boots."

The King looked down at his boots and sighed. "So, is that what gave me away?"

Ossian shook his head. "Well, not completely, no. You are also the finest groomed apprentice I have ever seen." Smiling more to himself than anyone else, he continued, "Most of us barely have time to eat and sleep, let alone having properly groomed hair, beard, nails and boots. Then there was the message seal. Magus Senoraske didn't immediately start screaming at you."

Magus Senoraske continued, "So, the Night Forest, there will be a semi-regular messenger sent to the village. Mage Mahler here will teach you how to create a message seal that only a specific person can open. You are to send a report with this messenger to Mahler regularly, with any updates."

"Has something changed to make the Night Forest a sudden priority? Surely Mage Mahler could study the village as a wizened old retired mage." Ossian could sense they weren't telling him something.

Mage Mahler's face turned up at the corners. He was clearly trying to hide a smile from these other two men.

"Do you know how many villages of the Night Forest there have been?" Magus Senoraske asked.

"No Head Magus."

"The records show at least twenty-seven. That's twenty-seven in the last thousand years. Before that, we know that more villages disappeared, but an exact number is unreliable."

"How have they disappeared?" Ossian could see why Mage Mahler wanted to study this now. His curiosity was peaking. Why did they disappear? Why around the Night Forest? Why did people form a new village?

Mage Mahler spoke up, "That is at least consistent." Glancing over at the King, he received a nod before continuing, "Reports always come back with the same information. There is no evidence a village ever existed. Merely a field where the village once was."

"Why would people return to create a new village than?"

The King spoke this time, "Freedom, coin, hiding. Everyone has something they want, giving it to them often results in enough people to start a new village." The king stopped for a second, thinking something over. "The latest report is that there is no evidence the village was ever there. No people, no animals, no buildings. The road stops several hundred yards from where it should. I'm tired of the lost resources, the lost people and the lost coin. I want to know what is going on. Mage Mahler can fill you in on the rest of the details."

With that, he waved his hand and Ossian was dismissed.

"Yes, my Lord." Ossian still had that niggling sensation that something wasn't being said, but one didn't directly question the man who could strip you of all titles, jail you or merely have you beheaded. He lowered his head slightly in a small bow, turned and made to leave.

With that, Ossian's life had been decided for him. Somehow, it felt normal. Or as normal as it came for him. A well prepared, yet somehow non-standard start, followed by a mage yelling. At least this time he hadn't been yelling at Ossian.

CHAPTER 3

Mage Mahler moved to usher Ossian out. As they crossed the threshold of the office, he started speaking, "Most excellent, congratulations Mage Ossian. I'd say this calls for a celebration." He placed quite a lot of emphasis on the word mage, which Ossian thought was over the top. Yet still it made his heart swell to hear his mentor, Mage Mahler, call him a mage.

"Oh, I think I could do with a stiff drink, and maybe some food. I haven't eaten all day." Ossian's stomach grumbled loudly as they walked down the corridor.

As they were walking to Isobel's, their normal haunt, they could hear the raucous drinking of the other eleven graduating mages this year as they got closer.

Before they got too close, Mage Mahler spoke up, "Let's try The Crown & Beaker. This is an auspicious day after all. How about something a bit more private?"

Ossian had never actually heard of The Crown and Beaker, but since Mage Mahler was suggesting it, he nodded and followed him down several streets further from the Academy. The further they wandered, the more and more Ossian realized that his last decade had been spent holed up in the Academy, focused either on learning magic or exiting the city via the east gate with the soldiers for physical training. Even when he snuck out to talk with the farmers, it had always been via the east gate. He did not know where Mage Mahler was headed.

Mage Mahler turned into what appeared to be one of the more disgusting alleys Ossian had seen. Ossian was just about to ask Mage Mahler about it when he noticed the smell of garbage was missing. After glancing further into the alley, he noticed the complete lack of refuse of any kind. The initial entrance looked grimy and nasty, but once they passed into the alley, it was poorly lit but upkept. It was also a dead-end.

Ossian was confused and every muscle he had was tensed for a fight as he followed Mage Mahler into the alley.

"Pay attention," Mage Mahler said as he raised his hand to a red painted door on the side of a plaster wall. The door looked out of place, as there wasn't a doorframe for it to sit in. It was merely lying against the wall. He didn't knock, merely placing his hand flat on the door and saying quietly but clearly, "Mages and sages."

A light glow surrounded Mage Mahler as like the sand in an hourglass, he slowly disappeared into the door. Then Ossian was alone in the alleyway. Mage Mahler hadn't exactly told him to follow, but it was clear he wanted Ossian to see what he had done.

Stepping up to the red-painted oaken door, Ossian stared for a bit. Nothing was particularly noticeable about the door, no runes, no markings of any kind. It looked like any door leaning on any of a dozen buildings they had passed on their way here. Other than, it looked like it did not belong here in this alley.

Ossian wanted to know what was inside, where had Mahler gone, how had he done that. He'd never heard of magic being used like this in any of his learning. Ossian spent another thirty seconds trying to figure out how the transmutation could move a living body through a door before finally deciding he would just have to ask.

Finally, he tentatively placed his hand on the door. It was colder than he would have thought, like touching a sword left out on a cold winter's night. Saying the words out loud, a shudder went through his body, his hand was sucked flat on the door. As a shock ran through him, he felt his body split into two halves. He wanted to jerk his hand back as his mind reeled in panic. Before he could remove his hand, his body split again into four and then faster and faster, his body was split again and again until it was thousands of tiny pieces.

That's when he felt himself sucked through the door towards the other side. As fast as he'd been split into so many pieces, he was spliced back together on the other side. First, thousands of tiny pieces placed together, then those were fused and fused again till he was one singular being.

Looking into a brightly lit room, he saw Mage Mahler. Barely registering several other people, as he noticed Mahler was holding out a wooden bucket for him. He cocked his head to ask what the bucket was for when his body convulsed. Snatching the bucket from Mahler's hands, Ossian vomited violently for several minutes.

After the bucket was taken from him, he was shown to a table with Mage Mahler, plus four people he didn't recognize. A mug of table beer was handed to him and a loaf of bread.

"We'd dive straight into drinking and congratulations on your graduation, but we've found that the door makes people queasy the first time as you become attuned to its unique magic." The person sitting to Mahler's immediate right said. His hair was long, shaggy and a shade of red that bordered on too bright to be real.

Ossian sipped carefully at the mug. It was a surprisingly bland beer which fit his currently empty stomach very well now. He broke off a small piece of bread and carefully chewed it. He was mostly recovered from the vomiting, but he didn't know who or what this group of people was.

Mahler finally started talking, "Sorry for the door." Then waving his hand around, he continued, "This here are the members of The Crown and Beaker." The flame red hair waved and smiled. Next to him was the prettiest man Ossian had ever seen. His face looked like the gods themselves had hand selected it. Third was a wizened old woman, who looked older than anyone Ossian had ever encountered. Next to the handsome-man, the contrast was even starker. The old woman was looking not at Ossian, but into him. He felt as if he was being studied more than looked at.

Finally, there was a young woman dressed in plain clothes. If Ossian had seen her on the streets, he would never have paid her a moment's attention. Even now, in this place with only six people in it, she seemed unremarkable. With no change to her face or expression, she wiggled her fingers at Ossian.

"Uh... hello." Ossian was still at a loss for words.

Mahler continued along, "The members of The Crown and Beaker are a..." Mahler paused, searching for words.

Red-hair broke in quickly, "Damnit Mahler, you think too hard about your words. We are a secret group of people who study crazy shit. If we determine it's too dangerous, we store the knowledge and try to protect that knowledge from getting out."

Mahler shrugged, "What Kiernan said."

"Isn't all magic dangerous?" Ossian said. He knew it wasn't the knowledge of magic that was dangerous, it was all in its application.

The old-woman smiled at that, her expression appearing more as a crack in a granite slab than as a warm or friendly welcome. "Well said."

Kiernan broke in, "Yes, yes, Izador. But Mage Ossian, certain magic is beyond just mere lightning scars and fireballs. Downstairs in the vaults here, we have tomes that describe how to..."

"Kiernan, he hasn't accepted yet," Mahler interrupted.

"He can't accept a position to which he doesn't understand." Kiernan spat back.

"Sorry, I already have an assignment from the King."

Handsome-man spoke then, "This position, it's voluntary. But important. Only the seven people in this room will know of your membership."

"Seven? There are only six of us." Ossian looked around the room for confirmation that there was not anyone else. He wasn't sure he liked the handsome-man now that he had spoken. His voice was smooth, with a singsong cadence to it. It made him think of a lure on a hook for fishing for some unknown reason.

"The seventh will join us soon. About your membership." The handsome-man continued.

"And if I choose not to join."

Kiernan spoke up, "Then we wipe yer memory and dump you at Isobel's, where you will wake up with a raging headache and no knowledge of us."

The non-descript lady spoke just then, "Or we wipe you from everyone's memory, like you never existed." She said it with such calm and poise, as if it was something she did casually every day.

"Can you actually do that?" Ossian's curiosity was getting the better of him, and he knew it. He was more interested than not in this strange group of people.

"We are not going to kill him, Unelma." Mahler slammed his fist on the table. "We are a group of people who protect knowledge that can't fall into the wrong hands. Knowledge of the magical that can alter the world as we know it. Bad things. We would like you to join us."

"Why me? And I meant, can you wipe someone from existence?"

The expression that crossed Unelma's face just then, Ossian imagined, was supposed to be friendly or maybe even flirtatious. All that Ossian could think of when he saw that sly smile spread on her lips, was run. And with the slightest of head tilts, she nodded yes.

If Mahler noticed Unelma, he didn't acknowledge it. "We are a unique group of people with select abilities. However, our selection criteria is singular, regardless of each of our specialties, we have one binding criteria. There is magical knowledge that can rock the very foundations of our world, that can alter reality and make it cease to exist. This knowledge can not become common knowledge. You either agree with that premise, or you don't."

"So I'm supposed to join you on the theoretical idea that there are magics that can undo our realities?"

Mahler waved a hand at Kiernan to stop him from speaking. "No, I guess we can each give you an example of a piece of forbidden knowledge we have discovered. Even here, in this place that is nowhere, none of us knows what all is in the vaults below. Only the Guardian knows."

Kiernan quickly spoke up than, "A spell that would ignite the sky, everywhere, all at once."

Handsome-man, who Ossian still had not learned the name of, went next. His sing-song lilting cadence giving Ossian the distinct impression he was being lured to his doom, "The dead can be brought back, but they are not what you think. It is a terrible, horrible thing that returns."

"So, not all of this knowledge is theoretical?"

The lilting-doom-song continued, "No, some of it was hard won knowledge that had to be cleansed first."

Izador spoke next, her voice ragged and aged. Ossian wasn't sure she would make it past the night. "Gateways to..." she paused, searching for a word, "places, I guess. Creatures, entities, unrealities, things that defy description."

As she said it, something inside Ossian shivered and he decided to not ask for any clarification from her.

Unelma spoke quietly, like she herself didn't want to hear what she had to say. "Yes, I can wipe you from ever having existed."

Finally Mahler spoke, "Magic always has a price. The scars on your hands are proof you understand that. Objects can be imbued with this power, this you will learn. Some objects, though, can trap people in them. Forever. Seeable, but just," Mahler's voice got very quiet suddenly, "out of reach." His hand reached for something before his eyes came back into focus and he pulled his hand back, lacing the fingers of both hands together in front of him.

Ossian thought about the terrible things they had revealed to him, even the thought of some of them was almost too much for him to think about for too long.

"How many people have refused to join you?"

A seventh person behind Ossian emerged into the room and spoke, "There have been some. None have left here with any memory of what it is we do."

"And you are?"

"The Guardian. Keeper of no where and old man."

"Say I join, then what? I search for knowledge that shouldn't be known?"

"The Night Forest is older than I am. It is an ancient, unknowable place. It would be preferential for you to be with us, rather than against us, if you discover something."

"So my membership is just in case I find something." Ossian said, somewhat deflated.

Mahler spoke at this point. "We are all in agreement. The Night Forest holds secrets, given how the villages disappear, so I was to study it so many decades ago. Since that was interrupted, and for some unknown reason, the King will not allow me to study it now. You are being sent. While I suggested to the group your membership before discovery, they all assented."

"Before discovery?"

"Membership in The Crown and Beaker is generally after discovery of knowledge that can shake the foundations of the world as we know it." The Guardian said.

"Wether, that's spells to erase people." Unelma whispered.

"Someone who wants to raise an army of the dead." Sing-Song-man said.

"Objects that trap people forever." Mahler pinned.

"Research that should never be completed." Kiernan blurted out.

"Or gateways to..." Izador did not finish. Her eyes drifting off to some unseen place.

Ossian knew he wanted to join. He'd known the minute it was suggested that this was a place he wanted to join. He was still wary, he wasn't convinced there was magic that shouldn't be known, but the way each of them spoke about their own discoveries. It altered each of them somehow.

"But we're trying something new this time. Instead of trying to convince you after you discover something world shattering. We would induct you in first. All of us believe something will be discovered in The Night Forest."

"And if I discover nothing useful enough." Curiosity got the better of Ossian again.

"Than we will have been wrong, and I, for one, will be grateful for that." The Guardian smiled weakly. Ossian knew then that the Guardian wasn't telling him something.

Ossian chewed a bit of bread as he looked at each of the members. All of them seemed genuine. He wasn't sure if Unelma or Izador were scarier, though. "I'm in."

No sooner had he said it than seven glasses and several bottles were placed on the table, and they all toasted a new member. Soon plates of food filled the table as well, and they chatted and talked about journeys and recent happenings in far-away lands Ossian had only read about in books.

Throughout the night, Ossian noticed one thing. They never again discussed what knowledge they had brought back to the vault.

CHAPTER 4

Ossian awoke with a pounding in his head. Glancing around, he was in his room, so that was good. His clothes were still on, that was neutral. It wouldn't be the first time he'd fallen asleep fully clothed. Then the poundings on the door came again. Not the gentle knock of the steward alerting you to breakfast—no, it was a shocking, deafening sound. That was bad. Ossian's entire head throbbed with each dissonant sound of someone trying desperately to send him to his grave.

Muffled through the door, Ossian heard the steward, "Mage Ossian, breakfast is in ten minutes."

Ossian tried to say thank you, but what came out was a groan. The steward must have accepted it, cause he didn't continue to torture Ossian's poor head back into submission.

It didn't take long for Ossian to fall back to sleep. The cacophony of the Academy was subdued, yet still there. Today the graduated would make plans for their trips off to places, having to figure out how to live by themselves. The still-to-graduate though, to them it was just another day.

By the time Ossian swung his feet out of bed, he was pretty sure breakfast was safely gone. Even the thought of greasy eggs made his stomach turn up in knots.

Eventually, he stumbled his way to the kitchen. The staff were in the middle of preparing supper. Still, there was a pot of porridge in the far corner. It was always there, slowly simmering at all hours of the day and night. Mages often kept odd hours, but the kitchen was sympathetic to a hungry mage-in-training in the middle of the night.

He ladled himself some porridge into a bowl and Desmond, one of the friendlier kitchen staff, placed a slice of pork on top of the bowl.

"Thank you, Desmond."

"Congratulations Mage Ossian, although I hear you travel to the Night Forest tomorrow."

"Tomorrow? Well, crap." He never thought to ask when he was leaving.

He snatched his spoon and gobbled up his porridge. Which was when he realized he'd just ladled it out of the simmering pot seconds ago. Scorching his tongue and mouth, he spat the porridge back out onto the floor.

"Damnit," Placing the bowl on the smooth wooden table behind him, he searched for the nearest cleaning rag.

"Don't worry Mage Ossian." He gestured to a small mousey boy, "YOU, clean this up," who darted over and cleaned up the porridge Ossian had spit onto the floor.

"Sorry Desmond," than turning to the small boy, "and thank you for cleaning that up. Apparently, my brain still isn't working. I best get packed up."

The mousey boy bowed and disappeared.

As Ossian reached out to take his porridge with him, Desmond leaned in. "You be careful in the village there, Mage Ossian. The Night Forest is not a good place."

Ossian smiled, while normally he trusted the staff to be interesting in their beliefs about superstitions, and sometimes it was a highly useful if somewhat colorful way of remembering local lore, he didn't have the time today to get into it with Desmond.

"Thanks Desmond, I will miss your generous food. And I know all about the haunted Night Forest."

Desmond stared at him blankly, something cold in his eyes, "It's not haunted Mage, they know nothing about it. No one has ever returned that has moved there. Only tales we have come from the soldiers who return...after." Then Desmond returned to slicing up pork for whatever dish the head chef was making.

Ossian was clearly distracted as he ate his porridge walking through the corridors, cause instead of returning to his room and packing, he ended up at Mage Mahler's office. Shrugging, he knocked politely. Normally, he would wait for an invitation in case Mahler was occupied. Since he was a mage now, he walked straight in.

The Head Magus was there, "—needs to prepare his own library—"

The tension in Mage Mahler's body and face showed he was clearly upset with the Head Magus. "Ossian, good to see you. Senoraske was just leaving."

Ossian could see the anger rising in the Head Magus. He was ready to explode. Instead, he turned, huffed and walked out in a rush. Ossian, using reflexes honed by years of avoiding upset mages, dashed to the side to avoid being overrun by Magus Senoraske.

"Close the door Ossian, we have a few things to discuss."

Ossian closed the door. "Sorry about that, Mage Mahler. I didn't think before entering."

Mahler, glancing around his office for something absentmindedly, then said, "No, no. It was perfect. Senoraske thinks he can tell me what I can and can't do with my stuff." Looking up at Ossian, he locked eyes with him. "And now that you are a mage, you need to understand, knowledge is yours. You can do with it what you want."

"So about last night..."

Mahler quickly raised his finger to his lips, silencing Ossian instantly. "Yes, yes, no worries. A young man only graduates as a mage once in a lifetime. Indulgences must be made. I've taken care of it with the bar."

Placing a large tome on the desk, Mahler then opened the front cover for Ossian. Inside was another book. The tome was a fake concealing another book. Mahler closed the cover and handed the book to Ossian.

"I've taken the liberty of stocking your personal library for your trip to The Night Forest. You will be far away from the resources you are used to. It will not be a massive collection, but I'm hoping they will be useful."

"You mean outside my grimoires?" Ossian had three personal grimoires, each of them his personal notes and modifications to spells. No mage could use them, they could learn from them, but only by transcribing the spells personally and changing them for each individual could the spells be useful to another mage.

"Yes, some of the books have mage locks, like the one we discussed last night. If you can remember it." Mahler had a conspiratorial look about him as he pointed most directly at the tome within a tome he'd just handed him.

Ossian thought Mahler was being a bit overly cautious. It wasn't like someone else was in the room listening to them. When Mahler looked down and pointed to a small, black raven feather quill. It looked completely out of place in Mahler's nearly spotless office. Ossian also knew that Mage Mahler preferred a more robust goose feather for his quills.

"I'll have the steward send over the books in your trunk."

Ossian blushed, he'd been living so long in the Academy, "I don't own a trunk."

"Nonsense," Mahler waved his hand absently in the air, "I had it commissioned weeks ago. The carpenter owed me a favor. To be honest, he outdid himself. You will have to deal with adding any— deterrents if you so wish."

"Mage Mahler, you can't—"

"Damnit Ossian, did you not just listen to me chide the Head Magus about telling me what I can and can't do? You have spent the better part of a decade learning the Mystical Arts from me. To be completely honest, I've never had an apprentice that was as useful or as hardworking as you. I will truly miss you, Ossian. Every damn'd day, I'll miss you as I train up a new batch of, at best, half-worthy apprentices." Mahler then let out an enormous sigh and slumped into his chair.

"Are you okay?" Ossian had never seen Mahler tired. Over-worked, sure. Under slept, sure. But tired, that wasn't something Mahler let show.

"I'm just tired Ossian, the last couple of months have been exhausting. I just need to take a day or two for myself. But that can wait till you leave in the morning." Mahler wasn't telling Ossian something, the way he avoided the question was practiced, but Ossian knew his master a bit too well for that to work on him.

Mahler brushed away the streak of a tear from his face. "Alright, duties of a mage in a village. Sit and we shall discuss them."

Gesturing to the chair Ossian had sat in many hundreds of hours, Mahler waxed on about the duties that Ossian was expected to do in a village. Occasionally, Ossian would ask a clarifying question, but to be completely honest, it sounded surprisingly boring. He would be the extension of the King, ruling in his stead in matters of dispute between the villagers. He would also be expected to provide what assistance he could to make the village successful, although Mahler was surprisingly vague on what that was. Finally, he ended with, his secret assignment, investigate the Night Forest and send reports.

There were other randomly uninteresting things he would be expected to do. Mahler looked like he was reading off a list as he hand waved each item away.

"Normally a new mage has an area that they are in charge of, traveling between villages, in order to better service the King. Given your post, we've decided that a single village should be more than adequate."

Ossian thought he was about to be dismissed when a knock on the door came.

"Excellent," Mahler sat up straighter in his seat, then yelled, "Enter."

CHAPTER 5

The oak door opened to reveal Sergeant Jorn. His lithe form looked ready to induce violence on anyone stupid enough to challenge him. Ossian had learned over the years of training with him that he was willing to induce violence quickly and swiftly.

"Mage Mahler," he said with the slightest of head nods, "I've been requested to bring you this." He held out a sword still in a scabbard, the gilding on the scabbard was beautiful, Ossian could read a spell in the gilding from here. The hilt looked beautiful, the leather wrapping dyed a deep blue, the pommel itself was a plain silver with a book engraved into it.

"Well, take the thing, Ossian." Mahler was practically leaping out of his seat with excitement.

Ossian stood there stunned, looking between Mahler and Jorn. "Mage Mahler, I can't take—" Ossian caught himself as he saw the joy in Mahler's face subside. Reaching quickly for the scabbard and taking it from Jorn's hand.

"Jorn, get in here, close that door," Mahler snapped.

Ossian stopped staring at the sword. He had spent the better part of a decade training with Jorn. There was no one in the army short of the King that could talk to Jorn like that without sustaining a beating in the training ring. Much to Ossian's surprise, Jorn stepped in and closed the door.

As Jorn's head turned around, he stared daggers at Mahler. A lesser man would have run screaming from the building, "Sorry, Jorn. I'm just so excited to see this weapon."

Jorn's ego assuaged, they both turned back to looking at the sword in Ossian's hand.

"You put your hand on the hilt, and pull," Jorn's cool dry sarcasm was always a biting commentary on how badly you trained in the sword ring with him. Ossian would not miss being soundly beaten physically, and then lambasted verbally, one bit.

Placing his hand on the hilt, a cool sensation flowed over Ossian's fingers as he gripped the sword tightly. Slowly pulling the sword from its scabbard, the blade emerged. Ossian couldn't believe it. The blade was completely blue. Etched deeply near the cross-guard, the blade had a spell etched around it. The circle forming completely around the base of the blade.

"Hoho, look at how deep that color is," Mahler was standing up now. He clapped his hands together. "I shall have to personally express my admiration to Master Naomi. She did a most amazing job on that sword. There are none other like it. It's a first of it's kind Ossian. Well, that any living person has seen. Here, put it back, put it back. I found mention of magical weapons in the histories and have been working to replicate them. This is hopefully the first of many."

Mahler raced around his desk and pushed Ossian's hands together. Forcing him to put the sword back in the scabbard. Then he grabbed the scabbard and handed it to Jorn.

Jorn stood there with the scabbard held away from his body, exactly where Mage Mahler had placed it. Ossian could tell from his body language he was becoming irritated at being here, let alone being treated like he was just some extra in a troubadour's skit.

Mahler settled down a little as Jorn stared him down. "Sergeant Jorn, please be so kind as to draw the sword."

Keeping his arm fully extended and the scabbard as far from his body as was possible while reaching his other hand out to grasp the handle. Sparks flew from the handle, shocking Jorn's hand.

Ossian fully expected Jorn to lash out and beat Mage Mahler to a bloody pulp. Instead, Jorn looked at the hilt, tilting his head.

Mage Mahler clapped his hands. "Oh well done, that's enough, though. It has a built in defense so that none other than Ossian here can draw it. The closer you get to drawing the blade, the more severe the reaction gets."

"So you knew it would shock me." Jorn's voice was calm and collected, and full of violence.

"I knew you were smart enough to stop drawing the blade at the first shock. I'm afraid I would want to see the full potential of the protection spell on the scabbard. Maybe I was misguided in my assumption you would find this as fascinating as me."

Ossian finally interrupted before Jorn could kill Mahler. "So that explains the first spell on the scabbard. What about the second? The one around the blade?"

"May I have the blade back?" Mahler's hand reached for the scabbard, and must have felt resistance from Jorn. "Please."

Jorn finally released the sword and Mahler placed the sheathed sword in Ossian's hand. Ossian glanced back at Jorn.

"Would you like me to leave? I do have duties to attend to." Jorn said.

"Yes, yes, thank you for delivering the sword, Sergeant Jorn." Mahler waved him off without so much as a sideways glance.

Ossian quickly added, "Thank you, Master Jorn. It's been a pleasure to train under you. Would it be okay if I stopped by before I leave tomorrow to say a proper goodbye?"

"No."

Turning, Jorn opened the door before adding, "I need to get ready to leave tomorrow. We can celebrate your graduation on the way to the village. I am to lead the escort to the new village." Exiting the room, he closed the door behind him.

Mahler continued, almost like the conversation hadn't happened. "The second spell has a trigger component. Do you remember your concentration rings?"

"How could I forget?" While Ossian thought back to the rings, his hands sparked with their own power again. He thought to the first ring, focused on the second ring, then guiding the power into the third ring. He pushed the power out through his feet and into the stone of the Academy.

Mahler explained how if Ossian targeted a spell at the sword while holding the hilt, he could use the blade to store some level of magical energy.

"That way, when you are holding the blade, you should be fully able to reuse that energy later to cast or embolden your spells. It's an idea I've had suspicions about for some time. Master Naomi has been trying, with my tutelage, to craft magic energy storage. So far, we've gotten close, but this is the first potentially successful try. Let's go somewhere more—grounded—before we try this."

Mahler and Ossian made it down to one of the practice chambers. The floor was basalt that traveled deep into the earth. It was a giant magical sink for when new trainees couldn't control their spells, they could ground the energy or be injured. Like what happened to his hands and the lightning scars running up and down his arms.

Mahler continued explaining the whole time, "Think about casting a spell, but instead of grounding into the rocks through your feet, use the blade in your hand to ground it. Nothing too powerful. The sword was only as good as the metal it contained. Still, it should be able to hold a decent spell or three. Mind you, this is all untested, till today, that is."

Mage Mahler grabbed a wood and sackcloth dummy at this point and walked into the middle of the room. Placing it down centrally, he backed away from it, looking as excited as a new apprentice about to try his first casting. He practically skipped back to where Ossian stood.

"Whenever you are ready, Mage Ossian." Mahler was standing to the side. A small journal and quill had appeared in Mahler's hands and he looked poised to take copious notes.

Ossian stared at the dummy. Why would he need a dummy if he was going to ground the spell? Deciding it didn't matter why, he took several deep and slow breaths, in through the nose and slowly forced out through thinly pursed lips. The world itself seemed to contract around him. Ossian drew the sword and the cold sensation swept up his arm again. It was on the edge of unpleasant, yet somehow Ossian knew he'd get used to that feeling.

Ossian decided on a shocking spell. It was one he practiced often. As the electrical spells always came the easiest to him. Moving his feet apart, he forced the image of the spell circle upon his conscious mind, adjusting it for the target in his hand.

He drew the power from deep inside of him. Feeling it course through his body, it lit up the spell circle. Each rune and character inside the circle became illuminated for a fraction of a moment as the energy traveled around the circle. It was heading to the culminating intersection of the circle, where Ossian would throw it out through his hand.

With the lightning spell clearly on its way, he could feel the lightning arc through his scars as it raced up his fingertips. He could still feel the original spell he had cast to obliterate a tree near his old farmstead. The one that had changed his life forever.

The sword rang out, the crack of lightning sinking deep into the blade. Then to Ossian's surprise, it stayed there. In the blade. He could feel the energy sitting there. Ready to be unleashed.

Mahler stood over to the side, scribbling notes furiously.

Ossian didn't even ask or wait. He squared up his shoulders. The feeling of the lightning energy singing inside the sword was powerful, the spell was sitting there ready to be used with only the barest of thought. He knew he'd still have to cast a shocking spell. Yet somehow he knew it would be almost too easy to do.

He forced the image of the circle inside his head, adjusting it for the target, the dummy this time. As well, for his and the sword's source of energies. His body's magical energies pulled from three of his limbs at once. Racing through his body, he could feel the energy being drawn to the energy already stored in the sword in his right arm. The energy was possibly one of the strongest spells he had ever cast, as if the energy in the sword was amplifying the energy he could draw out. He wasn't sure how that was possible.

The lightning illuminated the ring again and was arcing towards the sword as Ossian targeted the sack cloth dummy. The energy was pulled from his body and forcefully shoved through the sword towards the dummy at the center of the training circle.

The arc that flew through the air let out a buzz the likes of which nearly deafened Ossian. The bolt was immense, much greater than any spell he had tried before.

The dummy in the center of the training circle exploded as the lightning crossed the room. Splinters and shards of wood, straw and sackcloth flew everywhere, most of them on fire. The ozone smell was fresh in the air, followed closely by the burning of wood and straw.

A small splinter had embedded itself into Mage Mahler's forehead, but he was smiling from ear to ear. Ignoring the small flaming piece of wood, he was still scribbling furiously in his journal. Finally, throwing the quill into the air where it disappeared into nothingness, then snapping the book shut as it also winked out of existence right in front of Ossian.

"Excellent, that was a most—" Mahler than reached up and plucked the flaming splinter from his forehead, examined it briefly and tossed it to the ground, "excellent experiment, how did it feel?"

"So many things I want to ask about. I'm not sure where to begin."

Ossian's shoulders sagged. The casting had taken much more out of him than a simple, shocking spell should have. "The storage was easy enough to use, but it also appears to have amplified the next spell far more than I would have expected. I feel exhausted, like the energy in the sword drew more out of me than just I could have."

"Interesting," Mahler nodded and merely stood there.

"I think I'll have to practice quite a bit more with it. The sword drew the power out of me almost without me even trying." Ossian was pretty sure he'd just repeated himself. "I suspect it would be easy to draw too much energy. I feel very drained." Ossian then stumbled to the table next to Mahler and forced himself to support his weight with his arm.

He placed the sword into its scabbard and tried to lean against the table. Missing the table, Mahler grabbed for his shoulders as Ossian could barely stand. "Well, that is interesting, almost as if the sword itself drew the energy out of you. You shall have to see if that works with all the spells, not just your naturally inclined ones."

Mahler then lowered himself under Ossian's arm and, mostly supporting him, dragged him up to his room, which was missing everything except his bed and blanket.

"Hey where is—" which was when he remembered in the morning they would leave to make a new Village of the Night Forest.

"If you don't mind, I'm going to stay to observe you tonight. I want to make sure you're okay, Ossian. It wouldn't do for a new mage to get casting sickness."

Unbuckling the belt, Ossian tried to place the sword and scabbard on the table. Eventually, Mahler grabbed them and placed them on the table for him.

Crawling into bed, he grunted a kind of consent at Mahler and was fast asleep before he could notice Mahler summon his journal and quill from nothing and take notes.

CHAPTER 6

The next morning was a blur. He walked around the kitchen in a daze. He was pretty sure he woke up. Then he somehow dragged himself into the food hall before shoveling five or six people's worth of food into his face. The display of appetite awed even the enormously huge chef.

Then he somehow ended up in the castle's courtyard. The yelling of people, the smell of horses and mules and the sight of so many wagon's filling the yard, at least four dozen families. Ossian stood transfixed by the sight of so many people in a rag tag marching column, people he was now directly responsible for. The sobering thought of that responsibility, and then the first rays of sunlight, woke him up for real.

Jorn was sitting astride his skinny horse, Swift. It had always looked unhealthy to Ossian, but there was no horse that could outrun, or out maneuver, Swift. Two corporals were talking with Jorn, when he must have dismissed them, as they raced to their places in the rear of the civilian column.

Ossian walked over to Jorn. "You think these people can keep pace?"

"No, they can't keep pace. That's why the modified vee formation. The mage, if he ever shows up, and I can keep the column safe up front and the rear boys can keep a watch on stragglers and slow us down. Have you seen the mage who's supposed to travel with us? I heard a rumor he ate all the supplies this morning."

"Har, har. Master Jorn." His hand moving to his distended stomach, "I did eat a lot though."

Jorn's business tone came back. "It would be appropriate for you to call me Sergeant Jorn now. You outrank me Mage Ossian. Why are you on two legs and not four?"

Ossian never even thought they would ride horses. He was about to tell Jorn he didn't have a horse when a gentle cough came from behind him.

"Mage Ossian, I prepared a horse for you." A small boy of ten or twelve years held out the reins to a massive shire horse. It was just this side of honey in color and stood tall enough that Ossian was genuinely concerned about how he was going to mount such a beast.

Ossian glanced over at Jorn, whose facial expression to most people was neutral and unassuming. Yet Ossian could see what might as well have been a huge grin spread over his face. It showed only in the slightest upturn at the edge of his lips. "The farmers have agreed to allow you to ride one of their plow nags."

Ossian moved to take the reins when the horse stepped forward, lowered its massive head and snorted into Ossian's face. The head was the size of Ossian's entire torso. The warm breath blew out steam in the morning's chill. Ossian had the distinct impression this was no farmer's plow nag. He also wasn't about to let Jorn get the better of him in front of the entire new village of people he would live with.

Ossian was debating between threatening and trying to soothe the giant beast when one corporal screamed from the rear of the column, "Rear...Ready."

From the corner of his eye, Ossian saw Jorn look to the rear of the column. Taking the moment of distraction, Ossian focused quickly on a levitation spell. Releasing the energy in the spell, he took four steps. Each time his foot gaining purchase on a blank space of air, he leapt straight up to get on the back of the massive warhorse Jorn was trying to convince him was a plow nag.

Surprisingly, the horse didn't even budge as Ossian landed on his back, proving to Ossian it was a well-trained war horse who expected a rider. Not surprisingly, Ossian's legs couldn't be spread much further on the extremely wide back of the honey colored shire horse.

"Why am I riding such a massive beast, if it's a farmer's nag? Surely the farmer needs it to move their wagons and equipment." Ossian asked Jorn to draw his attention.

"The nag doesn't like to pull a wagon." Jorn said, then almost absentmindedly adding, "By the time we get there, you'll never want to ride a horse again."

Jorn flipped his reins and his horse moved to the head of the column. Without even glancing over his shoulder, he said, "You can ride anywhere in the column you want. Mage Ossian."

The week had started out so exciting; graduation, assignment, secret organizations and magical swords. So when Ossian kicked his heels into the shire horse, he was disappointed that the horse didn't move. Any well-trained warhorse of the King's army would respond to that heel kick in the same way, moving forward.

Ossian could hear Jorn chuckle as he moved further away from him, and under Jorn's breath, Ossian barely heard a soft, "Told you so."

Ossian panicked. How was he going to get a horse that outweighed him by at least ten times to move? A column of villagers replaced panic quickly as the wagons and carts, horses and mules, walkers and riders moved away from him. The two rear riders were politely waiting off to his right, probably scared of offending the new Mage. He hadn't recognized either of them, so they must be newer recruits.

Jorn forgot, or maybe he never knew that Ossian had started out on a farm. Jumping back off the horse, Ossian moved to take the reins and led the horse by hand towards the column. He didn't like his legs spread out so much, anyway. Quickening his pace to catch up with a wagon, he tied the massive shire horse to the rear. It would at least follow the wagon to the new, soon to be, village.

A well worn, sun tanned man looked around the wagon's front, "Sorry about that Mage Ossian. I told Sergeant Jorn that Honey won't move with anyone on her, but he insisted on it."

"Oh, that's quite alright, I prefer to walk anyway," Ossian smiled. The man reminded him of his father. He looked used to a hard life out in the sun. Thin and most likely one of the hardiest people in this entire group.

"Sorry, I don't know your name," Ossian jogged briefly so he was inline with the front of the wagon and offered his hand to the man.

"Names Deith, I'm but a simple farmer. Mage Ossian" The man's grip was rock solid, and Ossian's suspicion was confirmed. This man was as hardy as they came. Probably even an ex-soldier.

"First eight years of my life, I was a simple farmer. Not an easy life, but I have fond memories of that farm."

A smile crept up on Deith's face. He nodded slowly and flicked the reins. That's when Ossian remembered the King's words. Everyone was getting something out of this move. Probably quite a few of them weren't moving voluntarily.

It was midday before Ossian was greeted by the face of Jorn again. "Nag too much for you?"

"The horse preferred to be tied to the back of a wagon." Ossian would not give Jorn the satisfaction of knowing he couldn't convince the animal to move, but Jorn knew, as he sauntered off smiling at no one.

CHAPTER 7

The day was cool, and even with the sun high in the sky, it was just now barely getting warm enough for Ossian to think about it as spring. He loved the smell of the fields in spring. They passed farmers with their horses, plowing the land to prepare for when they could plant. The upturned dirt smelled of his first home on a farm.

Just around midday in the clearing between two copses of trees, Jorn called a halt to the procession. All the horses, oxen and mules slowly pulled into a circle and Ossian met up with Jorn and his two soldiers.

"You two stay in view. You know the drill."

"Can I help?" Ossian was used to being a soldier with these men. He could help keep watch.

"Mage Ossian, you have an entire village to acquaint yourself with. We have watch." And with that, Jorn distanced himself from Ossian.

Ossian wasn't sure why Jorn would be so direct. He'd basically chided him in front of the soldiers. Ossian guessed that meant none of them were staying longer than necessary to get the town started.

Walking back to the wagons, Ossian saw that most of the family units were staying to their own wagons. A couple of the families looked like they were pooling their food, or maybe they just knew each other.

He sidled up to the first family unit and introduced himself. Over the long lunch, he was offered food from nearly every wagon and family he talked with. He politely accepted small portions from each, so that no one was offended. He met several former soldiers and their families on their way to make a new life. Two of the families looked unfamiliar with their wagon outside of steering it, and Ossian asked a couple of the former soldiers to please spend the afternoon helping them become acquainted with the wagon and their animal.

No one refused and Ossian was very proud of his ability to convince the people to help each other. Then he realized he was to be the village Mage, no one here was likely to disobey his request, causing him to frown. He definitely had not done enough research on forming a village.

Luckily, they had a skilled woodsman, a blacksmith, a dozen seasoned farmers and a score of former soldiers, whose backs were strong. If anyone was from the dungeon or being coerced on this trip, Ossian couldn't tell.

Jorn sent his men in one at a time to pester one family for food. It looked like each soldier had been assigned a family. Ossian would need to ask Jorn later if those families had been given extra provisions for the soldiers. Plus, how long was the trip to take, given the first half of the day's time, Ossian was guessing eight days there minimum. He would also need to ask Jorn about convicts, or anyone else going unwillfully.

Jorn finally came in for a quick meal. Ossian gave him time to eat, but sooner than he thought, Jorn was standing up and shouting they would move out in ten minutes. Ossian noticed no one seemed to complain about that. Which Ossian thought meant that they were hiding it well.

As Jorn left the camp, Ossian caught up to him. "Jorn, wait up, please."

The sigh that came out of Jorn was unusual. Ossian had always thought Jorn, while not exactly loved him, tolerated his presence. Maybe that was all Mage Mahler's doing and Ossian was just a thorn in Jorn's side that would soon be gone.

"Yes, Mage Ossian."

Ossian just kind of stared at Jorn. He was even more succinct than normal. Now that Ossian was directly facing his old mentor, he couldn't bring himself to ask him what had changed.

"How long do you think it'll be before we make it to the village?" What Ossian really want to do was scream at Jorn and ask him why he was being so distant.

"Seven or eight days." Jorn turned and headed to his horse, signalling the guards already by their horses to head out.

By the time they setup camp for the first night, it was already dark. Ossian was pleased that the soldiers he'd asked to help show the obviously newer families how the animals and wagons worked were at least complying with his requests. He even thought he spied some of them smiling as they did it.

He was mostly wandering around camp checking that everyone else had everything setup for the night, when one of Jorn's men approached him and told him his tent was setup. As the man was walking him to his tent, it dawned on Ossian he didn't even know which wagon his stuff had been in.

Remembering to ask the soldier his name, the soldier replied it was Wendt. Ossian's tent was larger than the soldiers' tent next to it, but not by much.

"Make sure to add me to the rounds tonight. Four watches is always easier than three."

The look on the soldier's face told Ossian that the soldier hadn't been expecting Ossian to chip in on watch tonight.

"Or shall I tell Jorn that?" Given the look on Wendt's face. He, like most soldiers, had a hard time telling Jorn things that Jorn didn't want to hear. Ossian noticed that the soldier's face flashed between relief and worry that maybe he wasn't up to the standards of the new mage.

Ossian however, was too tired from walking all day to really care. He wandered off to find Jorn and tell him.

Wandering around the camp, three small fires kept the darkness at bay as the families sat around them conversing. The children had picked up sticks along the road that day and were fighting with them. Ossian was tempted to force Jorn to show them how to fight, then thought better of it. There was only so far he wanted to push Jorn, regardless of why Jorn was upset at him.

Instead, Ossian walked near to one of the older two kids and asked to borrow one of their sticks. Then he proceeded to instruct both of them in the finer arts of sword play, minus Jorn's usual beating. While Ossian understood the way Jorn taught, he was a different person. Gently coaxing one young man, Kamien. Then the second young man, Toffee, which Ossian thought maybe a tad sad of a name. He guided them through a single strike, block and parry.

"When you both have practiced those moves. And only those moves for the next two weeks, I'll instruct you further, or—," and Ossian added a wink he wasn't sure the kids could see, "I'll ask one of the former soldiers with us to teach you sword play weekly."

Both boys were giddy with joy. They made a very large point of practicing their strike and block and parry with each other in very slow, precise moves. Ossian looked up to see the farmer's wife frown at him. As she saw him looking at her, she changed her frown to a thin line.

Ossian would have to be careful with his advice. Mage Mahler had warned him that not everyone was as open with their teachings, or wanted everyone to have choices in life.

Ossian made his excuses and wandered off from the farmer's wife he was pretty sure he'd just made an enemy of. Finding Jorn, Ossian was on edge talking with what he used to think of as a mentor, if not a friend. "Add me to the watch rotation tonight, Sergeant Jorn."

Jorn looked up at him and a shrewd look overcame his face as he nodded and said, "Of course, Mage Ossian. As you wish."

Ossian had had enough of whatever attitude Jorn was dishing out. He stalked off to his tent and prepared to go to sleep. When he remembered, he could prep an alarm spell for camp. He needed to set certain parameters. He should coordinate with Jorn on that, but Ossian wasn't feeling cooperative at the moment.

Gathering the few ingredients for an alarm spell, he walked outside to find some charcoal from one of the cooler campfires. Reaching down into the campfire, he picked up a piece of charcoal. As he stood up, the heat stored inside the charcoal slowly penetrated the layers of his skin. Sinking down into his very bones, he tried to suppress a cry but ended up yelping out in pain as he dropped the still hot charcoal.

Most of the villagers came out of their tents at that point. As Jorn came up beside Ossian and said way too loudly, "Sorry for hitting you so hard, Mage Ossian, sometimes I don't even realize my own strength."

As Ossian looked over at Jorn, his blade had been out before Ossian could see it drawn. Ossian nodded and replied a little too loudly, "No worries, Sergeant, thanks for the lesson on parrying."

Then he side-eyed Jorn and whispered, "Thanks for that. The charcoal was not as cool as I thought."

The crowd, apparently appeased by the explanation or unwilling to challenge the new stupid mage and sergeant in charge, dispersed back into their tents and wagons. Ossian was hoping they thought Jorn and he had merely been practicing their sword fighting.

"What are you doing, Ossian?" Jorn sheathed his sword while he continued to whisper.

"I thought I might prep an alarm spell."

Jorn's face softened considerably, and he finally relented and acknowledged that this was a good plan.

Gathering together all the ingredients. Ossian moved to a central location of the camp and set up a small but complex circle to include all the guards and the people within their group. As he completed the circle, he spread the ingredients of the spell to the four corners of the spell circle.

Soon the air glowed reddish as the illumination of an alarm spell made a dome over the circle of wagons that was displayed over the collection of people, animals and wagons.

The red glow of the spell slowly faded away into the inky blackness of the night sky. Ossian just wandered if he had cast the spell wrong when Jorn signalled that first watch should start. Ossian had cast that spell many, many times, but never outside in the dark. It had always been inside during lessons. He was hoping first that the spell was unnecessary and second that if it was necessary that it worked.

Glancing down, Ossian looked at the wax tablet set on the outcropping of a portable table set out by Jorn. The table was a deep rich wood with streaks of yellow in the brown from far west. Brought back from the campaign that had made Sergeant Jorn's reputation as a formidable sword master capable of defeating entire squads of enemies all by his lonesome. The dark wood table was a sign that Jorn was here and he would not tolerate slacking during the watch. Jorn was known for walking around during other people's watches just to surprise them.

Ossian had once seen the next day's sword training when someone was sleeping on watch. As a shudder went through him at the thought of Jorn beating someone with a wooden sword.

Ossian could have stayed up, but that would have just resulted in him being tired. It was dawning on Ossian that these people were depending on him to be their rock in a new world that they all thought could easily and mercilessly make them all vanish. And with that, Ossian disappeared into his tent to sleep.

CHAPTER 8

Someone entering the tent woke Ossian up. He ripped his sword out of its scabbard and the blue glow that emanated from his mage flame torch showed him it was just Jorn.

"Good instincts. You always had good instincts, Ossian."

"My watch, I take it? I'll wake everyone up before breakfast."

Jorn nodded as he slowly turned to walk out of the tent. He paused. Ossian slowly sheathed his sword.

"Be careful of Yough and Bakker. They shouldn't be here. They had years left in their service."

"Excuse me, are you warning me of your own soldiers? What is wrong, Jorn?" Ossian didn't know what he would do if Jorn was genuinely upset at him, but at least he thought he should know why he was.

"This is the real world Ossian, the Night Forest is not a place to mess around with. The King has never sent a mage to the village before. Why now? Why is he sending soldiers in disguise? I'm worried for you."

"So you hold me at arm's length in front of everyone?" Ossian noticed he had stood up as he said this, but at least he'd kept his voice low.

Jorn turned around to face Ossian. "You are the new mage. I treat you with the respect you deserve. It's one thing for you to be friendly with them, but realize when bad things happen you will be the hand of the King in the village."

"I know my duties, Jorn." Was this the reason? Did Jorn not think he could do what would need to be done if justice had to be meted out?

"Knowing them and carrying them out, those are not the same thing." Jorn grabbed the tent flap and was about to open it. "I love sword fighting, Ossian, but I don't love killing people. Still, people die by my sword, cause it's what I must do." And with that, he opened the flap and walked out into the darkness.

Ossian pulled on his boots as Jorn's words echoed around in his head. He was warning Ossian about more than one thing. Why would the King send soldiers who hadn't finished their service? More specifically, why wouldn't he tell Ossian, since Ossian was here at the King's behest.

CHAPTER 9

As Ossian emerged from inside the tent, he paused for several seconds as his eyes adjusted to the darkness outside. As the low light level from the new moon slowly distinguished between the shadow and the deeper shadows, he saw Jorn waiting by his tent. Ossian waved a salute to Jorn, dismissing him from duty.

Jorn was the one that had warned Ossian many, many times that until you could clearly see in the current light level, you did not wave off the previous watch.

Ossian glanced around the campsite, wagons and tents filled a decent sized area. It would take him a while to walk across the camp. He could just barely make out the outline of the wagons on the opposite side of camp from him. The fire had been allowed to die out in the middle of camp. It would blind anyone looking into it, so first watch was responsible to make sure it was out before second watch woke up.

Around the circle, he spied at least four piles of wood that had been collected last night. Probably in order to start breakfast up in the morning. In his short jaunts around the city on patrol, the soldiers would have cold rations and be told to make fast time packing. When you added the families into the equation, he was guessing warm meals and polite words would be more effective.

As Ossian got further from his tent, he noticed there was a wagon behind him. He must have been preoccupied with being upset at Jorn last night and didn't notice that an entire wagon had protected him, from behind. Luckily for him, Jorn was looking out for him, even if they weren't currently having the best of relations.

Walking to the outside of camp behind the wagon, Ossian looked out into the farmer's fields. Stopping for several minutes, he waited to see if there was any movement. He gradually decided there was no immediate threat and walked to his left, scanning first the copse of trees, then more farmer's fields and eventually around to the other copse of trees. Finally, ending his circle of camp back at his initial position next to the wagon.

Deciding that the outside was clear, Ossian headed into the circle and walked around. Being extra careful to try and not wake anyone up, he explored the campsite that he hadn't taken the proper amount of time in the firelight last night to examine.

As the sun was near to rising, he was wondering who he should wake up first, when finally one of the tent flaps opened up and a woman stepped out. Of course, it would be the women who had been giving Ossian the stink-eye last night about showing her son how to fight.

Deciding he needed to diffuse the situation now, rather than let it fester, Ossian walked over to her casually.

As Ossian approached, the women bowed her head to him, "Good morning, Mage Ossian."

"I'm sorry I didn't get your name last night. And please call me Ossian."

"It's LeAnne. Mage Ossian."

"Just Ossian is fine."

The woman looked at him with her eyebrows raised. "Yes, Mage

Ossian." Her voice had a note that said she would call him Mage no matter how nicely he asked.

"I did not mean to offend you last night. I merely thought I would be of service and try to help the boys."

Her face went back to its scowl from last night, "Of course, Mage Ossian. They welcome any and all advice you'd be willing to provide them."

Ossian tried desperately to not allow his frustration to show. He was just here to help and everything he did just seemed to make someone more upset. This was going to be a long assignment while he learned about The Night Forest.

Sighing audibly, he walked away from LeAnne. "Sorry to have disturbed you, LeAnne."

"No trouble at all, Mage Ossian." Every word she said was pointed and direct, telling him with her tone that indeed he was the source of all her problems.

Ossian wasn't sure if he would have to watch out for her. He knew all too well from the Academy that some people kept grudges for the stupidest things. Regardless of if Ossian had given her a valid reason to be offended.

Continuing around the circle, more people were emerging from tents. Ossian was wondering if he would need to wake anyone up when the alarm spell sent a piercing screech through the camp. Well, he thought, at least that would do it.

Ossian spun around in a tight circle, trying to identify where the intrusion was. The alarm spell had a visual component, but that was being blocked by the wagons and tents currently in the way.

Jorn and the two corporals came flying out of their tents. Jorn was in full gear. Ossian knew he slept in his gear while on assignment. The two corporals were in various stages of undress and both had swords in hand.

"No visuals, I'm South." Ossian yelled it loud enough for the three guardsmen to hear over the screech, which finished just as he was saying south.

None of them replied, and with a practice born from daily drills, they separated into the four corners of camp and rushed to get a visual on what caused the alarm. Ossian, remembering his duties, dashed south, drawing his sword.

The sun's first rays highlighted the area around him as it crested up in the east.

Whizzing past his own tent, he quickly climbed the wagon behind it and stood at the top, looking for any movement or sound of something that shouldn't be there.

As the seconds dragged on, Ossian was certain that the guardsmen were dead, but he hadn't heard a single shout or sound of battle. He was just reassuring himself that it was just his imagination and nerves when he heard a rustle and saw several of the former soldiers push their families into the middle of camp away from the tents and wagons on the outskirts. They held daggers and Ossian was surprised they didn't have any swords among them. He guessed they couldn't afford them if they were choosing to head to the Village of the Night Forest.

That's when the sound of Jorn shouting and the screeching of an animal echo'd from the opposite side of camp. Ossian jumped down from his perch on the wagon's seat and ran towards the noise as it suddenly stopped. The former soldiers kept a tight circle with their families and let Ossian check out the danger. It was just occurring to Ossian he didn't know how many of the villagers were without families, like him, when Jorn walked through two of the wagons.

Blood was dripping from his hand. As Ossian was about to ask if he was okay, Jorn threw the biggest raccoon Ossian had ever seen in his life in front of him.

"Seems maybe we should recalibrate our alarm?"

The air in the camp immediately relaxed. The two corporals came back inside the circle and shrugged at Jorn when they saw the raccoon. Jorn gave them the hand signal for sweep camp a second time. Jorn was paranoid, but Jorn was still alive.

"Well, I have to keep it sized properly and there are children with us."

Jorn's face grew confused, "What do you mean sized?"

Ossian was still explaining to Jorn that the alarm spell would tell them if something entered or exited the circle when the two corporals emerged and called the all clear. Ossian tried to finish telling Jorn since the smallest kid was roughly two stones, he had to keep that weight in mind.

Jorn looked over at the soldiers with their families in the middle of camp and looked at the families that were just emerging from their wagons or tents where they had hidden.

"Should we drill them, Jorn?" Ossian knew it would take more than just seven days of drilling to get over the fear and be able to do what was best for the group, especially with people who had so much to lose. The desire to hide was strong in some.

"No time. You should explain what happened, though."

"I just did—" When it dawned on Ossian that Jorn meant explain it to everyone else.

It didn't take long for Ossian to gather everyone in the middle of camp and even less time for him to explain the alarm spell to everyone. One man asked if he could skin and dress out the animal and Ossian told him sure, since it was already dead.

Then that was it.

They just accepted Ossian's explanation of why the spell had gone off and since no one was heading back to sleep, breakfast was ready faster than he thought and before long, they were packed and heading on their way.

Ossian found himself oddly disappointed that no one seemed even a little bit interested in the spell, or why a raccoon set it off. He knew he didn't explain it enough and even Mage Mahler would have lectured him about how poorly he explained the spell. Shrugging, he fell in line with everyone else and moved out when Jorn called.

"Two stones?" Jorn said as he glanced around at the assembling caravan of villagers.

"The little girl." Ossian looked around the camp for her. "There her." Pointing at the smallest girl he'd seen in the caravan.

"Mage Ossian, she's three or four stones easily."

Ossian wasn't sure what to say to that. So he kept silent.

Today went much like the last.

CHAPTER 10

As the wagons circled that night. Ossian was even more tired from the walking. They had passed through the familiar territory of farmer's fields out into the more wild areas. Still, this close to the castle, there wasn't all that much chance of brigands.

That night, as Ossian was preparing to set the alarm spell, Jorn asked him if that was really necessary.

"Well, no, I guess not. But what if something sneaks into camp? Or what if someone sneaks out of camp?"

"As much as we teach you vigilance during the drills, the fact of the matter is, we are currently not at war with anyone. We are headed into an area that is unlikely to be populated by brigands, as there is no one to steal from around here." Jorn looked out past the wagons as they circled up for the night. "And you interrupted a seriously delightful dream last night."

Ossian smiled clear to his eyes. That was the Jorn he was used to. Well, not the part about not being vigilant, but making sly sarcastic remarks.

Then Ossian remembered what Jorn had said the other night, "Do you think this village is in danger?"

"Something feels off about this. Just remember, it's a forest. It's all made of wood if you need to burn it down."

"I'm better with lightning than with fire."

A sharp bark emanated from the man next to Ossian. Looking over at him, he was pretty sure Jorn was laughing. As Jorn continued to chuckle more quietly, Ossian was glad that he and Jorn were back on good terms.

That night, Ossian argued with Jorn about taking third watch. It was always the worst. You woke up too early. It was basically impossible to get back to sleep and very few people ever liked third watch. Ossian argued that since he was mostly just walking up and down a wagon column, there wasn't much for him to do. Jorn finally relented, more likely because Ossian wouldn't give in.

Jorn awoke Ossian from a deep slumber, shaking him awake. He'd definitely forgotten how much third watch sucked. Jorn must have moved himself to second watch so he could wake up Ossian.

"Get up, you fat lazy mage."

"Jorn, stop shaking me."

"You wanted to help with watch. And you wanted third. So get up. I'm tired and need to get back to that dream last night."

Ossian's eyes opened wide at that. "Oh really? And how lovely was this dream?"

Jorn placed his hand on the hilt of his sword, as a warning that Ossian was going too far. "Very lovely, and you will not talk about this again."

"Of course, of course. Master Jorn's secrets are safe with the fat and lazy."

It had been a long time since Ossian had pulled a third watch. He was bleary-eyed as he splashed some water into his face before emerging from his tent. As he glanced around the campsite, he was pretty sure either everything was just blurry or he wasn't awake. Rubbing his eyes several times, he finally saw mostly straight. There was actually some moonlight helping him see, then he signaled to Jorn.

Circling around the wagons and crossing through camp, he remembered how boring watch was. He thought about casting some spells to keep himself awake, but waking everyone up a second night in a row would not make friendly people out of the village people he was to attend to.

He eventually circled and crossed the camp twice more. Then, deciding he had nothing better to do, he placed his hand on the hilt of his sword and felt into the sword for the spells. There they were, a very complex example of a lightning bolt and a new spell Ossian was not familiar with. He would need to ask Mage Mahler about that one. It was large and complex, and Ossian couldn't hold it in his mind as he tried to concentrate. One side of the spell circle kept slipping from his mind as he tried to study other aspects of it.

He gave up the large spell and focused on the lightning bolt spell. He was hoping he could turn it off or disengage it somehow. Fiddling around with the runes in the spell, he eventually found a trigger word. Muttering the word to himself, the sound of a tent flap fluttering open came from behind him. Ossian was sitting in the middle of camp, so he rotated slowly so as not to startle whoever was coming out of their tent.

Ossian could just barely make out who he thought was Yough peering into the night. Yough must not have seen Ossian, as he started from his tent to the outside of the camp. He hated having to relieve himself in the middle of the night. You had to wake up, stumble around in the dark and try not to piss all over something important.

Not wanting to disturb Yough during his night break, Ossian sat quietly and counted to one hundred. When Ossian counted the second time to one hundred, he was getting worried. Could something have entered the camp?

Ossian quietly rushed to where Yough had passed through the wagon circle and glanced around for him. Not seeing him immediately, Ossian freaked out. What if he went missing or a bear ate him?

Deciding to sound the alarm, Ossian pulled his sword as he cast mage flame on the blade of the sword. The blue glow lit up the area directly surrounding him.

"What the hell." Someone behind him shouted as Ossian spun in a tight circle, keeping the sword in front of his body to block any sudden rush at him.

Yough stood there, smoking a pipe. Looking at Ossian, his eyes had been wide until he saw it was Ossian. Then they had settled back into a normal, bored look.

"Yough, what the—" As it dawned on Ossian, he had gone out for a smoking break.

"Wife hates the smell, and if she finds out, I won't hear the end for days."

Ossian's heart was racing. "I thought maybe a bear attacked you."

Yough's mouth cracked into a huge grin. "Jorn's been feeding you too many tales. And a bear would have made a mighty ruckus."

Not knowing what to say to the obvious issue Yough was pointing out about his idea being crap, Ossian sheathed his sword.

"That blue glow is interesting, seems handy for guarding, but it also lets the other side know exactly where you are."

"I cast it when I couldn't find you. And I won't tell the wife about the smoking."

"Then I think I'll keep the bear eating to myself as well, Mage Ossian."

"Yeah, I'd appreciate that."

Yough nodded his head at him as he continued to puff away on the pipe.

The rest of the night passed in a blur. Ossian was wide awake after Yough scared him half to death and he was too wired to work with the sword anymore. After waking up Corporal Yesmi and waiting diligently for her to signal her full awakeness. Ossian tried to sleep but couldn't. That was the real problem with third watch. He was too wired to sleep, and too tired to do anything else.

Ossian wasn't too sure how long he laid there before he finally heard the first sounds of people waking up and starting fires. Yesmi didn't trigger any alarm and have the entire camp up several hours early. So he guessed that was good.

As the day wore on, the newness of the caravan must have been wearing off. The children were playing around much less; the adults were more somber and the air even seemed heavy with anticipation of what they were heading out to do.

Trying to lighten the mood as they traveled, Ossian tried to engage several of the families. The conversations were muted and dragged out as he tried to get them to talk about their former lives by talking about his former life as a farmer.

Around lunch time he gave up trying to lift people's spirits. Cold morning left overs and two-day-old stale bread were what they ate. Ossian wondering genuinely at how long some tasks would take. He tried to engage a couple of the tradespeople with them and got at least a semblance of answers from them.

"Depends on the rocks, probably a week for a proper oven. If'n we want to only build it once."

Ossian could already tell the stale bread would get old fast and a working oven could be a central place for everyone to meet and chat.

He was sure he would have to convince some villagers to team up to build houses, which meant some of them would live in their wagons and tents for longer than others. Maybe they could draw lots. Or the ones with kids might get preferential treatment. He wasn't fully sure how he was going to handle that.

Jorn's whistling signal blissfully interrupted his thoughts and worries. Ossian jumped off the wagon he'd been sitting on and he located the issue. Barring the road was a downed tree.

Ossian glanced back towards the rear guard, who were spreading out. He also noticed that several of the wagons were slowing down and pulling off to the sides of the road. Those wagons belonged to the ex-soldiers who understood what they were seeing.

Rushing to the front of the caravan, Ossian monitored the surrounding countryside, looking for anything out of the ordinary. As he came up upon the downed tree, Jorn emerged from the area where the tree would have stood.

"Looks like the roots gave out, it wasn't cut down."

"How you wanna clear it?"

"It'll take us an hour or two to chop it up. We could camp here."

"Or... I could remove it."

"How dangerous is that?"

Glancing back at the wagons, he gauged the distance of the training hall he'd last used for a lightning spell. "Probably need to pull the front two wagons back."

"If you get injured, I'll be thrown into the dungeon."

Ossian looked over at Jorn with pleading eyes. "You know they want to see me use magic. After that alarm spell yesterday, I think they deserve it."

Jorn rolled his eyes. "Yes, Mage Ossian. Let's endanger everyone just so they can see you as their savior who flings fireballs."

"I could just move it. But you know lightning..."

"Lightning is dangerous, Mage Mahler was telling me last time he had a flaming splinter embedded in his forehead."

"Fine, fine, fine. I'll just move it with magic. Heck, I won't even gather them around and explain."

Ossian stood up straight, set his mind and imposed the levitation circle on his mind. Linking the spell into a form of the tree was easy, but how was he going to—ah, there it was. He added in a modified pushing spell that should shove the tree back into the forest on that side of the road.

As the symbols of the circle lit up, Ossian tried to ignore the complaints from Jorn, who was standing next to him. The wind picked up in the area as the tree levitated into the air. Ossian waving his hands in a large circle, when he realized the pushing component was a little more than he had expected. The tree shot off into the forest and crashed through it like an arrow from a bow.

"So, that was your idea of safe?"

"Are you on fire, Jorn?"

Jorn's face betrayed not a single emotion. His body language said otherwise. He was tensed, every muscle was ready to thrash something. Then just as suddenly, Jorn relaxed, shrugged and headed back to his horse, who still sat chomping on the grass only twenty paces away. Despite the magic and the sudden gigantic flying tree into the woods, the horse had not cared.

As Ossian turned around to head back to the wagon, he noticed that every single person from the village was standing wide-eyed and staring at him.

He could already tell some of the younger kids would be pestering him for more magic. As they were already bouncing on their feet and pestering their parents. He'd have to think of some simple spells to show them. Maybe he could mage flame them all some torches that night. He wondered how tired that would make him, probably very. Since there were at least twenty-three children.

CHAPTER II

Ossian had been correct, but most of the children were too scared to approach him, or their parents chided them when they got close. Then a little girl approached him and tugged on the side of his tunic. When Ossian glanced down, she almost bolted. Her eyes were like a deer caught out in the open, frozen and probably would scatter at the smallest of sounds.

Ossian tried to make it easier for her.

"Sorry, I'm not allowed to speak to strangers." Ossian said, trying to keep the sarcasm out and make it sound like he was being totally truthful with her.

She cocked her head slightly, then whisper-stammered, "They say you can summon demons?"

Glancing side-eyed at her, he tried for full formal.

"It begins with your name—let me show you."

Ossian stopped walking and stood before the girl. Bowing his head, he intoned, "Mi'lady, I am Mage Ossian of Stroik. I am pleased to make your acquaintance." At that last piece, he flourished his hand out in an exaggerated bow.

The little girl's cheeks flushed bright red, but to her credit, she didn't run. She grasped her tunic and attempted a curtsey. "I am Espeth." Looking up from her curtsey, her eyes told him she was looking for confirmation that she'd done it right.

"Good enough for a start. Next time, remember that you start with what is called an honorific. Such as Mi'lady, or to address me would be Mage."

Ossian continued, "Now, Espeth. Do you want to summon a demon?"

Her eyes grew enormous and she shook her head no violently. "No, sir—mage—sir."

"Well good, cause I can't do that." Then Ossian winked at her. "I'm not even really sure what a demon would be. There is a brief discussion of it in the magical literature." Which wasn't strictly speaking true. Ossian didn't want to frighten the girl with the realities of all the strange and magical creatures they were unlikely to ever encounter.

As the girl turned to flee from him, Ossian knew he'd played it all wrong.

"Espeth, would you like to see more magic?"

Her body betrayed whatever her voice was going to say as she hesitated in the half-turned away position.

"Fetch me a stick, and I can show you."

Espeth bolted off to the side of the road.

Deith, her father, had been watching this entire time from his wagon, eyeing Ossian with great suspicion. He couldn't fault him, though. What did these people know of him? He woke them up early, threw trees into woods and was responsible for their safety once they reached the village.

Espeth returned with a stick and two more children in tow.

As she approached, she curtsied. "Mage, I have brought a stick."

She was holding it out like Ossian imagined someone would do with a dangerously sharp sword, ready to run should the need present itself.

Ossian took the stick from her hand and was about to cast a mage flame spell to turn it into a heatless torch when he heard Jorn's horse approaching him from behind.

"Oh, I think we need at least two sticks. Do you want to see me magically turn this one into two?"

All three sets of eyes locked onto him as they nodded yes slowly. Ossian hoped that this would work, otherwise Jorn would likely pummel him to death. Spinning around, Ossian drew his hand sideways and whipped the stick at Jorn as hard as he could.

Jorn, who had been attempting to pretend to be looking off to the side, in an almost casual flick of his wrist, drew his sword, split the stick down the middle lengthwise and sheathed his sword again.

"Damnit Ossian, this isn't some playtime."

"See kids, I'm not the only person here who can do magic."

As Ossian turned towards the kids, all three of them were clearly disappointed.

"Fetch the sticks, right quick." Clapping his hands, Ossian startled the children to run after the sticks. Under his breath, he mumbled after them, "I'd like to see anyone else do that and escape Jorn's wrath."

When the children came running back, two were holding the individual pieces of the split stick and the third had found another stick to bring back.

"Alright, stand in a circle." Ossian placed each of the children in a circle so they would place their sticks all in the center. "Hold those sticks up. That's right. Good."

Ossian was thinking this would be the hardest part. Casting the spell was extremely easy. Getting the kids to not flee from the sudden appearance of fire. That might be a little harder.

"Now, if anyone runs, this won't work. So you have to stay brave and stay still. Just remember, the fire can't hurt you."

Espeth gritted her teeth and stood stock still. The other girl, slightly older and the biggest of the three, seemed less shaken, but the boy with them seemed ready to bolt like a rabbit realizing it was maybe the next meal.

Ossian had cast the mage flame spell so many times it was barely even a spell to him anymore. Raising up his sword, he powered up the circle inside his head and gently lowered the now flaming tip to the first stick. Touching it gently, he pushed the spell with his mind away from the sword into the stick where it caught.

Just as quickly, he cast the spell two more times, touching each of the sticks in turn. He could see the kids were nearing the end of their patience.

"Alright, that's it. While it casts a light, there is no heat." And with that, Ossian extended his hand into the mage flame as the small boy let out an eek and dropped his stick. Ossian picked up the stick from the flaming side and handed it back to the boy.

"Sir, I am Mage Ossian of Stroik. I am pleased to make your acquaintance." The little boy held out his shaking hand timidly and took the stick that now glowed blue at the end Ossian held.

Espeth finally chimed in, "Say, Mage, I am yer name."

The boy complied and told Ossian his name was Boa. Then Ossian repeated it and learned the other girl's name was Piaa, but with two a's.

As the kids dared each other to touch the flames, they ran off back to the wagons marching alongside them. Jorn on his horse pulled up along-side Ossian.

"You'll need twenty more before the night's out."

"Yes, I suspect I will." Ossian stared after the kids, trying to avoid Jorn's judgemental gaze.

"Throw a stick at me again, and we'll do some remedial training before I leave."

"Oh, come on Jorn, how cool was that? The kids might be taken with magic. But what you did there was beyond magic. It was the application of skill beyond what mortals can do."

"Try it again." With that, Jorn spurred his horse back towards the head of the column.

Ossian smiled. No matter what Jorn thought, that'd been cool. Ossian had tried many, many nights to do that trick, never with success. At best, he'd cut a stick, or make more kindling. Jorn could do it blindfolded with his back at the target. He knew. He'd seen Jorn do it once, drunk.

CHAPTER 12

The rest of the wagon trip that day comprised a group of kids running up to Ossian and begging him to magic their sticks. He'd complied with the first ten easy enough, but he'd forgotten how much so many spells in succession took out of someone.

Deith, the farmer, had been kind enough to allow Ossian to sit in the back of his wagon as they chugged along on the path to that night's encampment.

Ossian hadn't tried to cast that many spells in a very long time. Every student tried it at some point, or so Mage Mahler had informed him. The dangers of casting too much magic or too strong of a spell were real. Light-headedness, cramps and even unconsciousness he'd experienced when he cast too many spells, or too strong of a spell. Luckily, he hadn't suffered some of the other symptoms of overcasting. Like vomiting or bleeding from the eyes and ears, or death. Although the mages assured the students that death was an extreme example.

Mage Mahler had warned him that as his time and talents and experience grew, his ability to cast more and more magic would grow as well, or to be more precise he would get better at quickly substituting more accurate symbols for the spell circles. He could even hear Mahler now speaking to him in that voice of his that he used to tell him something he had better pay attention to. You must be careful, many a mage has died through willfully ignoring the symptoms of overcasting.

The next set of children did not like that they would have to wait till the next day. He wondered if they truly understood what he was saying when he told them he couldn't cast anymore magic today. He was well under his limit, as he'd just felt the first pangs of a headache. The caravan was also depending on him, and should something happen, he had to be ready. Twenty odd heatless blue torches were unlikely to scare off bandits. Although Ossian had to admit, any bandit attacking them would die by Jorn's sword long before Ossian could get a spell off.

As they sat by the fires of the night camp, Ossian had to ask Jorn for first watch.

"If yer tired, watch is covered."

Jorn's normal dry sarcasm was entirely missing as he looked over at Ossian. Ossian could see the mage flame torches flickering out on the edges of the encampment. The children were running around carefree. Ossian hadn't seen a group of young children playing in so long.

"Maybe you're right. I have another dozen torches to make tomorrow." And with that, Ossian gulped down the rest of his dinner, said his goodnights to the families as he walked past them to his tent. Opening the flap, the thought occurred to him that he should charge up the sword as he fell into the cot unconscious.

CHAPTER 13

As Ossian emerged from his tent the next morning, he was greeted by thirteen torches stuck into the ground immediately outside his tent. He couldn't help but chuckle, as it looked like what most peasants would associate with some magic ritual. Briefly, he thought about rearranging them and casting a spell in the middle, but it didn't do well to make fun of ignorance. He would need to locate one child and figure out why they left the torches outside his tent.

It didn't take long for one of the fathers, up early getting the cooking fires going, to walk over and mention that they didn't know how to turn the torches off. Many of the parents were also scared that an unwatched torch might burst their meager possessions into a raging inferno.

Ossian hadn't thought to educate the people on magic. He'd just been concerned with making some of them happier. Gathering up the torches, he spent his breakfast visiting every family with children and making sure each one had a torch, then he explained how the torch would likely only last the next week or two. Casually, he mentioned that anything put over the torch would hide the light and he demonstrated by placing his clay mug over it.

Some parents still had that look of disbelief on their faces. Ossian knew they would take longer to come around, or maybe they would never come around. Despite the world having magic, not everyone appreciated it. Even in the Academy, most of the students learning magic were high-born daughters and sons of nobles.

Ossian knew some mages took apprentices that were low born, cause the king demanded that everyone that showed talent be taught. That didn't mean they got the same level of education. Most of them ended up in villages like where he was destined before they decided to re-open a new Village of the Night Forest. Whiling away their days helping multiple villages eke out punishments or relay the King's judgement. The reason it worked was cause anyone that can throw a fireball or a lightning bolt was rarely ignored and if a war happened, they were some of the front line mages. Sparing the more elite mages of the realm from the war.

A young child tugging on his tunic caused Ossian to come back out of his reverie. The child handed him a stick and stood looking at him. He went back over the manners talk he'd had with Espeth and by the time he was done, another nine kids were standing around him, sticks held out eagerly.

The road march was much like the day before, except Ossian didn't have a headache this day. Either he was getting stronger, or more likely better controlled at using the mage flame spell.

CHAPTER 14

Three more days passed and before Ossian knew it they were looking out over the valley that lead to the Night Forest. Ossian could just make out the treeline from here. At the top of this hill, Ossian could not see the end of the Night Forest. It spread out and went on as far as the eye could see. He knew that on the other sides was the Kingdom of Levant.

Still, people didn't come out of the Night Forest. Or at least no one claimed to have been there and back again. The King claimed the Night Forest as his divine, but kind of like claiming a rabid dog as your pet, meant nothing if you couldn't use it.

The spot where the village was going to be was visible from here. Ossian could feel the energy of the group, both excited about their new lives and trepidation from looking at the Night Forest.

The caravan seemed to travel even slower than Ossian thought possible. It wasn't so much the downward path through the hills that was the problem. What with their future home so close, it was nearly impossible to not be excited and want to be there already.

Jorn was leading the caravan and Ossian could tell even from this distance he was on high alert. The Night Forest was not outwardly hostile. At least they didn't think so. Yet still, Jorn drilled vigilance into his troops constantly. Glancing backwards, the rear guards also looked on edge. They were glancing around actively, turning at the slightest sound.

Ossian couldn't help it though. He wanted to take off running down the road to where it ended. Which he was pretty sure he could see from here.

No old buildings, no foundations, no bodies or anything. There wasn't a sign that a village had ever been there. Maybe when they got closer, there would be smaller, more obvious signs. Judging from Mage Mahler's talk, though, he was pretty certain there wouldn't be any sign whatsoever.

Continuing to glance around, he noticed the children were being corralled by their parents, who didn't want their children running down to the new village site ahead of everyone. Ossian briefly thought about grabbing all the children and having a race down to the new site, then thought better of it when Jorn came into view again. Jorn would never approve, although Ossian was pretty sure Jorn wouldn't tell him off either. At least not in front of the entire village. It would be a private lambasting, just very loudly.

After what felt like an eternity, they finally reached the spot. Indeed, the road ended abruptly, like someone had just swept the road away from the earth at a line. Jorn, the two guards and Ossian scouted the area while the villagers set to work circling the wagons. They were a half-days' journey from the Night Forest. A couple of smaller woods, not attached to the Night Forest, spread out towards the northwest of the village and would be used by the woodsmen. No one would immediately go into the Night Forest, or at least Ossian thought at least for a couple of weeks.

In between the village and the Night Forest was what looked like perfectly acceptable farm land. Ossian had to admit he hadn't farmed in a decade, but the soil looked just the right type once it was rock picked, plowed and planted. A small stream, as wide as two of the wagons were long, ran from the hills, through the village and off into the Night Forest. Glancing in the waters, the fish could be seen swimming around. Ossian wondered how plentiful the fish would be.

They would need to build a bridge so that they could cross the stream regularly, but for now they could cross it at a point that Deith, the farmer, had found.

At some unseen signal, Jorn stood up from the stream, shook off his canteen and looked long and hard into the Night Forest.

"Did you see that?"

"Come off it Jorn, you can't sca-"

"Shhh," Jorn cocked his head sideways to place his ear closer towards the Night Forest. "Have you charged up that sword yet?"

"First thing tonight. Did you really see something, Jorn?" Ossian could barely see any actual trees from here. The forest was just a black line that met with the blue sky. He wasn't sure if Jorn was playing a poor joke on him, or genuinely being paranoid.

Jorn finally looked away from the forest. Ossian could feel those eyes burning into him. "I think we'll stay the week."

CHAPTER 15

The week blurred by. Several of the farmers plowed fields, watched over by one of the guards. Since they were the closest to the unknown dangers of the Night Forest.

The blacksmith started to set up a small shop. The woodsmen, their sons and the remaining guard took a wagon to fetch building trees from the nearby forest to the northwest.

Every single person worked from before sunup to clear after sundown. Ossian spent most of that time helping wherever he could. He charged up his sword that first night, but mostly spent the days working with his hands. Everyone either cooked, cleared fields in front of a plow horse, or went to get building materials.

His magic wasn't refined enough to do the delicate work of cutting down trees, or getting a fire going. At least not a fire that wasn't a raging ball of flame that exploded. That he could do easily. Controlling magic was always harder than releasing it.

Mostly he helped corral half the children as they picked rocks from the fields before the plow, they would race to find all the rocks and pebbles, run them to a collection site where Jorn or the guardsmen would pile them into a wagon and take them into town to be used as building supplies.

The second day, they split the rocks between two of the ex-soldiers and the oven to be. While Jayne, the baker and Bakker the potter, one ex-soldier and his partner, spent the time assembling all the ingredients for a proper mortar for a stone oven. Several of the villagers spent the first week building a mostly stone building from all the rocks they found in the fields. The other half of the children slept well that first week as they spent all day mixing mortar and running it between the blacksmith's building and the oven.

In between waiting for mortar to dry, they also built two complete houses from the woodsman's trees by the end of the week. Ossian was impressed with the entire village's work ethic.

Ossian knew he needed to cement the village together. Most of them were still living in wagons or tents. With this pace though, they would all be housed in four or five months, tops.

Cornering Jorn, Ossian asked him, "Do you think it'll be safe to hunt around here?"

"I don't see why not. Unless you mean in the Night Forest."

Ossian looked over at him. "What did you see the other night?"

"Movement near the trees. Whatever it was. It was fast and moved into the forest."

"We'll keep rotating guards at night."

"Those villagers will be tired, Ossian."

"We're all tired. Back to that hunt, though."

"Rumor is Deith is a skilled archer."

"The farmer?" Ossian had observed Deith a lot over the last couple of days, as he was one of the primary plow drivers. Deith seemed to be a genuine leader amongst the ex-soldiers and non-soldiers alike.

"Well, the rumor is poacher, but that doesn't matter out here."

"I'll ask him if he minds taking tomorrow off to hunt."

As Ossian was about to walk off to find Deith when Jorn started up again, "I have a bad feeling, Ossian."

"We do what we must." Ossian had heard Jorn use this line many times, when someone said something that made no difference to what they were going to do. Ossian didn't turn around, but he was sure he could sense the smile play over Jorn's face.

CHAPTER 16

It didn't take long for Ossian to find Deith in the field plowing away at the dirt with the huge honey colored Shire horse Jorn had tried to get Ossian to ride. Ossian was pretty sure that horse could use another couple of people on the plow to weigh it down and still it would just plod along, pulling the soil up and over. Stopping only when Deith pulled at the reins and clicked at it.

"Mage Ossian, what can I do you for?" Deith's face was streaked with dirt and his clothes were sweaty from the hard work of plowing field after field. It briefly occurred to Ossian that maybe Deith didn't have a change of clothes in order to wash out his dirty ones. He also wasn't sure how to ask that without appearing rude.

"Rumor is you are the expert hunter in this group." Ossian knew at once from the look that crossed Deith's face he'd said it wrong.

"What exactly did they say?" Deith's voice had gotten low. The low Ossian was used to getting from Jorn when he was warning you.

Ossian tried to sound nonchalant about it, tried to even add in a bit of hand waving over towards Jorn, "They said if I wanted a big feast tomorrow, that no one here could match your archery skills."

The creases on Deith's face became slightly less pronounced as he debated something in his head.

Thinking quickly, Ossian added, "I haven't told anyone else. If you want, we can forget this conversation happened."

"Well, no, it's fine. I can't expect my past to stay hidden. I was in the dungeons for poaching. Makes sense you'd know." Deith's shoulders sagged as he said this. Clearly, it wasn't his proudest moment.

"Uh—I didn't know. Jorn just said you were the archer to ask. I'd like to make a feast to celebrate the end of our first week." Ossian waved his hands over the village and the fields. "We've accomplished so much."

Then he held up his hands as Deith's mouth opened. "I understand we have a ton more to do, but if we don't celebrate occasionally, what's the point? And since I represent the King here, you can't poach."

Deith gave Ossian a small smile at that. "I'll need to find a bow. If I have to make one, it'll take too long. What with all this work we have left to do?"

"Oh, I'm sure Jorn or one of the others has one you can borrow for now. I'll find the bow. Tomorrow we can go hunting."

Deith raised an eyebrow at that. "Are you sure you want to go? Hunting is kind of a solo art."

"You can't just wander off into the forest alone. Someone needs to go with you."

"The Night Forest?" Deith sputtered at even the thought of that.

"No, no. The one we've been getting all the trees from." Pointing out over towards the northwest. "And I can sit still in a place you tell me to."

Ossian spent the better part of the day tracking down Jorn, who had taken one guard and gone patrolling closer to the Night Forest. Jorn shrugged his shoulders as he handed over his bow and a quiver of arrows.

"There aren't any footprints. Anywhere. No animal tracks, no human footprints, no strange indentations in the ground. It's like the forest is a wall." Jorn concentrated way too hard on the forest as he said this. Ossian was genuinely worried that Jorn might just charge off into the Night Forest just to prove it wasn't solid.

"Another time, Jorn. Tomorrow, I need you to stay in the village. Deith and I will go hunting."

Jorn shrugged again. Then turned around and walked back towards the village. Ossian was glad they would leave soon. He knew he was supposed to investigate the Night Forest. He was also certain that Jorn's idea of investigation involved nothing short of a full scale invasion. He was the King's right-hand man though, so that made some sense.

As they went to bed that night, Deith found Ossian and reminded him they would leave at the start of third watch. Ossian tried not to grumble or show his displeasure at that. While Deith explained if they wanted to find an animal, they would have to be in place before the animals awoke.

Taking a page out of Jorn's book, Ossian shrugged, then added, "Have second watch wake me up, I'll meet you by the fire. I assume we're walking the entire way."

Deith smiled at that. "We will be on foot. Yes, Mage Ossian."

Ossian didn't like the way he said that, then also remembered he had been the person to suggest that they do this.

Third watch came way too early for Ossian. Wendt shook him several times with him waving them off only once. Finally, flipping his legs over the cot, he sat up and the guardsman stood waffling in the tent's doorway.

"You can go, I'm awake." Ossian said through a full stretch and some yawning.

"Deith won't wait long. He's got a long run ahead of him."

"Run—what?" A frown formed on Ossian's face. Jorn had set him up again. Helpful hand here, then slap it down with the hidden hand.

"Deith is a scout, Mage Ossian. He'll make the forest faster than you could with the wagon."

"Thank you." And with that, Ossian waved the guardsmen away.

As the guardsmen left, Ossian dressed quickly and was mumbling to himself by the time he reached the campfire.

"Jorn forgot to mention we'd be racing to the forest."

Deith, to his credit, looked genuinely concerned at him. "Jorn didn't mention that I used to be a scout. Sounds like him."

Deith then, looking over, Ossian shrugged just like Jorn and handed over an oilskin and a waterskin. "We're traveling light. Rumor is that sword glows if it's unsheathed. You need to not draw it if we're to catch anything. I'll try to keep the run there easier for you."

"It glows when I cast a spell. And yes, I'll try and keep up. I trained often with the soldiers. I'm in better physical shape than most of the mages."

"We shall see." Deith then spun on his heels and hurried off towards their destination.

The pace that Deith set was a near full sprint for Ossian. He was on the verge of collapsing when Deith went from moving fast to a complete standstill. Ossian, being a full dozen meters behind him, took several steps to come to a stop as Deith knocked an arrow. Ossian couldn't believe his luck. He was surveying the area, looking for the animal that Deith had noticed, but he spotted nothing.

Then he smelled it, carried by the wind. The rancid taint of spoiling meat.

Ossian had trained with the soldiers enough to know to crouch, since they were in the open. Deith drew suddenly and let off an arrow that buzzed through the air. Deith had another arrow nocked before the first arrow must have found its mark, as a screeching could be heard in the darkness ahead. Ossian still couldn't make out whatever Deith was shooting at.

"We have a problem. How winded are you?" Deith whispered as he carefully tiptoed ever-so-slowly to where Ossian was crouched.

"I'm—fine—" Ossian couldn't even get out the words without

wheezing. He would need to ask Deith later if that was really his idea of a light pace. When he saw it running towards them.

"What—" is all he got out as Deith shot arrow after arrow into a charging shadow.

Ossian could just barely see the outline of the animal. He did not know what creature was running at them. He could also hear arrow after arrow's soft thud into the animal as each shaft embedded itself into the creature.

"Offensive spell?" Deith stammered out as he unleashed the final arrow in the quiver.

Ossian finally pulled his wits together. He sunk his mind into the lighting circle, targeting whatever animal was running straight at them. He'd charged up the sword, but he didn't need Deith to drag his unconscious body back to camp. Still wheezing slightly from the run, he stuck his hand out and summoned forth a lightning bolt.

The sudden blinding light that shot forth from his hand was visually overwhelming. There would be no way he was gonna see anything after that. Then the buzzing of the electrical forces as they raced through the air at the target. The smell though, that was always his trigger, that slightly off scent of burning air that singed his nasal passages. Just as quickly as all that happened, the lightning bolt impacted the animal as it shrieked into the night. The cry was loud and inhuman, but cut short as it fell to the ground, illuminated by the lightning.

Just as suddenly, they were plunged into darkness again.

"Holy shit. I'm blind. You?" Deith's voice was tinged with worry.

"Yeah, I can't see as well. The creature's dead, though."

"Well, luckily, grizzlies are solitary animals."

Ossian jumped as Deith put his hand on his arm. "I thought you said you couldn't see."

"There are other senses, Mage Ossian. Jorn is on his way. The horses are clomping their way here now."

Ossian tried to hear anything, but his ears were still ringing from the lightning's booming thunder.

"I'm guessing that means no more hunt?" Ossian couldn't resist saying it, then he chuckled briefly to himself.

"Well, at least we don't need to cook it." Deith slapped him on the shoulder, as finally Ossian could hear the stampeding of hooves that sounded like they were off in the distance.

~

BY THE TIME that Jorn and a few of the others showed up on horseback, Ossian could just about make out their outlines. The night blindness he had gifted them with was still not completely worn off.

"What the hell was that?" Jorn said as he flipped off what Ossian assumed was the massive honey colored Shire horse, judging from its sheer volume.

"Wow, you got that nag moving?" Ossian said as his vision was clearing up. He could almost make out the scowl that Jorn was surely wearing.

"Mage Ossian went hunting—and cooking—at the same time." Deith said calmly.

When had Deith moved away from Ossian, he'd heard and seen nothing. Of course, right now that wasn't all that surprising, as he could barely make out the men and horses around him still.

Jorn strode over to the grizzly bear and looked it over. Glancing up at Deith, he nodded his head in approval.

"Can't do anything simple. Can you—," as an afterthought Jorn added, "Mage Ossian."

Ossian walked over to the grizzly and looked it over. Eight arrows, one in the side, seven in the front of it, all in its chest. "Deith, how did that thing keep coming?"

"Bear's ignore most injuries. We would have left, but it was already charging when I fired the first arrow." Deith tried to pluck an arrow out of the carcass, but the lightning bolt had charred it. "Besides, no one outruns a bear." He said it casually as an afterthought, like one comments on a well-cooked meal. The taste of over and under cooked meat filled his mouth at the same time.

Pulling a knife from his belt, Jorn started into skinning the animal. "Hopefully, some of this meat is salvageable. Deith, see what that smell is, please. The one that isn't a charred bear. You three go with him."

Ossian moved to go with the men when Jorn said, "Not you. You stay with me."

The four men moved off into the dark of the treeline.

As soon as they were out of earshot, Jorn started into Ossian. Telling him how lucky he was. Even in the dark, Ossian tried hard not to roll his eyes. He'd survived and saved Deith as well. Jorn pointed out that neither of them would have been in danger if they hadn't been hunting.

"Sometimes, we have to put the good of the group ahead of ourselves and our wishes."

"Come on Jorn. How many grizzly bears do you think live around here?"

Jorn stood up and raised his hand in a silencing motion. Ossian had never seen him do that before. "Do you see these eight arrows? Each one of them was a killing blow. Yet still this bear charged—" Looking sideways towards the treeline he continued, "several hundred meters, not to eat you. To kill you. You are here to protect these people, which I will admit you did tonight. But lightning bolts won't always save you."

Ossian stood still for the longest time as Jorn bent over to continue skinning the bear. When he finally heard the men returning from the treeline, he spoke up, "I know that, Jorn. I'll try to be better."

For the first time ever, Jorn looked up at Ossian and smiled. "That's all we can do. Now give me some damn light."

CHAPTER 17

When Deith and the men returned from the forest, they confirmed the bear had been consuming some dead deer. Killed several days ago, judging by the state of the animal. They judged the animal sick and the bear had probably been feeding on it for several days. How it hadn't hunted down Anton, the woodsman and his axe, was beyond anyone in the group.

They all agreed that they would need to be a bit more protective for a couple of weeks with people. Traveling in larger groups and lightly armed.

After the quick reconnoiter, it didn't take the men long to butcher the bear. The pelt was barely worth salvaging. Deith kept suggesting they should make a mangy cape out of it for Mage Ossian as a trophy. Ossian refused politely several times and then, not so politely, told them under no circumstances should the pelt full of holes and charred flesh be made into a cape.

They made it back to camp before breakfast even. The smell of half roasted bear beat them to the camp, judging from the crowd gathered around. Deith spent several minutes enthralling the crowd with the tale of Mage Ossian and the gigantic bear that attacked them. When Ossian tried to interrupt and explain what really happened, half the village shushed him. Deith really knew how to spin a yarn. Ossian would need to remember that.

As the group broke up into their daily tasks, Jorn made sure there were fewer groups with more people in them today. Deith convinced several of the ladies to salvage what remained of Ossian's great kill into a feast for tonight. Ossian tried mostly to stay out of the way and not be too embarrassed.

Soon, most of the people were out of the way and headed to their daily work tasks. As they were leaving, Ossian could hear them all talking about the feast tonight. He smiled at that. It might not have gone the way he would have liked it to, but the result couldn't be argued with.

Suddenly someone tapped him on the back, spinning around and placing his hand on the hilt of his sword. Ossian knew before he even laid eyes on the person, surprised that he was being overly jumpy.

Deith had a huge grin on his face. "Mage Ossian, jumpiness is understandable."

"Oh, hello Deith. You could have toned down the tale you told. People think I'm a hero."

"Well, to me and my family, you are Mage Ossian. We avoided death and tonight we celebrate. Have no illusions, tonight that tale will be you alone, attacked by a twenty-foot giant of a bear. I bet you barely escape with your life. The blue sword of—Does the sword have a name?"

"No, and it better not have one tonight."

"Well, anyway, to the task at hand. The kids are gonna wanna see some magic tonight. Mage flame is perhaps a bit too tame for them now. And I'm pretty sure a lightning bolt will get you killed by Jorn and me by the wife. So got anything in mind?"

"I can't just throw magic around—"

"Mage Ossian, it's your celebration—Oh, and we need a better name than the Village of the Night Forest." With his proclamations over, Deith turned around and dragging the pelt with him, disappeared off into camp.

"Magic and a name...GAH." Ossian said, with no one around to hear.

The women, over by a very long and thin fire, glanced over at Ossian as he threw up his hands. They had managed to spit parts of the carcass and were roasting it over the fire. Ossian was hoping that they could salvage his toasted beast.

Disappearing into his tent, Ossian spent the morning pouring over his grimoire's. Most of his magic was combat magic. That had been Mahler's specialty because of his time on the front lines. Ossian's own lightning magic was almost unparalleled, even at the Academy. He couldn't control it as well as most of the Master's, but the sheer destructive force he could employ was nearly as good as any of the Master's felt safe using on their own.

The magic that wasn't combat magic was stuff he was trying to develop to help farmers. His obsession had been how to help people like his parents. He'd learned how to magic plants to grow with fewer weeds and less water. Managing a couple of successes with bug repelling, but then the bees wouldn't approach, so that was pointless. He could repair most simple wooden things like hafts and handles.

He even managed to repair a steel plow once. Well, before it melted into slag.

He wasn't sure what would be interesting for the village to see. The village he was now supposed to name. Mahler had never mentioned how difficult it was, let alone should he even be doing some of these things? The naming of a place usually resulted from a person who lived there, or a deed that had been done. Ossian wasn't fully sure there was anyone of note that had lived here. So that left the Night Forest and the strange disappearances.

There was the surprisingly amazing farming land here—that was it, something to encourage everyone for their assigned task of being here. Blooming Meadows, hrm...he wasn't sure how blooming they would be. Plenty Fields, nope, that sounded stupid.

New Meadows. There it was, something to tie them to the old villages that disappeared, but also something that hinted at what might come to be. It felt weird to make decisions that would become fact. Still, Ossian considered the naming done.

That left him back to magic. Ossian guessed he really didn't have to listen to Deith. Maybe Deith had even been teasing him about that part. Deep down, Ossian knew that even if Deith had been teasing him, it felt right. He just had to be careful, too much, and people would freak out. Too little and they would be kind of disappointed.

"Argh, finding the balance is just so damn'd hard."

That's when it finally came to him. Last morning, the torches had all been stuck in the ground. He could shoot them into the air that way. If he timed a fire spell right, he should be able to make all the torches burn out before they reached the ground again. Cause if they didn't, he'd burn the village down.

Still stepping outside of his tent, he clapped his hands together and yelled, "Children, I have a task for you."

The children were more than willing to collect sticks for him, he set a couple of them to cutting them into roughly the right lengths. Several of the others he explained the concentric circles he needed. The sticks pounded into the ground in and set them about their task. The ladies cooking the beast gave him more than a single surreptitious glance, but they weren't frowning, so he was gonna call that a victory.

By the time that lunch rolled around, the kids had almost one hundred sticks all stuck into the ground in a pretty good approximation of a series of wheels. Mage Ossian also had his papers out and was designing the air and fire spell that would shoot the sticks into the air, light them on fire and have them incinerate themselves before reaching the ground again.

Initially, he had thought to do multiple colors of fire in the individual rings, but the more things he added, the more complicated the spell became. The more complicated the spell, the more he really needed to experiment with it safely.

The children wanted to know what his plan was and he refused to tell them. Alluding to a display that they would have to wait to see. He thanked them for their help and promised that tonight he would show them some magic. Most of them dashed off with their friends, chattering excitedly.

When he turned to continue the spell in his tent, Espeth was standing there.

"Dad says you saved him. Thank you." Then, throwing her arms around him, she squeezed with all her tiny might. As she broke away, he could see her wipe away a tear. Before he could speak though, she dashed off behind a wagon and disappeared.

Looking up, Ossian spied one of the cooks looking over at him. She smiled and shrugged and returned to rotating the feast over the fire.

Ossian retired to his tent and resumed his spell research. Espeth's hug had made him feel great, so he decided to try maybe two colors in the fire. As he was scribbling out the proper circle in one of his grimoires, there came a cough at his tent flap.

"Excuse me, Mage Ossian?"

The yeasty smell of baked goods filled his tent with the lightest hint of dried fruit in them. His mouth was watering even before he could form the words.

"Please come in." Ossian moved to stand and was half-way through standing when a woman bearing a tray of scones came through the tent flap. On the wooden tray was also a metal teapot with steam coming from the spout.

"Mage Ossian, I'm Cara. Deith's wife, we thought. Well—" she was fidgeting with the tray and Ossian could tell she was nervous.

"Please, won't you set that down?" Ossian waved a hand at his portable desk that stood between them.

Glancing down, she gently placed the tea service on the desk, then suddenly embarrassed, she turned to walk out of the tent.

"Oh, is that for me?" Ossian understood, but also didn't want to eat so much all by himself. There was enough for Deith and his whole family. The fruit would have been carried with them for a special day. He knew how quickly people could take offense at you not accepting their gifts.

"For bringing Deith back home to us. He told me you saved him." Her eyes stayed cast down on the floor.

"Well, I put him in the danger to begin with. Do you think I should have asked him to hunt?" Ossian knew Jorn was certain of himself. Yet, Ossian also knew that bringing people together involved more than just hard work and more hard work.

"It's not my place to say, Mage Ossian."

"There is nothing you can say to me Cara that can cause punishment."

With that, Cara looked up at Ossian. Ossian saw the depths of fire in those eyes, fire that burned a mark into him. "You placed my husband in danger for a feast? A festival? I'll never forgive you." Just as quickly, the fire was gone and Cara continued. "However, my husband assures me the woodsman hadn't seen or heard the bear any in the last week. So maybe it wasn't your fault."

The sudden outburst and just as sudden contrition took Ossian aback.

"I apologize for placing your husband in danger. That was never my intention."

"Your intentions mean nothing if I have to raise those kids alone in this gods-forsaken land. Still, Deith asked me to bake you these as a thank you. So there you are." With that, she turned in a huff and stalked out of the tent.

Ossian had to admit the scones were amazing. Too bad he was on the wrong side of Cara now. He imagined getting scones baked from her ever again was unlikely to happen. The tea was a simple tincture of beebalm. Compared to the scones, the tea was barely flavored water. Ossian imagined it was gonna be hard to get proper tea out here. He had a brick of it from the castle, but he hadn't even broken it out yet as he'd been too busy to relax.

The initial conversation with Cara had shaken him, proving yet again he knew next to nothing about dealing with people on a personal level. As he ate the scones and sipped the tincture, though, his mind focused back on his spell. He added a third color to the wheel. Scribbling in his notes furiously, he hadn't much time before the villagers out in the fields made their way back from their various jobs today.

The wafting scent of the roasted beast brought him back to earlier that morning. It already felt like it was weeks ago. Back to when he wasn't sure they would make it home safely. After several minutes, he shuddered, then wiped the drool off his face. It also smelled far better than this morning.

After putting the final touches on his spell, he snapped the grimoire shut and clutching the wooden tray he exited his tent. Men, women and children were running around the camp every which way. There were several tables strung together and clay pots and plates filled the tables with all manner of cloth covered dishes.

Ossian briefly felt guilty that the children had placed the sticks in the middle of camp as everyone was avoiding going inside the wheel he had with the sticks. He looked out for Cara and finally saw her near their wagon. Walking through the middle of the sticks, he weaved in and out, trying not to disturb the sticks as he returned the wooden tray and set it on the back of the wagon next to Cara.

"Cara, that was lovely. Thank you so much." Ossian bowed his head at Cara, not wanting to be yelled at again.

"Of course, Mage Ossian. I'm glad you liked it." Cara looked out over the field of sticks. "So what exactly is with the sticks?"

"Well, I think I have an idea for a display of magic."

Cara looked him over with skeptical eyes. "We are always told magic has a price."

"Well, if the spell fails, the village will burn down."

Cara gasped at this and the fire came back to her eyes as she looked ready to slap Ossian.

"Sorry, sorry, that was a poor joke. I have a hard time with people-ing."

"Indeed, you do. Perhaps you should see about your feast." Cara's clipped tone doubled down when she turned her back to him and started cleaning the things on the wooden tray. Ossian was impressed with how quickly he'd been dismissed with just her body language.

Ossian walked away, certain yet again that he should just keep his mouth shut around everyone.

CHAPTER 18

The afternoon seemed to drag on, with Ossian looking here and there. He tried frequently to step in and help someone with something, only to be dismissed. His only saving grace was that he wasn't dismissed as rudely as Cara. Yet still, he realized his last decade of learning magic hadn't prepared him for the real world. None of these people needed his help in performing their daily chores and tasks.

Looking out past the horizon, he could just make out the line of trees of the Night Forest. His mission was to explore them. Deep down though, his goal was to protect this village from whatever happened to the other villages.

Lost in thought about his mission, he finally looked down to see one of the young children standing at his feet, looking up at him.

"Hello Boa, what can I do for you?" Ossian found it easiest to talk with the little ones. They held no judgement and you could usually speak pretty plainly to them. Although as he thought of that, he looked around and observed that at least three of the wives were staring daggers at him and he was pretty sure a couple of others were glancing at him without directly looking at him.

"What are you doing?"

"I was contemplating the Night Forest."

The child turned to face the forest and appeared to be mimicking Ossian. Staring off into the distance. Ossian had to admit the kid had the mimicry part down pretty well. All he needed was clothes like Ossian and he'd be a spitting image.

"Are we going to die?"

The question was so sudden it took Ossian by surprise. The child didn't look up at Ossian, and said it so matter-of-factly that he was certain the child was much older than even Mage Mahler himself.

"Well, that's what I'm here to prevent." Ossian wasn't so sure, though. Technically, he was here to investigate the Night Forest. He was confident the King wouldn't care about the village or him, as long as the intel returned was useful.

Suddenly, Piaa and Espeth appeared, shouting over at Boa about a snake they found. Boa took off like a streak, his concerns with this mortal coil forgotten in the carefree way that children can be oblivious to the surrounding dangers.

"You'll have to forgive Boa, Mage Ossian."

Ossian jumped at the sound of someone next to him. He really needed to work on his skills of staying present and in the moment.

Wiping her hands on a section of her apron, Cara was standing next to Ossian. "He says things that pop into his head."

"I think the children lack the filter we have for what is proper to talk about. I find it easier to deal with."

Cara stared at the ground for quite a while. "I'm sorry for my outburst earlier. I was upset, but it isn't my place to tell you off, either."

Ossian could feel how much it took for Cara to apologize to him. Her body language spoke volumes of the self control she was holding in, trying so very hard to act as the adult in the situation. "I prefer what you said. As you've seen, I have a hard time with real people. Probably from the last decade spent with books. You have nothing to be sorry for. I would appreciate it if you would always tell me what you really thought."

Cara looked at him like she didn't really believe him.

Ossian added, "Then maybe I can at least understand one of the adults."

Cara smiled at that. "Well, you might have picked the wrong person to tell that to."

Ossian wasn't fully sure what to say to that and was rescued by Deith returning from the fields.

"Heavens above, that smells good." Deith grabbed Cara around the waist and kissed her.

Ossian flushed red at the open display of affection. The Academy frowned on open displays of affection, even though behind the scenes the apprentices did plenty of it.

As Cara broke from the kiss she added, "Mage Ossian here was trying to convince me to leave you for him."

Ossian sputtered, "—I most certainly—"

"Well, I guess he should have let the grizzly have me then." Deith was smiling the whole time. He finally punched Ossian gently on the arm. "Come on Mage Ossian, you're redder than a beet. Maybe I need to watch my wife around you, eh?"

Standing there just staring at the two, Ossian had no words for the what was happening, was this some kind of cruel joke? The noble sons loved to play jokes on the low-born at the Academy and while it wasn't exactly sanctioned, there wasn't a lot a low-born could do. If you struck a noble son, there were punishments. So you either had to learn to be above it all, or retaliate in subtle ways. Ossian had oscillated between the two. He admitted that on more than one occasion he had stooped to swapping a noble son's ingredients or changing out their inks.

Cara made to leave. "Be nice to Mage Ossian, Deith. He saved your life."

"Oh, right, the feast? That still smells amazing," Cara had walked off to attend to the table of food, as Deith yelled after her. "When are we eating?"

Cara didn't turn around, ignoring his question completely.

"They'll tease us with the scents of food, till we revolt. Then they'll finally let us eat," Deith grumbled as he stood next to Ossian.

"I have no intentions towards your wife."

Slapping Ossian in the shoulder, Deith continued, "Come off it man, Cara was teasing. She only teases people she doesn't hate. Which is surprising. This morning, I thought she might have poisoned you with the scones."

"Oh, she had a few proper words with me. Admittedly, nothing I didn't deserve."

"Yep, that sounds like her. So are mages not allowed to marry?"

Yet again, Ossian wasn't prepared for the question as it spilled out of Deith. Maybe that's where Boa got it from. He stood there for a bit, reeling from so many questions that jerked him in different directions. "No, it's more." Ossian tried to recall the way the Mage Mahler put it. "Magic is all-encompassing, and a fickle mistress. It doesn't share well with others."

"So, just a life of drudgery and frustration?" Deith placed his arm around Ossian's shoulder and slowly turned him to face the middle of the camp.

"You are awfully talkative today." In the limited time that Ossian had known him, this was already more words than they'd spoken together and all of them in such a short period.

"Got the necessary fields plowed and sown. Worst case, we can struggle through winter, on a meager diet of gruel."

"Wait, did no one tell you about my specialty?"

"Does it have to do with this here ring of sticks in the middle of camp everyone is afraid of?"

"No, that's for tonight's celebration, but it'll need to be dark first."

"A man of mystery, interesting. So this specialty?"

"Farming."

"Well, that is convenient. When are you gonna pitch in? We could use all the help before the spring rains come."

"Magic Deith, I've been researching farming magic."

Deith had that same look Cara had earlier, like he didn't quite believe Ossian. So Ossian continued to explain how he could magic plants to grow with less water and in poorer soil, not that this place needed the less soil part. He was pretty sure he could keep out larger animals, but the insect spell hadn't worked. He thought maybe he could extend the growing season by a couple of days, but that would be the hardest.

"So this is all one giant magical experiment?"

"Well, no. It's my personal field of research. My parents were farmers. I was hoping I could make it easier on people like them."

Dieth's smile hid something. "Anytime it's made easier on the lower folk, they find something else to keep us down." With that, Dieth patted Ossian on the back one last time, "still, keep up the good fight." As he wandered off into the camp.

CHAPTER 19

A large slab of roast meat was brought to the end of one of the tables. While almost everyone from the village milled around the tables and watched the children run around screaming and playing. Ossian was just about to ask someone where Jorn was when he rode in on his horse, quickly dismounted and bee lined it to Ossian.

Ossian put all his mental defenses up as Jorn sped towards him. His rigid mannerisms and speed told Ossian something was wrong.

Jorn finally sidled right up into Ossian's personal space and whispered in his ear. "We found the bear's cave. Nothing was amiss."

Then Jorn turned around, laughing loudly. He slapped Ossian on the back. "You look like I was going to kill you."

"It crossed my mind. Is this confuse the mage day and I missed it?" Ossian could believe the sudden attitude turn in Cara and Deith, but Jorn. Jorn had been a rock in Ossian's life for the last decade. Never cruel and viscous, well not too cruel or viscous and usually only to people who deserved it. Ossian knew he'd deserved several of the beatings Jorn had given him.

"What are we waiting for, let's eat." Yelling it out loud, then Jorn glanced over at the sticks in the ground. "Do I want to know?"

"Needs to be dark first."

A plate was thrust into Ossian's hand with a slab of the roast beast.

As Deith stepped away, he said far too loudly. "For the Mage who saved my life this morning."

Ossian stared down at the beast, the scent bringing back the charging beast from the morning. The thawp of the arrows as Deith sent them. The burst of light and the ozone as the lightning streaked from Ossian's scarred hands.

Jorn shook him gently and mumbled under his breath, "Say something, man."

Ossian hadn't thought to prepare a speech. Come up with a name, design a new spell, make up a speech. When would the demands end? Then it crossed his mind. They wouldn't. He was responsible for all these people.

"I've been thinking a lot today about all the hard work you've done. And I'm tired of calling this place the Village of the Night Forest." Ossian saw most of them flinch at the name, and several of them crossed themselves to ward off evil.

"So I propose we rename the village." At that, most of the villages changed from hesitation at his words to interest and curiosity.

"I think we should call it New Meadows." He saw several of the heads nod assent, and no one seemed in disagreement with him. "Then I shall inform the king of his new village's name, on my next missive."

"When it gets dark, I have a demonstration for the children, as so many of them want to see magic. Meanwhile, please eat and let's celebrate what we've built so far."

Everyone swamped the tables at that. There was an order to it, a dance of people, arms, plates and utensils. The children rushed in like a pack of wild dogs and were brought to bear by several of the fathers and mothers to watch their manners, or they would be given to Jorn for guard duty. Ossian couldn't stop laughing at the face Jorn made at that. He also saw that at least two of the older boys thought maybe that wouldn't be a punishment as much as a fun training.

From the far end of the table Yough shouted down, "Mage Ossian, to your credit, you hunted a bear. But I must say, the cooking you should leave to the experts."

Several of the other men and women added in their hear-hear's to that. As Jorn rolled a barrel out of a wagon, cracked the top of it, and started to disperse beer to everyone. Ossian noted that Jorn himself didn't partake of any.

Several long hours of food and drink and fire and talk. By the time it was dark enough, Ossian was growing tired and grateful that he'd charged up the sword for his spell casting. He knew already he would sleep like the dead and he hadn't even cast the spell yet. About every ten minutes, the children would convince one of their own to run up and ask Ossian if it was time for the magic. Each time, Ossian would casually mention, "Not yet."

Finally, he stood up and moved towards the center of the circle. "Good people of New Meadows. Are...you...ready?"

The children stood stock still, all gathered in a group. Looks of vague apprehension were scattered across their faces. Ossian didn't want magic to be so foreign to them. He wanted them to respect the magic, that was necessary, but he also wanted magic to be more mundane than it currently was. The noble sons spoke like magic was everywhere in their houses. It enraged Ossian to hear of something that made their lives so easy, wasn't shared with more people.

Shaking his head, he needed to concentrate. Ossian moved into the center of the circle and brought his hand down low. Strictly speaking, he didn't need such large and sweeping gestures he was about to use. Yet, he felt for the kids he might want to make it something more.

As he focused into his inner mind, he concentrated on the spell circle with his mind. This wasn't the most complicated spell he'd tried, but it had a lot of components and he'd never practiced the spell before. He saw the air component and the fire; blue, red and yellow. He started the pressure of his mind, filling the runes of the circle as the sticks wiggled. He needed to finish the air component before any of the sticks fell over.

Pressing the runes to finish faster in his mind, he shoved both hands into the air high above his head as the sticks shot out of the ground into the air. Little puffs of dust were the only things left to show the sticks had been there. He heard several people gasp at that. Good, hopefully this next part would be even more impressive.

The three fire circles were tightly woven like a braid. Ossian snatched his sword and pulled it from its scabbard, shoving it high above his head, pointing it towards the middle stick. The braid inside his mind was lit on fire as the runes flowed through his hand into the sword and were driven upward into the sky towards the sticks.

The middle stick ignited into a red flame so quickly that it burst into a shower of small, ashen cinders. Something he hadn't expected, but it gave off an interesting effect. The next ring of sticks lit up blue and also exploded into a shower, followed by the third ring of yellow.

The grin on Ossian's face was probably larger than the rest of the village together. He was quite pleased with himself at that display of magic. He'd have to make a point of sending a message back to Mage Mahler about that one.

Suddenly, something was tugging at his mind. A vacuum was pulling on him when everything went black. There was nothing around him, just a black void. Ossian was getting worried when, just as suddenly, he was back in the circle. The yellow sticks were still just on the edge of burning out as Ossian spun around in a circle.

He was still in the village. Maybe he'd add a bit about the sword sending him to a black void to Mage Mahler's message.

Sheathing his sword, the village children ran around clapping and saying do it again. The adults were more subdued and clapped, with whispers spreading through the adults, much like the fire Ossian had just set loose.

Jorn, on the other hand, was walking away from the feast

towards Ossian's tent. As he got to the tent, Ossian saw the real problem, one of the sparks was embedded in the top of his tent. Jorn looked over at Ossian as he emptied a mug of beer on the spark. Smiling the entire time as he poured the spark out.

THE NEXT MORNING came all too early for Ossian. His bedding, soaked in beer, had been left hanging outside his tent. He'd need to wash it tomorrow. Jorn couldn't stop being happy that Ossian had nearly burnt his own tent down. Jorn had also added that the magic was indeed very pretty.

Sleeping on a cot with a random assortment of clothes usually wouldn't allow Ossian to sleep much, but the spell had yet again taken more out of him than he'd expected. He'd slept like the dead, after also consuming maybe a bit too much beer.

Jorn coughed from the tent flap. "We'll be leaving shortly, Mage sleepy head."

As Ossian rolled out of bed, his head came pounding into place, "I don't think I should have drank so much, Jorn."

Jorn shot an eyebrow up at him, "You had like two beers."

"Oh. I'm gonna need to use the sword more, I guess. It takes a lot out of you. I need an hour to prepare a message back to Mage Mahler, if you can wait."

"An hour." With that, Jorn left.

Ossian got up and cracked open his chest. He'd need some ingredients. Practicing the individual message spell wasn't tricky, but the modifications to his message needed to be exact.

He found it odd to be talking to a pile of melted wax while holding the spell circle in his mind. Finally, with the message completed, he poured the wax onto the brass plate. As the wax cooled, it formed into a thin round disc, with the symbol of a plow sowing a field in a book. Mage Mahler had explained that the symbol was specific to the plate.

He also said he thought the artist had taken certain liberties with the description that Mage Mahler had given him.

Ossian's head pounded. The sword's use with the fire spell had taken more out of him than he thought. The message spell was pushing him into the feelings of casting sickness. He'd need to be careful for the next couple of days.

Picking up the cooled wax symbol, he headed out of the tent to find Jorn and the two guards waiting for him. He handed the wax seal over to Jorn, who placed it in the leather pouch on his belt.

"Good travels Jorn. Stay safe and we'll see you again someday."

"Wow, eloquent. Where'd you read that from?"

Ossian smiled, "Some story in the library. It sounded appropriate."

Ossian then extended his hand and clasped Jorn's. He would miss Jorn, but it was time New Meadows got along without Jorn guarding them. Ossian wondered if the village would listen to him, or if he'd have to convince them he was worth listening to.

Jorn and his men mounted up and headed off back whence they came.

CHAPTER 20

The mid-day sunlight shone through the oil canvas of the tent as Ossian sat on his bed. The tent was humid from where the beer had pooled under Ossian's cot and the patch Ossian had made yesterday was, at best, amateurish.

Once he saw Jorn off, he wandered the village aimlessly when Cara finally spotted him.

"Mage Ossian, you look restless."

"Well, yeah, I'm actively avoiding magic today. I think the sword took too much out of me the other night. So yeah, I guess I'm just wandering."

Handing over a bundle of oilcloth, Cara continued, "Excellent, take this out to the south field. It's Deith, Boa and your lunch."

"Why is Boa out in the fields today?"

The look that crossed Cara's face told Ossian to stay out of it.

"Nevermind, deliver lunch, check."

Cara smiled weakly and waved him away.

Ossian took his time wandering out to the south fields. He passed three different groups of farmers, plowing, sowing or weeding.

He finally found the honey colored Shire horse out in one of the furthest fields. Waving at Deith, he didn't want to walk over the newly plowed field. Deith stopped, unhooked Honey and walked over.

"You don't hobble her?"

"She's never wandered more than maybe twenty feet, and never over an already plowed section."

Ossian could see Boa off in the distance, hauling rocks out of the field ahead of Deith. Ossian shouted over to Boa, "LUNCH."

Ossian then sat on the ground and placed the packaging down, waiting for Boa to join them. Deith apparently was not in a talking mood and merely sat down, gazing off towards the Night Forest.

As Boa took his time walking up, Ossian grew bored and drew in the dirt with his fingers. He let his mind wander as his fingers sketched out the spell for mage flame.

Boa finally reached them, inspecting the symbols in the dirt he ask Ossian, "What does it say?"

Ossian came out of his stupor and looked over. "Oh, it's the spell for mage flame, the blue heatless torches."

"So it doesn't say anything?"

"No, the symbols are representative, but it's not a language. They are conduits of power. They shape and guide the power into specific paths, then out of the circle with a specific purpose."

"Why aren't we taught to read?" Boa was apparently very melancholy today.

"Boa, Mage Ossian has better things to do than to teach you how to read," Deith snapped. Ossian hadn't seen Deith snap before. It put Ossian on edge.

"Actually, if it's okay with your parents, swing by my tent tonight. I can teach you to read. I can't teach you magic, but I can teach you to read and write."

Boa's face brightened at that. "Dad, dad, can I do that? Please."

Ossian realized what he'd just started and thought maybe he should have asked in private first.

"That's Mage Ossian's problem, you ask your mom. Now, if you don't help with this field, there will be no reading."

Snagging a hunk of cheese and a roll, Boa grabbed at the reins of Honey and dragged it over to the plow. The horse casually walked over with a nine and one-half year old leading her. Ossian liked that horse. It was one of the calmest animals he knew. Maybe being that big lent oneself to knowing other things couldn't hurt you.

Deith looked at Ossian. "Do you know what you're getting into? Do you know how to teach twenty kids?"

Ossian shrugged, "How hard can it be? I can kill bears with a spell. Kids can't be that hard."

A sudden bark of laughter came from Deith, but it did not give Ossian any confidence. "You, my friend, have no idea what you are in for."

CHAPTER 21

Word of reading lessons spread before the darkness came with dusk. The children ran around whispering. Several of the adults came over to speak with Ossian, each of them checking to make sure it was okay with the mage if their children could join. Ossian assured each of them he had indeed told the children he would teach them to read and write. LeAnne insisted that the lessons not interfere with their work.

Ossian didn't think to ask how many of them could read or write, till he was lying in his cot that night. He was recalling his first lessons with Mage Mahler. He had a chalkboard.

Ossian was trying to think of all the supplies he would need to teach the kids. They could scratch in the dirt with sticks for a while, that would save paper. He knew how to make charcoal sticks. They could write on most things with that. Parchment was in short supply though, and teaching them with quill and ink was going to be an issue.

He'd see if Mage Mahler would send down a supply of chalkboards and chalk. Paper was very expensive, ink on the other hand,

Ossian could make from several things. It wasn't like any of the pages they were making needed to be long lasting.

Then there was the problem of when to teach them. Most of the non-adults worked the fields or harvesting trees. Ivy had taken up pottery with Bakker. Ossian would need to wait till after supper to teach them, but with only a few hours before dusk, it was going to be brief lessons.

As he was just falling asleep, it occurred to him he didn't have to teach them all at once. He could show the youngest during the day. Following up with the older at night. Smiling, he rolled over and fell blissfully to sleep.

The next day started out pretty easily. He showed the children the sticks he'd collected and the dirt area he had them sweep out. Then walking them through the first five characters, asking them to draw them in the dirt and commenting on them, showing each child how to adjust holding the stick. The sticks were harder than Ossian thought. They were nothing like holding a quill or a piece of chalk. Before the next lesson, he would talk with Bakker about making some charcoal to use.

When the older kids showed up, Ossian explained about the charcoal. Kay suggested they do it by the stream, as they could use the water to wash off the charcoal to reuse the surface. Initially, Ossian thought this was a good idea, when Kamien pointed out what that would do to the stream. Pointing out both boys' good ideas, Ossian added buckets of water and large flat rocks to the list. Luckily, he was a mage and finding rocks was the harder part. Moving them would be a snap once he could cast again.

As Ossian was explaining the day's lessons to Yough and LeAnne over dinner, Yough pointed out the fields of large rocks on the road into town. They thought they were at least a mile away, but Ossian didn't think that a horrible distance. He'd just need to be careful with the spells he used.

They continued drawing in the dirt for an extra day, till Ossian felt confident the worry of casting sickness was absent. When he told

Deith and Yough his plan for getting the rocks, Deith merely shrugged and said good luck. Then he was promptly smacked upside the head by Cara.

Ossian was saddled with Piaa and Boa. It was Cara's suggestion, not subtly said to Deith in front of the group. Those two, of course, begged that Espeth could join them.

It was explained in no uncertain terms that they were not to be in the way, by their parents. After Ossian and his bodyguards assured Cara, LeAnne and Alisha, they would be careful and Ossian promised he would keep them safe. They headed off to find some large rocks they could practice writing on.

The road out of town was prairie fields that lead up towards the low-lying hills that surrounded the village on the way deeper into the Kingdom. The three children ran around Ossian like a flock of birds, scattering this way and that. Exploring the ground, the grasses and the random bushes that popped up. Then they would scream at something and they would all scatter and flock back to Ossian, just to disappear again in a couple of moments when they their curiosity won out.

After about an hour, they came across a grouping of rocks that were the size of the children, not massive, but probably big enough to write on if they could find a flat surface. None of the sides facing them looked likely, but Ossian could turn the rocks over as well. Shooing the children back, he told them they needed to stay back as he prepped his mind to turn over the first rock.

The earth spells were always the hardest for him. Several of the mages at the Academy tried to explain the relationship of magic affinities to Ossian and how, since air spells were easy for him, earth spells would always be hard for him. He assumed they were right. Still, it did nothing to help him with the earth spells. Frequently, he even used air spells to do things that would be easier with an earth spell, merely cause air was that much easier for him to cast.

The forms of the earth spell circle formed in his mind slowly, the rock and the earth, the turning of the rock and the stopping of the turning. It was a pretty simple spell, still it took several minutes to form it in his head.

He reached out to touch the rock. The air spells didn't require a touch component to them. The earth spells, though, they preferred direct contact for the optimal or at least a less taxing casting.

The spell circle formed. Ossian forced the power into the circle. It flowed like molasses as he tried not to push the power too fast. He wanted the rock to turn over, not to continue rolling over to the next hill. Slowly yet surely, the rock rolled over, revealing a pock-marked rock-like face on the bottom as well.

Ossian ceased powering the spell and could feel the perspiration beading underneath his shirt. That had taken quite a bit more than he'd expected out of him.

Turning toward the next rock, he repeated the cycle again. The churning dirt reminded him of the freshly plowed fields he'd so recently been in. Underneath the turning rock was a whole other world, worms and pill bugs, many legged long things, bits of mud and bark and lots of tiny tunnels in the mud. Yet this rock too revealed a pocky, unsuitable rock-like face.

Ossian's mind wandered to the chances of finding a smooth rock face. Maybe the type of the rock mattered. He knew there were smooth hexagonal rocks on the other side of the kingdom where he was from. Juts of columns of smooth rock that sprang from the dirt fields, some they labored over removing, most they merely plowed around. Those would have been perfect.

Walking over to another rock, he made to turn it over. It also revealed a non-suitable rock like texture on all sides.

Ceasing the casting, Ossian sat down on a nearby rock. He was already breathing heavily and the children were looking at him like they should all run to the village now.

Ossian plastered a smile onto his face and tried to reassure the children, "I'm fine."

"You don't look fine." Piaa said, always the blunt one.

"Yeah, he's all sweaty." Espeth added.

"Should I run back to the village?" Boa was already on the balls of his feet, bouncing back and forth, like he wanted to sprint to the safety of the village. He was always antsy, the most impulsive of the three.

"Not yet. I just need to take a rest." Ossian looked up at the sky. It wasn't even mid-day yet. He'd turned over just three rocks. Even with them being earth spells, that was not a good sign. But he probably just needed more practice. Even at the Academy, the mages warned him of neglecting his earth spell practice.

Which he did frequently.

After a long silence, Piaa finally asked, "None of these rocks will work?"

Boa reminded her, "He wants flat ones to write on."

"Right," Espeth was looking around, "We could search for rocks in the area, while Mage Ossian, uh..."

Piaa smiled and added, "Thinks."

Boa chimed in quickly, "Yeah. Takes the time to think. Go."

The three of them each ran off in different directions, running around in zig-zag patterns. Ossian wasn't sure there was any organization to it at all, but they were buying him time to rest. He pulled an apple from his pack and munched on it. Espeth was the furthest away when Ossian finished the apple and looked at the core. Deciding he was more hungry then normal, he ate the apple core as well.

Espeth was jumping up and down towards the north, shouting. From here, Ossian couldn't make out what she was saying. So he pushed off the rock and walked over to Espeth. The other children, through some mind-link they all shared, zoomed towards her like lightning strikes.

Boa, tripping on something, fell. Jumping up as fast as he fell, he shouted, "I'm good!" But remained looking at the ground before bending over to pick something up. Then continued his full headlong sprint towards Espeth.

As Ossian walked closer, he saw what Espeth had found and his blood ran cold. On the ground was a rock the size of his fist. The shiny black rock stood out starkly against the dry brown dirt. Sticking out of the rock were six legs that jutted straight out, each leg was made of a smooth, dark wood Ossian did not recognize. Each leg was in two sections, with a black metal link between the sections.

Ossian was reminded of a spider, its leg splayed out as if dead.

"What is it?" Espeth asked. "I didn't want to touch it. It's creepy."

Ossian had to agree with Espeth. As he looked at the body of the creature, the color was strange. The black looked unnatural, like it was absorbing the surrounding light. Giving it a slight halo of distortion.

Ossian picked up a nearby twig and poked it at the creature, "I don't know what it is, but it's solid." The rock-like body had no give. This was no organic creature.

Boa finally reached them and showed everyone the coyote skull he found. "Can I keep it, Mage Ossian?"

Distracted, Ossian had to smile. "You gonna hide it from your mom?"

Boa grew silent at that, as Ossian knew he would. Cara would never let him keep a coyote skull in her house. Something young in Ossian understood though, the skull was interesting and captivated some younger piece of him as well. "Maybe we can try to convince her."

Ossian backed away from the rock-like spider, trying to think about what to do with it. Espeth's observation was sound. It was creepy. It set off every nerve in his body. He wasn't fully sure what to do with it.

"Can we touch it?" Piaa finally asked.

"I don't think we should."

Boa glanced away from his skull and noticed the rock-like spider for the first time. "Oh, what is that?" Then before Ossian could stop him, Boa kicked it with his barefoot.

The rock with its spindle legs sailed four feet in the air, spinning loosely, until it reached the apex of its flight, then the legs snapped alive, preparing the creature to land on its legs.

Everything Jorn had drilled into him kicked into high gear. Ossian's hand went to his sword and drew it with his right hand, as an air circle formed in his mind, sweeping the children twenty feet away with a sweeping motion of his left hand.

"Run, NOW."

As the spider touched the ground, its legs bent and the middle black section dipped slightly, like a cat preparing to pounce. When it sprang upright and lept straight back at Ossian, now the only target close enough to jump at.

Ossian's sword swung down of its own will, the years of training with Jorn making it a muscle memory instead of a conscious action. As the cold metal touched the spider, Ossian could feel the surge of magical power from the sword explode into the spider. The spider creature detonated, sending shards of rock everywhere.

A second spell circle had formed in Ossian's mind as his hand swept down, a torrent of wind sending the three shards traveling towards him into the ground in front of him instead of into his body.

Ossian stood there, stunned. It had all happened so fast. The kick, the creature coming alive, the children—

Ossian looked around to see where the children were, but like he'd told them to, they were already halfway to the village. He smiled to see that Boa had dropped the skull before running away, probably when he'd swept them out of the conflict zone.

The sword still hummed with the magic that had so recently left it, the energy stored inside it was gone. The sword, like Ossian, was still hyped-up, ready for a longer engagement with the enemy. The enemy lay in pieces scattered around the field, though.

CHAPTER 22

Standing in the field, Ossian watched the wind blow around the prairie grasses. The grasses were still growing and green in the early stages of spring. Everywhere you could see the browns of last year's grasses lying on the ground, ready to be recycled. The black shards of the rock creature stood out starkly against the still dry dirt. The rains of late spring hadn't come yet.

With the rains, the grasses would grow tall and upright, coating the prairie in a knee-high blanket of grasses. Making the rocks and dirt impossible to find.

Heck, even two or three more weeks and Ossian thought it unlikely they would have found the rock-creature. He worried there were more, but he couldn't easily search the entire prairie for them. No one was going to like his suggestion that the entire village help him search the area.

He shuddered at the thought of what would happen to a villager if they accidentally tripped over it one summer day. The rock creature had come to life. Then it had lept at them. He didn't actually know its intentions were bad, maybe it just wanted to—No, Ossian knew from the moment it had activated, that it was unnatural and harbored ill will.

It had activated when Boa had touched it. Was it a warning?

Ossian used his air spells to gather the shards of the creature and put them all in roughly the same area. He still gripped his sword and wondered if he should take the time to recharge it when he heard the clump, clump, clump of a horse. Still staring at the rocks, he listened as the horse got closer. Off in the distance, he could hear the villagers continue to shout at him.

Somewhere nearby, a horse stopped and someone slid off it.

"Mage Ossian, are you okay?" It was Cara.

Ossian finally looked away from the rock-creature and saw that she had a sword in hand and had beaten most of the rest of the village out to him. A dozen men and women were running towards them. Some strange inner feeling made Ossian happy that so many people seemed to care enough about his well being.

"Yes, I'm okay. The creature is dead. I think it was a creature." Ossian wasn't really sure what to call it.

"We came as fast as we could. The kids say a spider attacked you?"

"It's okay Cara, let's wait for more people. I need the entire village. We need to look for more."

Cara nodded, mounted the horse and spun around, heading into the village. She shouted as she passed the ones running, and they slowed to a walk.

It was mid-day before the village was assembled. The wait had been like sitting in a classroom, waiting for an absent minded mage to remember he had students to teach, while the entire classroom dared each other to go tell him.

At some point, while waiting, he'd finally bent down and touched the shards of the creature. The rock shards were colder than he thought they should be, but they also didn't reform into an attack spider. He wasn't sure what he expected, he just had to be sure they were safe before he gathered them up and placed them in his pouch.

"We need to search the area." Ossian started straight into it. They were losing daylight and he would prefer this done today if he could. He'd sent several of the older children off to collect the sticks from the collection he used for spell practice, one for everyone.

"Is that wise?" Bakker asked.

"It did not activate until it was touched. Everyone come close and look, please. This is the black rock we are searching for." Ossian wasn't about to tell the village Boa had kicked it. He was sure they would know by the end of the day. Then again, the trio might be tightlipped enough to keep it to themselves.

As the older children arrived with the sticks, Ossian didn't need to explain about fanning out. "Do not touch it under any circumstances. If you think you see something, I need you to call me. Even if you're not sure, call me. These creatures are dangerous, but only if you touch them with skin." Ossian hoped this was true.

The village spread out. Ossian asked them all to mark behind them with a line. It wouldn't last more than a few days at most, but it gave them somewhere to start again if they needed to. Then they walked the distance back to the village, with everyone searching the ground for the stark black rock of the creature.

The first person who shouted, "Mage Ossian." Caused Ossian's blood to spike as he ran towards Cath. The rock that was visible was black-ish, but dull. Not the bright glossy shine of the creature. "Good job, Cath. Please Continue."

Cath looked ashamed at having called him over. "Cath, please, these creatures are dangerous. Don't for a minute feel bad about calling me over."

"Sorry, Mage Ossian."

Ossian could feel the situation slipping out of his hands. Cath wouldn't call him again to see a rock as easily, and he wasn't sure what to do about it. As he was trying to figure it out, another shout went out and Ossian ran off to see another dull rock that was roughly fist sized in shape.

Ossian ran from shout to shout for the better part of the day as they closed in on the village. As the village got closer and closer, Ossian wouldn't admit to himself that he was getting happier. Not finding another of those creatures meant maybe it was a fluke. Then the idea that they weren't searching a big enough area came unbidden into his head and his shoulders slumped. Would the village listen to him if he asked them to search another area tomorrow?

Finally, they were close enough to the village for Ossian to admit they would find nothing. "Thank you everyone. I'm happy we didn't find another of these. Please, if anyone spots one, I need you to find me before touching the creature."

Murmurs of assent mumbled from the village as they disappeared into their houses. Another fruitless day spent helping Mage Ossian.

"We should talk." Deith was a foot away from Ossian. Ossian was at least happy he didn't jump from the sudden appearance.

"Tonight, after first watch."

Deith walked away without saying another word. Ossian wondered if Deith thought he was crazy for what he'd done, but he didn't care. He'd known what had happened, he'd seen it. Now he needed to recharge his sword. The wind that blew through the village did not comfort him as he stood staring out towards where they had been searching for rocks. It sent a chill through his bones.

Something was coming.

CHAPTER 23

The tent's closed flap felt oppressive tonight. The blue flickering of the mage flame, normally a comfort to Ossian, provided him with nothing but an increase in his trepidation. He'd swept the floor and had shaken the shards of the creature onto it. The shiny black rocks stood out starkly against the dirt floor. It was probably his imagination, but Ossian thought the rocks were leaking malevolence.

Collecting up the rocks, he tried to place them together like a puzzle, trying to reform roughly the shape of the creature. As he placed the last piece, the tent flapped ripped open and Ossian surged out of his crouch, drew his sword and was soaking in sweat before he knew what had happened.

"So, Boa was telling the truth." Deith's words did nothing to soothe Ossian's heart hammering in his head.

Ossian didn't reply.

He was trying to calm down his entire body from the sudden surge of fight mode. Jorn had described it to him many times, yet this was the first time Ossian had ever truly felt it. He did not like it.

Staring at the creature, Deith finally asked, "Any ideas?"

Ossian was still panting. As the sweat was drying, the tent was getting uncomfortably cold. "None. I know objects can be imbued with magic. This one, though, it attacked."

"Boa said he kicked it. Do I need to worry?"

"It activated after he touched it with his skin, but it took a bit."

Ossian then walked through the entire situation from finding it, kicking it and battling it to when Cara showed up.

"Thank you."

Ossian looked over at Deith. "If we weren't looking, we probably never would have found it."

"Someone would have found it, eventually. If not today, next month or next year. Then they would be dead, yes?"

Ossian shook his head back and forth. "I don't know." Standing in the tent with Deith, he was now doubting his reaction to the creature. It hadn't actually harmed him. Maybe he'd overreacted. "I think so. I didn't give it a chance to find out."

"So the sword, is it supposed to do that?"

Ossian shook his head, "No, the sword is a like a grain silo. It stores magical energy till I need to use it later."

"Do you have any way to find out what it is?"

"There are things I can do. I'm not sure if they will tell us anything."

Deith stood still like a statue, the man so rarely moved even a muscle. Ossian wondered if maybe he was also a rock creature. Ossian finally voiced his real trepidation. "I'm scared."

"Good, that means you'll be careful, then. Will you allow someone to watch?"

"Do you want to watch while I sit, casting spells?" Ossian knew the spell casting fascinated the children and even some of the adults. He also knew the spells he was going to be casting would look like him sitting in a circle with his eyes closed for hours at a time. There was nothing showy about magical research either, sitting alone with books reading for days on end.

"I think someone should be with you. What if it attacks again?"

Ossian was going to protest Deith's suggestion that he could not handle himself with the dead rock-creature. Then the memory of the creature's legs snapping into place, it touching the ground for a fraction of a second and leaping back at him. It had been so fast, the only thing that saved him was his reflexes. None of it had been conscious thought.

"I don't want to put them in danger." Ossian loved that the village wanted to help. He was also sure Deith could convince the villagers to take turns watching over him.

"Just the former soldiers, then?"

"You're not going to let this one go, are you?"

"Do I need to take the rocks away from you tonight?"

Ossian smiled at that. Deith had read his mind.

He indeed was going to start directly into researching the creature as soon as Deith left. Ossian didn't fight it though, technically he was in charge. However, like Jorn, he was fully sure Deith could take him in a fight, magical prowess or not.

"Not tomorrow. I need to do some research first. But I promise I'll let you know before I cast anything."

Deith moved to the tent flap before speaking again. "Thanks for protecting the kids. Jorn would have been proud."

Ossian was glad that Deith left then, as his eyes began to water. He got up and laid down on the cot, sobbing silently to himself as the reality of the day finally collapsed on top of him like a pile of shiny black rocks.

CHAPTER 24

The nightmare he had about the spider woke him up. Ossian was sweating yet again in his clothes, breathing hard and waiting for his heartbeat to stop pounding in his head. The tent was just brightening with the first rays of lights. He twisted in his cot to look down and was glad to see that the glossy black shards of rock hadn't reassembled themselves in the night.

Since no one was depending on him to protect them, he took his time calming down. As he took deep breaths, the pounding in his ears slowly faded. Yet another set of sweat soaked clothing, he guessed he would wear them today and they would probably dry out by mid-day. He should ask Deith if that part ever went away.

Swinging his legs over the side, he made sure not to step on any of the shards. Moving to his desk, he pulled his five magic reference tomes out of the chest and set about trying to find out what spells he could use to glean any kind of information about the spider or its make-up.

There was talk of animated creatures in the records. Most of what he'd heard about was in tales from distant times, before the Times of Tribulation.

Ossian's mind grasped at that single thought. Could this spider be that old? He wasn't really sure how long ago the Tribulations even were. They were just mentioned as cautionary tales. The only thing he'd ever seen that was supposed to be from the Tribulations was Thorne.

He'd seen the undead horse that the Knight of the Rose rode several times, usually visiting Mage Mahler. During those times, Ossian wasn't allowed in the office.

He dove back into the books, searching for something that could verify the creature's makeup, or age, or even its origin.

CHAPTER 25

Ossian was poring over his books when something scrapped against the opening flap of his tent.

Then Espeth's voice could be heard, exasperation in her voice, "How is anyone supposed to knock on this stupid thing?"

That's when Piaa's voice could be plainly heard, "Mage Ossian?"

Then the tent flap opened with Boa peeking his head in. "He's in here."

Ossian had spent the entire day with his five magical tomes cracked open searching their cramped tiny writing for something, anything he could use to dig information out of the black glossy shards of rock that were left over from his fight with the spider thing.

Piaa and Espeth poked their heads in with Boa, but it was Piaa who spoke up, "We brought food. Mom said we should leave it outside the tent and not bother you."

Boa had a look on his face, like he had no intention of doing that. "You find out what it is yet?"

Ossian realized he'd been sitting hunched over all day. "Come in." Standing up, the yawn overtook him as he stretched his arms high and his entire body tightened into a full stretch. Then, bending over, he touched his toes as the kids entered his tent.

Each of their eyes was glancing around everywhere, taking in the mage's lair. Boa eye's finished on the chest where Ossian kept his ingredients and grimoires, Piaa's landed on Ossian as she held out a tray of food but Espeth's eyes did not stray from the black shards on the ground.

Ossian saw the worry in her eyes. "They haven't reformed, Espeth."

Her head nodded that she heard him, but her eyes did not stray from the shards.

"Would you three join me outside?"

The three kids backed out of the tent like the spider might attack them at any moment. Ossian stepped over the spider and joined the children outside in front of his tent.

He could see the pain on Boa's face as the tent flap closed behind Ossian. He wanted to look more and see what was in the tent. Ossian understood. It had taken him years to not be fascinated with everything new and exciting in the city, let alone all the strange and wonderful things in the Academy. Most of them were things he could never afford.

"So, food," Ossian's stomach rumbled as he said it. The sight of the cloth covered tray sending all thought of magic from his mind. "Care to join me?"

Boa looked to Ossian at the sound of that. "Yeah."

Piaa and Espeth both chimed in at the same time. "No."

When Piaa continued, "This is for Mage Ossian."

Then Espeth chimed in, "Mom says he has eaten nothing all day."

It was like they had rehearsed it, but Ossian had heard enough of this trios conversation to know they were just in sync with each other at a level he'd never had with anyone his age. By the time he'd ended up at the Academy, most of the students his age had already formed their small circle of friends. He was pretty sure that's why it had been so easy for him to work harder than most of them. He had no one to distract him.

"Let me get a blanket." Ossian disappeared into the tent again and brought out a blanket to spread out on the ground. There was no sense in sitting in the dirt if one didn't need to.

As the children settled onto the blanket, Piaa lifted the cloth. There was enough food for three meals and Ossian finally had to look up to notice the lateness of the day. "Oh, I missed the day, didn't I?"

Boa said, "Dad said we weren't to bother you." Then he switched to a whisper as he looked around. "He also said if you were casting spells, we were to annoy you till he got back."

"Well, I promised him I wouldn't cast spells today, but that was easy cause I was researching what I need to cast."

Boa clapped his hands together as his eyes strayed to the food. "What did we learn?"

His hand reached out for a dried cherry as Espeth slapped it away from the tray.

Ossian had to chuckle at that. Reaching out, he grabbed a chunk of bread, some ham and a piece of cheese. He purposely left the dried fruit for the kids. "Dig in and help me with all this food."

The ham was salty with a hint of sweetness and the cheese was nutty. He realized how hungry he was as he tried to force himself to chew slowly.

He swallowed before he filled in the children. He'd found it helped to talk things out with someone. It would have been helpful if that someone was a mage who knew more than him, but he also found that talking to anyone, or anything, often helped his mind find connections that his pure study just didn't connect.

"Well, I can't date the rocks. I would need something to date them against. And I don't have any reference items with known ages. Well, I have some, but I doubt the rocks are younger than twenty years old."

"You need things of a known age?" Espeth asked.

"It's called a similarity spell, and it can compare one thing to another and you get a general feeling of how similar it is."

"And you think the spider is—"

Ossian needed to be careful, he didn't need to scare the kids. "Older than anything I own. Well, anything that I know the age of."

Ossian took another mouthful of ham and cheese and chewed it thoughtfully. He was about to raise the bread to take a bite out of it when that thought occurred to him, "However, we have rocks from around here. Does anyone in the village have any black jewelry?"

All three of the kids thought about it as they continued to chew on the dried fruit pieces. Ossian noticed they were being very purposeful in their slowness and was certain they had been warned not to eat all his food. In turn, each of them shook their heads no.

"Ah, just as well. I'm not sure knowing when it came from would help."

Espeth spoke up, "So it can compare any items?"

"Yes. The mage has to alter the spell for the knowledge they seek, like age or composition. But they have to start with a known."

"But it can tell you how different they are?" Espeth was thinking of something and for some reason, didn't want to say it out loud.

"Well, you get a feeling of how different they are. Like if I compared you and Piaa, I'd get a tiny sense of age difference. Whereas if I compared you and Anton, I suspect I'd get a much larger feeling of difference."

Espeth seemed to nod at that.

Ossian was trying to figure out how to get Espeth to tell him her idea when Deith walked up.

"Casting spells then?" Deith said.

"No. The kids volunteered to join me for dinner." Looking over at Espeth, Ossian continued, "The problem is, I don't know what to cast?"

Deith just opened his mouth when Espeth spoke up. "What about your sword? Isn't the sword a magical object? Would that tell you anything about the shards?"

Ossian thought about that. What would it tell him? Was it the same type of magic? "Yeah, that might help Espeth. Good idea."

Ossian realized everyone was staring at him. "Those spells can also wait till tomorrow. Maybe some more research tonight will shed light on something I'm missing."

Deith chimed in, "Alright, you three head home, leave Mage Ossian to his books."

Waving his hand goodbye as the children each grabbed one last dried fruit, they headed off towards their houses with Deith still standing around.

"So, what is the plan?" Deith's voice was low.

Ossian lifted the tray of food and carried it into the tent as he replied, "You just heard the plan. I've spent the entire day digging through the tomes I have available. I'm afraid I'm at a loss. Researching magical items is not in the normal repertoire of a mage. Magical items are actually exceedingly rare." Ossian placed the tray on the bed. Deith brought in the blanket after shaking it outside for him.

"The sword?" He pointed at the item with an upraised eyebrow.

"Despite evidence to the contrary, they are rare. Before my graduation, I can honestly say I had never seen a magically imbued rock creature. Hell, I'm not even sure what to call the damn thing." Ossian could feel his heart beating faster, his voice was rising and he had to take a moment to collect himself. "Sorry, it's just I feel like I know nothing, and everything I learn answers one question and poses six more."

"It's okay Mage Ossian, we're here to help."

"How can you help with this, Deith? Do you know anything about that thing?" He pointed down at the shards of rock. He would need to deal with those before he stepped on them and injured himself.

"It's Fireglass. The Northern tribes make arrowheads out of it, sometimes daggers. It's wicked sharp."

"Oh." Ossian hadn't expected Deith to know anything about it.

"Actually, that helps." The more Ossian thought about it, it didn't actually help him know what kind of rock it was. "Well, not really. I'm not sure how that helps us. But it is something, at least."

"Is there not a way to learn what spells were on it?"

Ossian's bark of laughter was much too loud for the tent. "Normally, I would touch an object and you can feel the spells inside. It's not instant, and it doesn't always work." Ossian didn't want to explain to Deith how, of the four objects he now owned, he understood only one of them, and that had been made and attuned directly for him. "I can try, but since the object is broken, I'm not sure what it will reveal. Plus, when that specific object was touched, when it was whole, it was instantly activated."

"Maybe a good night's sleep will help? Get a fresh start in the morning."

"Indeed, here, give me a second and you can return the tray for me." Ossian moved to grab the bowl of dried fruit and pour it into his own bowl. As the last bit of fruit stuck to the bottom of the bowl, he shook the bowl to dislodge it. The bowl slipped from his fingers and fell to the ground, shattering. "Damnit."

"It's okay, it's just a bowl."

Ossian stood staring at the bowl. It was only in four pieces, simple enough he could use a mending spell on such a simple piece of pottery. When a thought popped into his head. "Oh, now there is an idea."

He picked up the four pieces and placed them back on the tray. "Sorry, I'll need the tray for another day."

"I'm sure Cara will miss it drastically. What was your idea?"

"We have a mending spell. We don't use it much cause it only works on simple things. Like a bowl, nothing complicated like the plow. Although that is the spell I altered to perform the plow repair. That is a much more complicated—nevermind. The problem is that I need to understand the process and or materials being worked. That's why I can use the wooden repairing spell. I understand making the plow, and the nature of the material, wood."

"You think you can try that mending spell on the rocks? Is that a good idea?"

"I am pretty certain it won't regain any magical powers. I don't understand the creation process enough to repair that kind of damage. If that kind of damage can even be repaired."

"And you'll wait for tomorrow, when several of us can be present."

"Oh gods, yes, Deith. And we probably shouldn't be in the village for that. I think that's much too dangerous."

"So tomorrow, we attempt to reawaken the strange rock spider that only Mage Ossian's sword Rock-Breaker can destroy."

"Did you just name my sword?" The corners of Ossian's mouth formed a very large frown.

"Well, it will need a name at some point. That is how these things work. Rock Shocker? Boa said it was more of an explosion. Said he could see it even though he was turned away and running."

"It was bright."

"Tomorrow it is Mage Ossian." Deith nodded his head ever so slightly and headed out.

Ossian picked up the shards one by one and placed them on the wooden tray that so recently had held his breakfast, lunch and dinner.

CHAPTER 26

The next morning, Ossian had Deith, Yough, Mira and Taro, all four former soldiers, accompany him out of the village proper. All with armament in tow. All the children were warned to stay away, and several of the mothers took it upon themselves to watch from a distance and observe the children. Which Ossian was pretty sure meant watching his group just as well.

Earlier that morning, he had charged up the sword just in case. He didn't want to do any of this if he could avoid it, yet he saw no other way to gain much useful information.

Lugging the rock shards, along with the broken bowl, out of the village towards the west. He set Taro to sweeping a clearing so that he could prep a proper full circle. Doing the mending spell from his mind would work just fine for the pottery, which he intended to practice on first to refresh his mind on the mending spell.

For something so complicated as the rock-spider, he wanted the reassurance of a fully prepared circle. He would have preferred one of the wooden and metal inlaid circles from the Academy that the students used to practice their spells while they were still learning. That would take weeks to make, and he wasn't comfortable enough with woodworking or metalworking to make one reliably.

So a circle of dirt and powdered charcoal would have to do. Powdered charcoal being the nearest pure substance he could get out here in quantities.

After Taro swept the area clean, Ossian himself laid out the circle. The heat of the mid-day sun was bright overhead by the time he wrapped up the circle. None of the soldiers complained about standing there for hours. Ossian hadn't thought to summon them after the circle was ready.

Mira's shifting showed her restlessness. Ossian could hear her saying why are we here? Get this over with. Or maybe that was all in Ossian's head, and Mira was just tired of standing in the same spot.

"I'm going to practice on the bowl first. Should be a simple spell, but I want to practice. I haven't used this spell in so long." Ossian said it as much to himself as to the group.

With a fully formed circle in charcoal, the spell took nothing to power up. As the four pottery pieces levitated in the air, they slowly floated to each other, rearranging themselves as needed to fit properly. As they touched, a small blue light emanated along the cracks before the pottery bowl was floating, fully repaired, in midair. Ossian inspected the bowl and while the cracks were clearly visible, they were repaired and a single piece of pottery, again.

By the time Ossian was prepared to cast the mending spell on the glossy black rocks, the sun was high overhead.

"Do you want to eat first?" Ossian asked the collected soldiers.

Yough spoke first, "Do you need to, Mage Ossian?"

"No, I'm prepared."

Deith answered, "Then let's get this over with."

"Okay, if the creature activates, keep it contained until I can help fight it. The only thing we know for sure can harm it is my sword."

Mira piped up, "Why doesn't one of us hold your sword, then?"

The corners of Ossian's mouth twitched up ever so slightly as he tried to stop them from moving. "It only works in my hands." He didn't want to reveal too much to too many people. No one here currently in the village knew his sword had a built in defense mechanism.

All four soldiers took up spots around Ossian at regular intervals. If they hadn't agreed to come with him, Ossian was sure it looked like he was being robbed. The soldiers each had their swords drawn and each of them looked determined to not let the rock-spider out of their sight.

Ossian placed the wooden tray of rock shards near him in the center of the circle. Sitting cross-legged in the middle, he placed his hands over the shards and started up the circle. The energy quickly flowed around the circle and Ossian guided the power into the shards in front of him. The glossy black rocks fought the entry of the energy at first.

Vibrating and humming something fierce, the rocks refused to accept the power he was trying to channel into them. Switching the energy from a sudden burst into each rock into a blanket of energy surrounding the rocks and the rocks started to shift, moving slowly, yet closer together.

When the first two rock shards fused themselves back together, Ossian almost lost the spell. The sudden surprise of the spell working shocked him. He really had expected the spell to fail miserably. His hands were shaking, yet the power continued to flow through him. Rock shard after rock shard slowly moved to within touching distance of each other, then fused back together with a small bright blue light. As the final two pieces touched, fusing back together, Ossian finally turned off the power flowing through the circle.

A sudden splash caused him to jerk back reflexively. The sweat that had beaded up on his forehead splashed into the dirt in front of him. Taro and Mira, the two soldiers that Ossian could see, winced when he jerked back.

"Is it?" Taro asked.

"Shhh." Deith hissed.

Ossian didn't dare take his eyes off the rock. It was whole again. Kind of.

Even from an arm's length away, Ossian could see the fractures that littered the small rock body of the spider. The sweat on his forehead continued to form into rivulets and splash repeatedly into the dirt directly in front of him. Now, instead of magical effort, it was from the sudden reappearance of something that had so recently attacked him.

Ossian hesitated, self doubt crept into his mind. He'd defeated the spider the first time, but that had been as much reflex and luck as any actual skill he himself had. It hadn't involved planning or knowledge.

The rock creature showed no signs of movement. Then again, it had shown no signs of life till Boa had kicked it with his bare foot last time. That thought froze Ossian. Had it been the skin contact, or the violent kick that had awakened the creature?

Deciding he had better test out one theory, Ossian reached his hand out. Ready to touch the creature, when Yough spoke up, "Maybe one of us should touch it, Mage Ossian."

Behind him, Deith said, "Yough is right. Draw your sword and be ready."

Ossian slowly rose to his feet, a slight breeze blew through the area, sending a chill through Ossian as it evaporated the sweat quickly forming everywhere on his body.

Yough appeared on Ossian's right. Kneeling down, he extended his non-sword hand out. To Ossian, every inch his hand moved felt like an eternity. Then, just as quickly as the spell had been over, Yough's hand was resting on the rock.

The sigh that emanated from everyone was loud and made Ossian glad he wasn't the only person who had been nervous.

Taro spoke up first. "Is that it?"

"Well, I was pretty certain it wouldn't restore any magical properties of the creature." Ossian wasn't really sure what to say. They weren't being attacked. He wondered briefly if he should apologize to Taro for not endangering her life.

The sounds of swords sheathing themselves were quickly followed by the four soldiers milling around. Ossian was still staring at the rock, it was crisscrossed with what looked like scars to him, rock scars but scars none the less. Reaching out, he picked up the fist size chunk of rock with six dark wooden legs sticking out of it. Even the small metal links in between the legs had reformed. It was a small, heavy jet-black puppet like the traveling show brought to the castle occasionally.

Something was stuck in his mind, though. Ossian rotated the creature repeatedly, trying to get a feel for the rock or the magic. He could sense no magic left in the creature, but the scars formed a pattern. He was sure of it. The pattern just wouldn't come to the front of his mind. Somewhere deep in his mind, though, he knew there was a pattern to the cracks.

"Mage Ossian? You okay?" Mira had noticed the sudden interest he was paying to the creature as he continued to rotate the rock.

"I can't feel the spell used to create the creature. I'd been hoping something might be left, some small vestige. Some clue." Ossian couldn't keep the disappointment out of his voice. Some not so small part of him had hoped to discover the animation spell used on the creature.

"Is it safe to bring back?" Deith, the ever practical, brought them all back to the reality of the situation.

"It's just a rock now, Deith." Ossian bent over and placed the rock back on the tray. "Mira, can you—" Ossian stopped as he looked down at the creature with its legs splayed out, the scars formed a symbol he'd seen many times. The creature's scars formed an older version of the symbol for transmutation. It took the legs being splayed out and all flat in a single plane for the lines to match up. Yet, there it was, clear as day.

"Damn."

CHAPTER 27

The next few weeks rolled by fast. Ossian spent every waking hour searching for something that just didn't appear to be there. The transmutation symbol was the only visible sign of magic from the creature and all his investigations into the rock-shards left him with nothing.

The rest of the village continued with planting, building and arranging for what family's house they would build next. Those were the toughest decisions anyone had to make. Ossian had suggested after the initial blacksmith shop that the rest of them should draw lots. The villagers tried to convince him they should build his abode second, which he promptly vetoed and said his would be built the very last.

The children constantly pestered him to show them magic. He had to fight them off more than he'd had to fight even the grizzly, when one day, a plow support broke. One carpenter said they could build a new one, but it would take two or three days. When Ossian, welcome for the distraction, asked if he could try to repair it.

One of the older farmers told Ossian that since it was already broken, it wasn't like he could hurt it more. So at supper, Ossian told everyone that they were welcome to watch him, but he also admitted he'd never tried it in such a complicated shape before.

Supper came and before the sun set too deeply in the sky, Ossian had the plow placed in the square that was forming in the village. Sitting down next to it, Ossian brought out one of his grimoires. He had a spell he'd been working on that made the wood like clay for the duration of the spell. He'd studied with a woodsman for six months, learning about wood and the fibers in it. The lignin that bound it all together and how best to search for a piece of wood that was mostly already in the shape you wanted.

He drew a rough circle on the ground and explained to everyone they needed to stay outside the circle. "If you don't want to melt."

Most of the kids gave nervous laughter at that. They'd grown more accustomed to Ossian's sarcastic ways. Still, they stayed outside of the circle like Ossian asked. Bringing the spell circle into focus in his mind, soon he was shaping the splintered wooden form of the plow back to what it had been before. Feeling the fibers of the wood stitching themselves back together as he moved his hand over the broken section. He thought about fixing a couple of other spots that felt like the tree hadn't grown perfectly straight, but decided that repairing what was broken was good. He could experiment later and not on one of the few plows they had.

As he wrapped up, he noticed he wasn't even feeling worn out. The thought that he was getting stronger, or perhaps just more skilled, pleased him more than we could have put into words.

After Ossian finished up, he mentioned to the plowman he could inspect it. The plowman, hesitant at first, came forward and was twisting the plow this way and that way. Eventually, nodding his approval and hefting the plow onto his shoulders, hauling it off to do more good work tomorrow.

The kids scattered to the wind as they always did. Only to be seen again tomorrow as they pestered Ossian to show them more magic. Helping build the houses, and occasionally plowing the fields or carting off rocks from the fields, had left Ossian with almost no spare time for his studies. He needed to practice with the sword, as it took too much out of him when he used it.

Then there was the actual worry that his spell skills would atrophy if he didn't actively use them. He initially thought about contacting Mahler and asking, but he would just respond cryptically about how an unused dish gathers dust or some such nonsense.

Thinking back to his days at the Academy, he wondered if he could satisfy the children and practice his magic tomorrow at the same time.

CHAPTER 28

The next morning, he was up early. He needed to work on his focus and control more than anything else in his magical repertoire. Lightning was the hardest for him to control, as he had a natural affinity for it. Which really just meant, if you wanted something toasted and fried by lightning, he could do that. If you wanted a small spark to start a fire? That he had a problem with.

Heading outside, he moved outwards towards the hills on the outskirts of the quickly forming village. Picking a place, he drew out a large V pointing towards the village. That way, if a bolt went errant, it would disappear into the hills. Next, he needed several volunteers. He knew that would be the easiest part of his tasks.

Walking back into camp, he was set to eat with Deith's family today. Luckily, after several attempts at cooking for himself, the village had taken it upon themselves to disperse him around. Each meal was taken with a new family. It allowed him to talk with them, get to know them better and not starve to death on his poorly cooked meals.

When Boa asked if he was going to show him magic today, he

winked at him. Ossian could never have guessed at Boa's reaction. He lept up and ran away from Deith's wagon.

"Uh, sorry, I didn't realize." Boa's reaction genuinely confused Ossian.

"You promised him magic. He's alerting Espeth and Piaa, who will alert the others." Cara said calmly, like it was the normal reaction to a show of magic.

Deith chimed in then, "So what are we showing the kids today?"

"Well, I need to practice my spells. I've been neglecting my studies and my practice in favor or helping the village get started. So today is going to be target practice."

"Oh, and yer gonna use the children as targets." Asked Cara.

The last couple of weeks had Ossian pretty comfortable with Cara's sarcasm by this point. She was often blunt and to the point, but laced it frequently with sarcasm that, if you knew her, was pretty funny.

"Well, in a manner of speaking, yeah."

Deith looked over at Ossian at this. Deith was the more serious of the two, and still didn't know how to take Ossian's joking as much as Cara did.

"I need them to throw targets for me. They won't be in any danger."

With that, Boa returned and scarfed down his food like a dog starved for weeks. In between mouthfuls of breakfast, he stuttered out, "Mage Ossian, what are we going to see today?"

"BOA!" Cara's temper had a hard side, and all Ossian cared about was that it wasn't directed at him.

Boa slowed down and chewed his food carefully. Swallowing completely, he added, "Sorry, mom."

"I did not raise a hyena, did I?"

Boa smiled largely at that, weighing his chance of getting hit if he answered yes.

Deciding to spare the boy, Ossian chimed in, "Stick throwing, so I can practice my aim."

Boa looked from his plate to his mom. His small body shook and quivered with anticipation.

"Off with you then," Boa streaked away a second time before Cara could even finish, "Be back before—"

Ossian looked down at his plate as he tried to hide his amusement. Cara snatched his plate from him and put another sausage on it.

"You keep that smile on the inside, Mage Ossian."

"Thank you for the wonderful breakfast, Cara. It was delicious, as always."

"Gideon and Alisha are lunch today."

Ossian also didn't have to keep the schedule. The cooks of the village took him under their wing and made sure he knew where to go for his next meal. They also kept his tent stocked with various cookies and pastries. Well, not stocked, but at least there was always a spare one for him whenever anyone took the time to make them.

Finishing up his sausage, Ossian handed his plate back to Cara. Turning around, he encountered all the children who weren't required to work the fields, waiting for him.

"Today shall be target practice. We'll need as many sticks as you can gather. You know the boundaries."

The children scattered into smaller groups as they fled off into the distance. Not quite like a flock of birds, that had a grace as they reformed into a flying mass. Still, it had an order to it. Espeth, Boa and Piaa moved off towards the Night Forest, searching the fields and surrounding area. Maria and Ivy headed towards the Bear Woods, as the children had dubbed them. As Kay, Karl and Victor ran towards the stream. That was the trio to watch. Ossian knew if anyone was going to find trouble, it would be those three.

Mage Ossian did the rounds this morning while he waited for the kids to determine how many sticks would be enough. They had most of two dozen houses built now. The blacksmith, whose house they had constructed first, it's lower half built solidly from rocks they found in the surrounding fields. The blacksmith had finished the top half of the house in wood when they ran out of enough stones. Ossian had warned against it, but the blacksmith had merely said he had enough to be getting on with without waiting for more rocks.

Two of the laborers had drawn the first lots for their families to be housed in the newest houses. Ossian could tell pretty quickly that didn't sit well with some people. Yet over the weeks, most people forgot about it and moved on.

Five other farmers' families. Yet Deith and Cara still didn't have a house. Bakker, the potter and his partner Jayne, the baker, had been housed. At first they had insisted someone with kids take it, but everyone told them they had drawn lots.

Anton, the woodsman, was still living in a wagon. He'd refused to draw lots and said since he was comfortable living out of his wagon, he'd wait till last. Since he didn't have a wife or kids, no one argued with him, except Ossian.

Ossian and he had long discussions about whose house would be last. Anton arguing that his house would probably be the simplest and easiest to make. Ossian would counter it with the nicest tent belonged to him. It already almost felt like a house. None of the arguing had resulted in either giving in.

Today it looked like they would finish house number twenty-six. Yough and his wife LeAnne would move in with Kamien, Victor and Piaa. Yough was a former soldier, Jorn had claimed that Yough's service hadn't been complete when he'd joined the New Meadows caravan and traveled with them. LeAnne hated Ossian, at least in private. She used polite words, but her tone and body language constantly reminded Ossian he wasn't welcome near their table. When it was their turn to share their meals, she'd cooked the blandest, most boring gruel that Ossian had ever eaten. Still, one did not complain about food, lest one be forced to cook for oneself.

Walking up to Yough and LeAnne's wagon, Ossian hailed them. "Good morning. Ready to move in soon?"

"Of course, Mage Ossian. We can't wait to have a solid roof over our heads again." Yough was friendly enough. His tone, though, said that Ossian had interrupted yet another fight. The two always seemed to argue about something. Which explained why Victor was always getting into trouble. Kamien was almost an adult and Piaa, somehow Piaa, ended up being the opposite of her family. She was nice and polite and either hid it better than them, or was genuine in her sincerity.

Deciding that he didn't need to get into their personal affairs today, Ossian walked on.

Bakker, the potter, was outside near his kiln that was already smoking and he could be seen nearby in his vats of liquid. Ossian had spent many days talking with him about the clay making process he was using. It was a fascinating business. Ossian was always curious about the processes and procedures that each individual used to make, create and design things.

He was just about to ask how the kiln was going when two of the three groups of children appeared simultaneously, carrying bundles of sticks in their arms. Ossian noted they had more sticks than he could safely cast spells at, but that would work.

"Shall we head to the practice arena?"

The kids all shook their heads yes.

As they walked off towards the area he'd already laid out, the third group joined them with far more sticks than the rest. Apparently the stream had been the stick gold mine today. Ossian smiled at that. It was the more obvious of the area's that should have lots of sticks, given the trees and surrounding bushes that called the stream home.

Ossian stopped at the point of the vee and explained the very serious situation to the children. Asking them all to throw their sticks into a central pile. He used specifically grown up language this time. The kids quickly got a very somber tone as Ossian explained how dangerous the spells he would use today were.

"No one is to cross the lines into the range. For any reason. Is that understood?"

Head nods all around.

Ossian went on to explain that he wanted the kids to throw their sticks into the air, so that the sticks would end up inside the range. He didn't have the endless resources of the Academy and its seemingly unending supply of straw filled dummies they used.

It occurred to Ossian just then how many people must make dummies for the Academy. Surely the number had to be staggering. It wasn't uncommon during lessons for them to go through close to a hundred dummies. Especially after a more spectacular spell or two reduced a dummy to just sticks that were on fire.

Pulling himself back to the moment, Ossian repeated his warning one more time. Trying to set the importance and danger to the children properly. Last thing he wanted to do was injure a child.

Setting himself at the vee, he turned around and decided that practicing what they were about to do was probably the easiest way to make sure everybody understood the assignment.

"Alright, everyone pick up a stick and we'll go through a practice run."

Each of the kids selected a stick from the pile as Ossian directed them to form two lines.

"When I shoot a bolt, I want you to count to at least three, then throw your stick into the area and go get a new one. Alright, Victor, start us off."

CHAPTER 29

Spell practice went wonderfully. Each of the kids got to throw two or three sticks and Ossian hit most of them with a quick lightning bolt. He was working on accuracy and by the time the practice was done, he was missing very few.

Dinner ended up being a regular meal with Bakker and Jayne. Then Ossian found himself alone in his tent, bent over the secret tome, for the first time since Mage Mahler had given it to him.

He glanced at the book and tried to open it, but it refused to budge. Looking at the book, Ossian was certain it was one gigantic block of vellum that happened to have a book cover on it. If vellum came this thick, he might genuinely have thought that Mage Mahler had played a joke on him.

Instead, he laid his hand on the book as he repeated the words, Mages and Sages. He could feel the pages in the book unbind themselves from a single mass, into multiple pages. The book fluttered open and Ossian stared at it. He quickly flipped through the pages from first to last. Confused. Was there something else that he'd missed? Every page was blank.

He re-examined the outside of the book, but could only find the transmutation spell that bound the pages together. He placed his hand on the first page and said, Mages and Sages again. Only to find that the book snapped shut, as he quickly jerked his hand back and the book sealed itself.

With the sword, Ossian had been able to feel the spell when he spent enough time in contact with it. So he tried just sitting there holding the book in his hands. He sat there with his eyes closed while the sun set on him. Nothing, not even an inkling that a spell was bound to the book. Yet, he knew there was one. What kind of magic was this that Mage Mahler had shared with him?

It was already dark outside by the time Ossian realized how late he had stayed up. Since he hadn't checked the duty roster, he walked outside and saw that Deith had organized the watch and Deith himself was pulling first watch.

"Mage Ossian." Deith nodded his head.

"Sorry, I didn't realize how late I'd been studying my books. Who has watch tonight?"

"Bakker, Yough and myself. We decided on three. That should leave most people to only have to pull watch once every two weeks."

"You'll add me to the roster somewhere." Ossian said.

"If you insist."

"I do, and goodnight, Deith."

"Sleep well, Mage Ossian."

Ossian disappeared back into his tent and promptly fell asleep.

SOME TIME IN THE NIGHT, a noise woke Ossian up. He'd fallen asleep fully clothed, just like when he'd been an apprentice and couldn't be bothered to lose a single minute of his precious sleep. It'd been too long since he'd cast so many spells. Stretching, he found he needed to relieve himself before trying to finish his sleep for the night.

Exiting the tent, the moon was in full view and the night was almost as illuminated as the day. He was about to walk-off, away from the village, when he heard the noise again. This time, it was clearly not his imagination and coming from just behind the blacksmith's shop, which admittedly was the most isolated building in the village at this point. Everyone was scared to death that the village would burn down, which Ossian couldn't fault them for.

Weaving his way between two of the houses, he gradually snuck around till he could see behind the blacksmith shop. Yough was talking with a man that Ossian couldn't get a good look at, but he knew for sure he'd didn't recognize the man at all. Ossian didn't know what to do. Should he confront Yough and this stranger immediately? Should he wake up other people? Which people?

While he was standing there, hidden from view, paralyzed with indecision. Yough and the man finally ended their conversation and Yough walked him to his house and let him in. So it couldn't be that nefarious, could it? A strange man, in the middle of the night. Jorn had warned him that something might be going on.

Ossian snuck back to his tent to wait till the morning. He wasn't exactly sure how he would bring it up yet, but he'd find a way to quiz Yough. Entering his tent, he remembered he'd left to go to the bathroom in the first place. Pacing back and forth in the tent to the count of a hundred before he allowed himself to head back out and walk out of the village. Still, he found himself jumping at every noise, peering into every elongated shadow.

On his way back to his tent, he tried several times to catch sight of Yough or this new stranger. Alas, he was looking in the wrong direction when suddenly Yough came out around a corner. Ossian jumped and let out a gasp. His heart tried to leap out through his throat.

Yough also must have been surprised, as both men's hands went for their hilts. Finally, Yough stammered out. "Sorry, Mage Ossian, didn't see you leave your tent."

"Yough…" Ossian was still catching his breath. He'd genuinely been looking for Yough and it seemed as if Yough had materialized from nowhere to ambush him. "If I hadn't just peed, I'm pretty sure it'd be all gone now."

"Second watch usually is the most boring, but at least you made tonight exciting. I'm more awake now than I've been all night." Yough removed his hand from his hilt and with the slightest of bows said. "Sleep well, Mage Ossian."

"Night, Yough."

Yough hadn't mentioned the stranger at all. Ossian found that extremely odd. How hard would it be to say, oh yeah, some stranger came into town while everyone was sleeping? Ossian briefly considered walking over right now to pound on Yough's door, but LeAnne, his wife, popped front and center into Ossian's mind. She really hated Ossian, and he didn't need to give her anymore reasons to dislike Ossian than she already imagined she had.

Heading back to his tent, he decided that sleep would not happen. His heart was still racing from Yough surprising him. Pulling out the Crown and Beaker tome, he opened it up again and tried to find out why it wouldn't tell him what it said.

CHAPTER 30

The sounds of morning came far too early to Ossian's sleep deprived mind. He'd spent the better part of the night sitting with an open book that he concluded was blank. Maybe Mage Mahler meant it as a safe way to store his investigations into the Night Forest. Then again, how many of the villagers of New Meadows could possibly read? It wasn't exactly a skill that most had been taught. Ossian knew that if he was still just a random farmer, he probably wouldn't even know how to read or spell his name.

Then again, he was teaching most of the children to read and write. Maybe Mage Mahler was appropriately paranoid after all.

Closing the book, he got up and splashed water on his face. The cold shock of water on his skin woke him up not a bit. Today was going to be a long, long day.

Most of the village was still just stirring as he made his way outside. Walking next to the stream that went through town, he wound his way down the fields they had already plowed, heading toward the Night Forest. He felt the overwhelming need to explore. So far, he'd spent most of his time helping the villagers create a village and the occasional spell, but he'd failed to investigate anything about the forest.

They'd discovered the rock-spider, that was at least something interesting. There wasn't much else to add to his first real report and it would be due soon.

Ossian groaned out loud. Obviously, that was probably who the stranger was. Was the messenger early, or was Ossian late? The stranger didn't bring any supplies or appear to have a horse or cart. The king was supposed to send monthly supplies, at least till the farms could produce, then the village would send a monthly supply the other way.

Ossian froze at the sound of something large splashing in the stream ahead. Almost no one was up from the village except Ossian, and possibly Bakker, who should be pulling watch patrol. Several more splashes sounded ahead as Ossian took a tentative step forward, making sure his foot didn't fall on anything that could make noise.

When suddenly Honey, the shire horse, came shooting up the stream towards Ossian. Flailing his arms, he fell on his butt as the horse shot past him, towards the village.

He stood up, wandering how or why the horse got clear out here. Especially that horse, she hated being away from the other horses. That's when Ossian noticed the blood in the stream. A streak of blood came around the bend where the horse had come from and led away, following the horse.

Ossian placed his hand on the hilt of his sword and felt for the magic stored there. Several tentative steps led him around the bend, where a human sized but green skinned creature had its head kicked in. Apparently by a very large honey colored horse.

The stress that Ossian didn't realize was in his shoulders relaxed as he saw the creature there, dead. He didn't recognize the creature. In all his studies of goblins and orcs, trolls and fish-men, none of the drawings looked anything like this creature. His entire body was covered in a green leather armor in the shape of leaves that flowed down his extremities.

Stepping into the water, Ossian approached the creature carefully, in case it wasn't truly dead. Although, given that most of its head was now pulp, he wasn't sure how it could survive.

They weren't in the shape of leaves, they were actually leaves. The creature was humanoid and covered completely in leaves. Its face, neck and chest, even its arms and fingers, legs and toes, every single space had leaves on it. Ossian reached out and touched the leaves. They were as soft as a maple tree leaf at full bloom, with the slightest fuzzy feel to them. He tugged at one and it came off the body.

The sheer amount and density of the leaves made it hard to see where Ossian had plucked this leaf from. He grabbed a couple more to see if it was a suit or something else. After plunking a couple of leaves he could see, just under the leafy outer covering, there was a hard brown bark like surface.

Ossian didn't know what to do. He grabbed underneath a foot and lifted. The creature weighed far more than a man would have. He couldn't carry a body this size all the way back to the village.

Stuffing several leaves into a pouch on his belt, he headed back to the village quickly to see if someone or several someones could help him recover the body. This was definitely something new and exciting, although sad, cause the creature was dead.

As he turned to head up the stream back to the village, suddenly everything around the stream got quiet. The hairs on the back of his neck stood up as he slowly turned in a circle in the water. He could feel something nearby watching him. As his eyes carefully scanned the surrounding area, the stream, the trees and the bushes.

With his hand on the hilt of his sword, he carefully took several steps back, away from the body. His legs, still in the cold moving water, could feel the pressure against them. Every step was an effort just to move. Ossian realized how exposed he truly was out here, away from the village, with no one knowing where he was.

After a dozen excruciating steps, he rounded the bend and the body went out of sight. That's when he turned and bolted for the village.

As he cleared the treeline around the stream, Deith and several villagers were heading his way. Ossian silently cursed himself. Even Deith knew enough to bring reinforcements.

"Honey has blood on her. She has a scrape down her flank. What happened?" Deith started before Ossian could catch his breath.

"Body..." Still breathing hard from the sprint, he pointed more than said anything that made sense. Ossian made to head back into the stream towards the body, when he noticed no one was following him.

Deith looked at Ossian's boot. "What is that?" His hand pointed to a leaf that must have fallen when he plucked them from the green creature. Finally, Ossian noticed that the leaf's green was unlike any color he'd even seen on a tree, it was too light to be a tree in full bloom. As Ossian moved his foot back and forth, looking at the leaf in the early morning sun, it almost looked blue.

Realizing he was standing there, moving his foot back and forth, examining the leaf, Ossian said, "There is a...body in there, covered in leaves. Honey killed it."

Everyone went silent when Ossian said leaves, and several of the villagers' faces went ashen.

Deith finally spoke up, "You should let dead bodies lie."

"I need to study the body. I've never even read about a creature like it."

Deith turned and addressed the three ex-soldiers with him. "You each have to make your own call on this one. I'm going to help him, but no one here is currently enlisted."

Bakker and another villager looked from Deith to Ossian, then to the leaf. Then turned around and walked back to the village. Ossian couldn't blame them, strange and unusual wasn't everyone's cup of tea.

"Are you going to help me?" Ossian directed it at Dieth.

"As long as you realize, I think this is a terrible idea."

Kamien stood next to Deith. Ossian knew if he came with them, his mother would never let him hear the end of it. "You should stay, Kamien."

Kamien must have not trusted himself to speak, as he just shook his head no and walked towards the stream.

Ossian tried to lead the way, but Deith overtook him quickly once they were in the overgrowth and bushes around the stream. Deith moved quickly in the direction that Ossian had come from, without asking where he had gone. Ossian knew there really were only two directions he could have picked, but Deith seemed set on the exact path that Ossian had taken. That's when Ossian remembered Deith had been a scout.

Following, Ossian kept Kamien in between himself and Deith at the lead, who made no sound as he moved through the bushes, despite all the detritus on the ground. Ossian's wet shoes squished more as he tried not to make any noise.

At one point Deith stopped. Ossian, who had practiced enough with the soldiers, stopped in his place, crouched and watched their back. Kamien walked up to Deith. As he spoke, his voice seemed unnaturally loud. "Why did you stop?"

Deith silenced him with a hand over his mouth, looked about and finally glaring at the young man. He whispered something in his ear, then continued down the stream.

As they got nearer to the bend, Deith slowed down his pace as he walked through the heavier underbrush. Ossian watched in awe as Deith still made nearly no sound nor did he leave any trail in the dense heavy brush. Ossian, faced with the heavy brush around him, had taken to the stream, as it was the easiest path and he hadn't minded getting wet, since he was still wet from before.

Deith stood still for several minutes, looking into the surrounding trees and undergrowth. Ossian thought from Deith's position he should easily be able to see the dead creature's body. Yet still, Ossian waited like he'd trained with the soldiers to do.

Kamien's patience finally gave out and he made to move when Deith threw out his hand behind him. Kamien froze and with it, Ossian's heart raced. He found his hand on his hilt again. The magic stored in it was coursing through him and he had to will the power back into the sword.

They stood there for another very long minute, when Deith, just as suddenly as he'd thrown his hand out, lowered it. Raising his arm up, Deith pointed to where the creature should have been. Barely a whisper on the wind came out of Deith's mouth, "There is no body."

"What? I saw it for myself." Ossian walked up, as he passed Kamien, the boy unfroze and they both joined Deith near the stream. The noise both of them made was enormous and even Ossian's untrained eye could see the path of destruction they were leaving in the brush.

Coming up next to Deith, Ossian could see the spot where the body had been. There was still a spot of blood from Honey on the ground. As well as a thick viscous liquid that wasn't blood. Still, Deith was right, there was no body.

"It was dead. Its head was pulp. I even lifted its foot." The words spilled out of Ossian before he realized he even said them.

"We should leave. Something is here."

"What is that liquid on the ground?" Ossian was entranced. If this was a new creature, he needed to know as much about it as possible. Surely Deith understood that as a scout.

"Does it matter? We should leave, Mage Ossian."

Ossian couldn't take his eyes off the liquid. There were no other leaves around the area, though. Luckily, he'd already taken a few, they were safely stowed in his belt pouch.

Removing a handkerchief from his pocket, "I just need to get a sample, then we can leave."

"This is a bad idea." Deith's voice told Ossian that he disapproved.

As Ossian stepped further into the waters, his legs were getting colder the longer he stayed in the water. A bird cawing caused

Ossian to flinch, which then made him misstep and he fell into the water. As he was flailing about in the foot deep water, a hand grabbed him and hauled him out by the scuff of his neck.

"Hurry up!" Deith's mannerisms had left polite behind, and Ossian knew he was soon to be abandoned to his own luck.

Taking the final step towards the liquid. Everywhere that it touched the dirt, it was already disappearing. The only spots still left were puddles on the stems and leaves of whatever plants the creature had trampled as it fell in its death throes.

Ossian placed the rag on a spot that looked as good as he was going to get and he let the liquid absorb into the rag. Grasping the rag with both hands, he cupped it more gently than he would a newborn child. "Do you know what this is?"

Ossian was about to turn around and face Deith when a leafed face came into view. Deith hissed through his teeth and took a step toward Ossian. The splashing of the waters caused the face to blink.

"No Deith, stop." Ossian felt the creature meant him no harm. Deith was just going to scare it away.

That's when Ossian heard Kamien gasp, and Deith swore. Yet, Ossian couldn't take his eyes off the face in front of him as it stood up. The creature was easily a couple of heads taller than Ossian.

Ossian finally decided he had to say something. "We meant no harm, our horse got loose. I think whoever this was got in its way."

Deith took another step, so he was touching Ossian and whispered in his ears, "We are surrounded."

That's when Ossian finally looked around. He saw at least four of the creatures on the bank near Kamien. Who was wisely holding his hands up. None of them were as tall as the one on the bank near Ossian.

Wondering how many of them they couldn't see, Ossian understood Deith's earlier warning now. He'd have to pay more attention to Deith next time. For now, it was too late.

The creature on the bank next to Ossian looked down at the ground where the body had been. Then looked into Ossian's hands.

Extending a hand slowly, he plucked the rag from his hand. The soft, furry leaves of his fingers touched Ossian's skin, and if he hadn't been so terrified, he might have giggled from the tickling sensation that ran up his arm.

The creature dropped the rag into the water, and Ossian watched as it floated down the stream. He envisioned the stream making its way carefully, yet surely deep into the Night Forest.

Ossian was struggling between bolting and wanting to talk with the creature when curiosity won out. "Can you understand me?"

The creature gave no sign that he understood, or, for that matter, heard Ossian. His gaze casually drifted up towards where Kamien and the others were, then he took a step backwards. On his second step backwards, he disappeared into the forest.

"Shit." Deith grabbed Ossian by the arm and waded back through the stream.

"Can't we try to follow him?" Ossian desperately wanted to know more about the creature.

"If you head after them, it's without us." Deith's tone caught Ossian unaware.

Ossian finally looked at Deith. His face was white. Ossian decided that alienating Deith, who the village trusted, was probably the wrong move right now. So he allowed himself to be dragged back to the shore, where Kamien still stood, just staring off into the trees around the stream. "They just disappeared. Like magic."

"Nonsense. They are just good at stealth, like Deith here." Ossian had seen what Deith could do. It wasn't strictly magic, but his skill was astounding.

Deith looked at Ossian. "No, that was magic. Whatever they are. I have no idea where they went. They are nowhere near here."

The walk back to the village was nearly in silence, only the squishing of Ossian's shoes and the rustling of leaves and twigs from Kamien made any noise.

As they approached the village, Deith stopped suddenly.

He turned towards Kamien and held out his hand. "Mage Ossian, what do you want to tell the people?"

Ossian didn't understand, "Uh, that we found a new creature who lives in the woods. They didn't harm us. I don't think we have anything to worry about yet."

Deith just stared deeply at Ossian. Ossian was pretty sure he was being weighed and measured on some scale he wasn't aware existed before today.

"I think we should say we saw something, and that the woods should be avoided."

Shaking his head no, Ossian didn't like the idea of lying. He never liked to lie. Especially to a group of people he was responsible for. "Why should we lie?"

Kamien was the one who spoke up now. "Half these people will leave. They already fear this place."

Ossian was shocked. "What if they are the reason this place keeps disappearing? What good does it do to remain, just to be killed?"

Deith started into him next, "Any villager leaving before their service is up immediately becomes a criminal. Mage Ossian, as the king's emissary, you will be tasked with finding them and or charged with preparing warrants for their arrest. Are you prepared to jail and possibly kill some of these people if they choose to leave?"

"Do you really think people will leave?" Ossian wasn't in the same situation that most of them were in. He really hadn't thought about life for them, what deals they had been offered in return for going to a village known for being wiped out.

"I think strange leafy creatures appearing from the forest will make several of them consider an outlaw's life again. Although, I am surprised no one has left of their own accord yet."

"I don't care. I think we should tell them the truth. They need to know what to be on the lookout for. If they choose to leave, they know the consequences. I wouldn't be able to bear it if something happened to someone cause of those creatures." Ossian said.

"Honey was hurt."

"Did you look at the wound? Was the creature trying to injure her?"

Deith stalled before answering. "No, I think she hit a branch or something."

Kamien chimed in, "I didn't see any weapons, and their fingers looked all soft and leafy."

"I think we should have a town meeting. We should warn everyone about what happened. And I will remind people that as New Meadows, we can stand together. I was sent here to determine what happened with the last villages. I will also send a message to the king asking for soldiers. No messengers ever came from the village claiming harm was happening to them."

"If that's what you want." Deith bowed his head and continued on into the village, "I'll round everyone up. We should do it sooner rather than later."

OSSIAN RAN TO HIS TENT, his shoes squishing the entire way. Holding his hands up and away from his body, making sure not to touch anything. When he got to his tent, he kicked at the tent flap until it opened up slightly, then bent over as much as possible and shouldered his way into the tent.

Looking around his tent, he finally spied an empty cup sitting on his portable desk. "Perfect." He muttered to himself.

He scraped as much of the substance off his hands as he could into the cup. There wasn't much. He could already see the viscous fluid pooling at the bottom of the cup. Then he wiped his hands on the tea towel next to his bed. Placing the cup and the handful of leaves into his chest, he locked it.

CHAPTER 31

As the villagers gathered, Ossian saw the stranger from last night. He'd been so engrossed in the new creatures that he'd completely forgotten about him. He would have to corner him after the town meeting.

The talk with the villagers went less smoothly than Ossian had hoped. After presenting the situation, several of the ex-soldiers said we should storm the stream area, cut down all the trees and eradicate the area so close to us.

Until Deith spoke up. Deith commented they didn't just emerge from the forest, they appeared out of it. Apparently, Deith understood how the soldiers worked, cause most of them quieted down after that.

Ossian said he thought they should either increase the guards or double the number per shift. Everyone grumbled at that until Yough mentioned Ossian was on the watch list as well. That seemed to mollify most of the villagers, although Ossian noticed that LeAnne was not among those mollified.

Ossian did agree to cut down the nearest fifty feet of stream area. To give them a line of sight, he also warned that anyone going that far into the stream would need to be in groups. Contact with the creatures would need to be reported immediately.

Finally, Cara asked what was on everyone's mind, what would the king do. Ossian told her he would address a message directly to the king today. Then, when that didn't seem to mollify them, he added that someone or some group from the village would have to ride hard to take it directly to the king.

That's when the stranger finally spoke up.

"I am the messenger from the King. I arrived late last night, having rode ahead of the caravan, which should be here." He glanced over towards the hills and continued, "Well, as soon as they come down those hills." He pointed towards the road into town and everyone saw the caravan, or more appropriately, the two wagons, cresting the hill.

"I'll wait for everything to be unloaded, and then we shall ride hard to get the message to the king as soon as possible."

Ossian thanked the messenger and dismissed the assembled villagers.

Yough and the messenger didn't wait for the crowd to disperse as they made their way towards Ossian and the makeshift box he was standing on. As Ossian stepped down, the messenger stuck out his hand.

"Mage Ossian, the names Clarke, I have supplies from the king." Waving his hand towards the wagons. "I'm afraid I have little news for you. Mage Mahler gave me this." And he held out a purple message seal.

Ossian took the seal and placed it in his belt pouch. "Thank you, Clarke. Why did you arrive ahead of the caravan?"

Clarke's face blushed at this. "I'm afraid I got excited to see the Village of the Night Forest. I apologize for arriving late in the night and not coming to see you immediately. Yough said by the time he knew you were awake, I was already asleep."

"I need time to prepare my message for Mage Mahler and the King. Unless you have other news to tell me, I'll excuse myself."

Ossian felt he was being overly formal, but he wasn't liking something with Clarke.

"Of course, Mage Ossian. I'll be around the village when you have the missives."

~

Searching the crowd for Deith, Ossian wasn't able to find him as he turned to head back to his tent.

Flipping open his tent flap, he wasn't surprised to see Deith already waiting there for him. "I understand you disapprove of the message—"

Deith was already holding up his hand. "The meeting was fine. Something is not right with Clarke. I think you should be careful in the missives you send with him."

"Magic will protect the message to Mage Mahler. To the King, I'll just be asking for soldiers to protect the village from what I can only describe as unknown green creatures."

"Magic can be bypassed. I wouldn't trust anything with Clarke." Deith repeated himself.

"Thank you for the warning Deith, I'll be careful. I don't trust him either."

Whatever stress was in Deith's shoulders relaxed at that. Ossian hadn't realized how hard this must be on Deith, choosing between his kingdom and his family. "You know nothing you say to me will ever be used against your family."

"As the emissary of the king here, you shouldn't say that. Although, I appreciate the sentiment." Then Deith stepped past Ossian and left.

Ossian had been prepared to send a leaf back to Mage Mahler, but now he wasn't so sure. Something about Clarke unnerved him. It was probably just nerves from the encounter with the green creatures. He would need to think up a better name than that.

Cracking open the seal from Mage Mahler, there wasn't much

information there either. They'd been gone what, two months at the most.

As Mage Mahler's form appeared in front of him, Ossian was happy to see his old mentor. He knew it wasn't a two-way communications but even the sight of him brought Ossian much joy that he wasn't aware he needed. Mage Mahler told him about some news from the western side of the kingdom, but it was all extremely boring and nothing important. However, the message ended with Mage Mahler saying wait till Clarke is gone for the rest of this.

The purple, glittering form of Mage Mahler should have dissipated into the air. Instead, it coalesced into a small bowl with a single drop of what looked like ink inside of it.

Ossian was giddy enough to see the magic, let alone experience it. He glanced around his tent, looking for any spies sitting inside the tent watching him. How had Mage Mahler done that? He'd hidden a transmutation spell inside a locked message spell. Ossian was almost upset that Mage Mahler hadn't shown him how to perform it. Then again, how much time did they have at the end?

He placed the bowl carefully in his chest, and got out the ingredients for the message seal, and some normal ink and parchment for a missive to the King.

CHAPTER 32

As he wrapped up the locked message seal to Mage Mahler, he poured the molten wax mixture over the brass plate. The red seal formed the same round shape, with the same symbol of a plow sowing a field in a book.

After spending quite a bit of time folding, he finally got the parchment missive for the King into the right shape. The tail on the parchment was always the hardest part. He struggled quite a bit with the thin piece of parchment till he got it in the slot and could make it so that if anyone opened it before the King, it would be ripped.

Although it occurred to him, maybe Clarke could bypass it. He didn't want to be rude to Clarke and ask him how one could open a letter like this and read it without slicing the tail.

Then Ossian had a thought, preparing another batch for a locked message seal, he altered the formula slightly for the King, putting a simple message of, I hope this finds you well, Ossian placed the parchment on the brass plate and poured the wax seal over it. The wax initially spread out over the parchment, which made Ossian frown. Then, as it finally touched the brass plate, it shrank back onto itself, forming a perfect round wax seal. He wasn't sure if Clarke could bypass the magic and a securely folded parchment missive, but it was better than just giving Clarke the information.

As he pushed aside the tent flaps and walked out, he saw it was already noon, and the supply wagons had arrived hours ago. They looked to be unloaded, but the supplies sat in the middle of the town with a few men Ossian didn't recognize and Clarke, Yough and Deith sitting amongst them chatting.

As Ossian walked up, all the men glanced at him. Clarke stood up to take the message seals as Ossian handed them over. He placed them in a tooled leather pouch that looked extremely well made to Ossian.

Clarke, seeing Ossian stare, said, "Courier pouch, technically it's death to open one if you aren't its owner or the recipient."

"Technically?"

"Well, you have to be caught opening it. It's not bewitched or anything. Mage Ossian."

Ossian was pretty sure he still didn't like Clarke. Yet, the idea of bewitching a pouch to a person, Ossian's mind was already working through the implications, trying to figure out if the idea was doable. "Now there is an idea."

"I'm sorry Mage Ossian, what?"

"Sorry, I was distracted by your idea."

Clarke looked at Ossian for a while, then said, "The supplies have been offloaded, but I was specifically informed that you were to handle the dispensation." Then he extended his hand, holding out a piece of parchment.

"Thank you for delivering them."

"We do what we must."

The thought of Clarke saying Jorn's words bothered Ossian. Then he wondered if the saying was older than Jorn, or probably more widespread than just the castle. To Ossian, Jorn was the only one who really seemed to say it as a solution to most issues that really didn't have a suitable answer.

Ossian didn't know what else to say to Clarke. Was he supposed to dismiss him? Was it rude to ask him when they would leave? Clarke at least already knew about the stream.

"I assume you warned your men about the green creatures and the stream?"

Clarke nodded assent, then added, "A most interesting discovery. If I may be so bold. A new creature, and so near the Village of—," Clarke stopped and looked over at Deith, "Sorry, New Meadows. Most intriguing."

Ossian nodded the entire time as he glanced through the list of supplies. That's when it occurred to him, "Clarke, I thought the supplies were supposed to be once a month. Isn't this a bit late?"

"I am but a humble messenger. I don't question the King."

Not having anything to say to that, Ossian continued to read the list till he got to Supplies, Magical. His head glanced around, looking for a box from Mage Mahler. Clarke must have sensed what Ossian was looking for and pointed to a box. Ossian wasn't sure how he hadn't noticed it immediately, as it stood out from the rest of the simple plain boxes and crates and sacks in the piles.

It was a dark, heavy wood, bound with iron. Symbols were carved into every inch of the wood and a gigantic padlock was on the front. Ossian was confused. He didn't have a key to a padlock. His confusion must have shown as Clarke held out a key.

"Sorry, I thought you knew how this worked. Magical components are expensive, the key stays with me. You can open it in private in your tent, but I have to take the box back." Clarke almost sounded apologetic this time.

Ossian looked at the assembled men. "What's in it? I wasn't expecting any ingredients."

Clarke gave him a puzzled look. "We're not privy to everything we haul around these lands. I'm sorry, Mage Ossian." Then, pointing at two of the men, he shouted, "You two, take the trunk into Mage Ossian's tent so he may open it in private."

"Thank you, Clarke."

Ossian then followed the men carrying what looked to be a very heavy trunk into his tent, carrying the key. As he entered the tent flap, both men were standing holding the chest. The strain on their faces showed clearly as they held the heavy chest.

"Where would you like it, Mage?"

"Right there is fine, thank you."

They carefully set the chest down with considerable effort to not jostle the contents, then promptly exited the tent.

Ossian was left alone with a chest full of magical ingredients. He was surprised at how giddy he was, like he'd gotten a present.

CHAPTER 33

Turning the key, the padlock did more than just unlock. Ossian could feel a spell behind the key and lock. They acted as one to allow the spell to be complete. He reached out with his mind and found the fire spell. When suddenly he jerked his eyes open, not just any fire spell. This box would have obliterated anything within a thirty-foot radius. What could be so special in the box, or were magic ingredients just that expensive?

On top of the contents of the box was a note from Mage Mahler.

Enjoy the ingredients. I know the outside villages can get lonely. Remember to experiment. Mage Mahler.

Ossian couldn't believe that Mage Mahler continued to provide him with things, or maybe the King paid and Mage Mahler merely suggested what he should get.

He took ingredients out of the box. Iron gall, lavender and what looked like powdered amethyst. He continued to pull small wooden boxes labeled with their symbols on them, placing them on the surrounding ground. Smiling, he wondered how many people would be surprised to learn that most magical ingredients were pretty mundane things.

Then he saw the last couple of boxes. Removing one of the boxes, he opened it to a bright burst of orange light leaping out of the box. Inside of it was a phoenix feather. It glowed with a power all of its own. Some ingredients, on the other hand, were just strange and curious objects.

Removing another box, he found a wooden bowl with a silver rim. Etchings along the rim looked to be for a seeking spell. It wouldn't take someone long, or use much effort, to use the spell with all the etchings on the rim.

Last, he opened the largest of the boxes. Inside was a statue of some kind of creature. A weasel, maybe? Ossian looked over the statue. It was roughly the size of a cat. Carved out of what looked like a solid chunk of red jasper. As he lifted it out, it was heavier than Ossian thought it should be. He wasn't even sure what it was for.

The rest of the supplies were ingredients he knew what to do with. Well, everything except for the phoenix feather, the only mention of a phoenix feather Mage Mahler had told him about, was a way to minify and reconstitute information. The weasel, though, it must have weighed fifteen or twenty pounds. He could tell just from the touch that it was magical. Maybe Mage Mahler was experimenting with other objects. Then why send it to Ossian?

Taking out the red jasper statue, he placed it at the foot of his bed. Maybe it would scare off intruders.

Closing the box, he carried the chest back out to Clarke. Curiosity got the better of him, as it always did.

"Do you know what happens if that chest is opened improperly?"

Clarke's face grew serious quickly. "Indeed, Mage Ossian, I know of its protections."

Ossian was tempted to try it out. Instead, he just asked. "Have you seen one go off?"

The two men with Clarke crossed themselves. Clarke said, "Luckily, no. And let's pray that it stays that way."

Ossian wondered at the man who choose to carry such destructive things. Maybe that's why Clarke arrived so early. Maybe he didn't like to be near the box. "Do you need any of the rest of the crates or packaging back?"

"Nope, the rest is yours to enjoy. Good day Mage Ossian. If you have no further need of us, we shall be on our way." Then Clarke bowed to Mage Ossian and gave a nod of the head to Deith and Yough.

OSSIAN, Deith and Yough spent the rest of the day separating out the supplies evenly between all the families. Some supplies were for the blacksmith or the potter, but most were merely wheat or sacks of flour, salt, sugar and beans, plus various other foodstuffs. Deith opening a largish box, pulled out a large hunk of salted meat. The smell, even from ten feet away, assaulted Ossian and all he could think of was the bear.

"We'll need to cut this up. Yough, can LeAnna take care of that?" Ossian hoped that maybe she'd be happy with being assigned what he thought of as an important task. Making sure everyone had an even share of meat.

"I'm sure she'd love to." The sarcasm in Yough's voice couldn't be missed.

"If it's too much for her, I can have someone else do it."

Yough's shoulder slumped. "No, Mage Ossian, it would be just fine. I'll get Kamien and Kay to help me carry it over." With that, Yough walked off.

"Am I missing something?" Glancing over at Deith, Ossian continued to forget that he didn't really understand people.

Deith shrugged and kept on pulling bags and putting them in spots, then cracking open crates and pulling out more things.

In the end, everyone got a sack of flour, sugar, salt and a generous portion of beans. Several sacks of dried fruits were assembled, but there wasn't enough for anyone to take an entire sack. There was even sausage and a fair chunk of dried meat for each villager.

However, there wasn't any tea. Ossian knew there was unlikely to be any, but he still had hoped. He'd have to break into his personal stash soon.

Deith finally asked Ossian had been wanting to say out loud all day. "Why did they come so late?"

Ossian shook his head. "I've no idea. The ingredients Mage Mahler sent were nothing special, and it's highly unlikely I would have run out of them so fast."

"I mean, I appreciate the dried fruit. We'll run out of that fast here. And no one's spotted any good patches of fruit, trees or bushes around here. Although one of the woodsmen said he spotted a fig tree."

"I'll add that to my next missive that more fruit would make for a…" Ossian thought harder about his next words. "Morale boosting. Maybe I'll need to think of a better way to say that."

Ossian waited with the foodstuffs, as Deith and Yough went around and informed everyone it was time to pick up their lots. Every family brought their own bowls for the dried fruit, yet all of them handed their bowls to Ossian to portion it out.

When the families had all picked up their supplies, Deith looked over at Ossian. "What about you?"

"What about me? I don't even cook anymore."

With everyone gone, Deith looking off towards the stream, finally broached the one subject Ossian had been avoiding. "What are they?"

"I have no idea. They weren't hostile, though."

"Yet. They weren't hostile yet," Deith said.

"How do you think people will handle doubling the guard?"

Deith just shrugged. "If anyone says anything about it, you can have them flogged."

Ossian knew Deith was joking, yet he needed to know for certain. He couldn't guess with over half the families. He knew them all by name, but they were all overly formal with him. "I'm serious Deith. How will they handle it?"

Sighing, he said, "The families will be worried. You only talked to them this morning about the green men. I doubt anyone will mind the extra guard duty at first. You won't have as many issues with the retired soldiers. But vigilance is hard to maintain in civilians."

As Deith walked off towards his house, he said, almost to himself, "We should get ready for first watch."

CHAPTER 34

Ossian noted that as the village was preparing itself for the next day, he saw most of the former soldiers were wearing their swords and scabbards openly, but he hoped they wouldn't need them. He could already feel the itch to dive back into the woods to see if he could contact the Greenmen as Deith had called them, which he thought was a good name.

Back in his tent, he collected the ingredients and placed them slowly and carefully in his now almost full trunk. He still had his three magical grimoires, a half dozen reference books from Mage Mahler, and now a trunk overflowing with ingredients. Now he just needed something to do with it all.

Glancing at the red weasel, he was about to touch it when he remembered the drop of ink from Mage Mahler's message.

Clearing his portable desk, he set out a brand new sheet of parchment. Then collected the small bowl that held the drop of ink, placing it carefully next to the parchment. Grasping a quill he was just about to dip it in when he his mind wondered back to the phoenix feather. He vaguely remembered some old tale Mage Mahler had told him about a way to communicate pages of information using a phoenix feather.

Putting the quill down, he emptied his trunk of most of its boxes to find the carved wooden box that held the phoenix feather. Opening it up, the flash of bright orange light was less blinding this time. Or maybe he'd just been expecting it. Even as he glanced into the box, his eyes were drawn to the luminous colors in the feather. It glittered and shimmered as he rotated the box, watching the colors of a fire dance around the feather.

Finally, Ossian dragged his eyes towards the shaft of the feather and indeed, it had already been carved into a quill's nib for him. Placing the wooden box on his table, he grasped the phoenix feather by the shaft. He could feel the warm, welcoming hearth of a fireplace emanating from the feather in his fingers.

Dipping the feather into the bowl, the phoenix feather sucked up what little ink there was. Then, gently lowering the feather, Ossian slowly tried to touch the parchment with the phoenix quill.

Nothing happened.

Ossian stared at the feather. He tried to write his name on the parchment, he could see the ink try to flow out and every time the phoenix feather sucked it back up.

On the edge of panic, Ossian paced his tent. He had a phoenix feather loaded with a magical drop of ink. It refused to let the ink onto the parchment. What else did he have that Mage Mahler knew about?

Slapping his forehead, Ossian pulled out the tome Mage Mahler had given him. Opening the fake book, he withdrew the smaller tome and set it on the desk in front of him. He could feel it in the air as if the book and the phoenix feather knew each other.

Ossian, yet again, gently lowered the feather to the page of the book and gasped as the ink flowed from the feather. It coursed over the page, filling in words and diagrams and several spell circles. It flowed over the edge of the page and down further into the book.

Ossian flipped through the pages as words and diagrams continued to appear on the first three pages.

Flipping back to the first page, Ossian read. It was from Mage Mahler. He was glad that Ossian remembered the phoenix feather. Then briefly explained how the feather's innate magic reconstituted a set of pages consumed by another feather. Then it outlined the spell that did the consuming of the ink.

Ossian was giddy at learning secret magic. He'd always just thought of magic as utilitarian. He never really considered the subtle and important application of such magics.

The next two pages were more updates from Mage Mahler, a brief update about how he'd found very little to no new information about the Village, even in the deepest vaults of the Academy.

Finally, on the last page, Mage Mahler hoped Ossian would enjoy his new familiar. It was an old family heirloom from Mahler's family. It then outlined the awakening and binding spell that would last till the Mage's last breath.

Ossian was certain he would be giving the weasel back, and as he thought this, another section of words appeared in the book.

I am the last member of my family Ossian, there is no one to inherit this heirloom. Please accept it as a token of my appreciation for your hard work and dedication.

A tear splashed onto the page next to Mage Mahler's appreciation.

Then Ossian reread the awakening and binding spell and hurriedly collected the ingredients. He'd have to wait till tomorrow to actually cast the spell, as it looked like a pretty long and convoluted binding process, but the ingredients themselves were pretty mundane.

CHAPTER 35

By the time Ossian emerged from his tent, there was a small covered clay pot next to his tent and a chunk of stale bread. He guessed not everyone was as willing as some to interrupt the mage in his tent. Uncovering the pot, breakfast was cold gruel with a sprinkling of what used to be dried fruit, which now was swollen from the moisture in the gruel.

Bringing out a stool, Ossian ate his breakfast and some of the bread as he watched New Meadows head towards mid-afternoon. Several mothers were out of their houses commanding the smaller children to always come back when they edged too far away. Ossian assumed this was because of the Greenmen, as he'd never seen the children corralled like that before.

Finishing up breakfast, Ossian walked over to the stream that ran through the edge of New Meadows and scrubbed the pot and its lid with sand from the stream's bottom. Looking towards where the trees and shrubs sprang up wistfully, he knew he shouldn't just march in there and hope to encounter them again. Yet, the desire was strong, pulling on him like a new spell waiting to be cast.

He walked back towards his tent when he realized he didn't know whose clay pot this was. He spotted Cara and found out that it was from Muriel's house. Dropping the pot off, Ossian remembered to thank Muriel for the food. She smiled and took the pot away, saying no words. Maybe he would need to learn to cook for himself. Not all the families seemed glad to share their meal with him, even with extra food.

Walking back to his tent, Ossian decided. He grabbed the new wooden bowl with silver etchings on the rim, a tin needle and stalked off into the woods. Several of the children watched him walk towards and finally into the trees as they whispered and their mothers kept them back.

The scrub brush was closest to the village, and as he came towards it, even Ossian could see many tracks from the villagers walking around, but none of them walked in further than a couple of feet. Ossian tried to identify where Deith, Kamien and he had entered the treeline, but he was not a skilled tracker. It looked like dense brush, trees and dirt to him. Even the water mocked him with not a single footprint to show for his staring into it.

Ossian then dipped the bowl into the stream, taking just a small amount of water into the bowl. Placing the tin needle on top of the water, he sat down and formed the spell circle in his mind, then focused on a picture of the Greenmen that had surrounded them. Finally, he chanted over and over the words that activated the seeking spell.

At first, the needle spun lazily in a circle, which increased rapidly until the needle was swishing back and forth rapidly, swirling the water that was in the bowl. Staring at the water, Ossian was confused. He focused his mind on the first thing that came to mind. Muriel was back in the village. The needle snapped into position, pointing directly behind Ossian towards the village.

Ossian then focused on an image of Deith in his mind. The needle shifted out towards the fields to his left. He didn't know where Deith really was, but the fields made sense. Then Ossian focused back on the image of the Greenman's face, the one who had taken the handkerchief from his hand and let it float down the stream towards the Night Forest.

The needle moved slightly, not pointing out towards the trees around the stream, but somewhere between the stream's trees and where Deith was. Looking out over the fields, the only thing that Ossian saw out that way was the distant line that was the Night Forest.

Ossian then tried to concentrate on the rest of the Greenmen and the needle started swishing back and forth again, always towards the Night Forest, but it swung back and forth rapidly. The only consistent thing was, it never pointed back towards the Kingdom, only at the mysterious line that was the Night Forest.

Ceasing concentration on the spell, Ossian picked up the bowl and walked into the scrub brush, heading towards the treeline. Every shadow of the trees held a secret and every movement of a leaf, or a branch, caused Ossian's attention to focus on it till he was sure there wasn't a velvety green leafed body emerging silently from beneath the scrub brush.

Each step he took felt like an excruciating endeavor. The closer he got to the actual treeline, the more and more Ossian's heartbeat increased. The sweat formed on his skin and he could feel his body heat dissipate as the sweat evaporated.

Normally, this is when Ossian would turn around to the safety of the Academy. Head to his refuge and wait to ask Mage Mahler about something. He wasn't at the Academy anymore and the mage in residence was him. Squaring his shoulders and telling himself that he was being an idiot. Ossian took his first step into the treeline.

Nothing snagged him or dragged him screaming into the forest. Although where that thought came from, Ossian couldn't guess. The forest was quiet, but it was the quiet of knowing that he was there. The chirps and clicks slowed to a nearly imperceptible level but still were present. None of the shadows, except his, were moving. He could hear the stream burbling next to him, which was a good thing.

Bringing up the bowl, he picked up the tin needle and wiped it off, placing it gently back on the surface of the water. Holding his concentration on the singular Greenman that had stood in front of him, the needle pointed off where the stream did not go, out into the Night Forest, off to his right. Focusing back on the group of Greenmen, the needle kept swishing back and forth, pointing at everywhere that was the Night Forest.

Dropping his concentration, he moved deeper into the treeline, following the stream to where they had been just yesterday. While Ossian tried hard to be silent, he knew he was failing. The trees seemed to echo with every single one of his footsteps.

The trees around the stream parted near the bend where earlier he had stood in the heavy brush with Kamien. Several trees up ahead hid the spot where Ossian had found the body, and it had been removed before he could investigate more. Crunching through the brush, he came to the trees and was about to go near it when Ossian felt something around him.

The bowl was in the wrong hand. He'd been carrying it in his dominant hand as he walked into the forest. He wasn't sure he could draw his sword with his left hand, still he put his hand on the sword as he tried to discern what had suddenly made him stop moving.

Ossian nearly jumped out of his skin when he heard Deith's voice.

"At least you have good instincts."

Spinning around, Ossian glared daggers at Deith, "You can't—" but he stopped speaking when he noticed Deith was within a single step of him. He could easily have killed Ossian and walked away.

"How do you do that?"

"War." Deith didn't elaborate, then continued on another line. "Why are you back in here without an escort?"

"You know no one wants to come in here with me. My job is to protect New Meadows, and I need answers."

"Hurry then, no one is here yet."

Turning around, Ossian headed out towards the stream and looked over where the Greenman's body had been. The spot where he had lain didn't look trampled, it didn't look tossed or that a dead body had been there just yesterday morning.

In its place was a lush patch of flowers, a wild variety, each bigger than Ossian had ever seen.

"Do you see this, Deith?"

"Yes, the body is gone."

"No the flowers, there is no sign that the body was even here. Look at the size of those things."

Deith said nothing more. Merely stood looking out into the surrounding treeline.

Ossian, for the third time, waded across the stream to the spot where he'd found a body just yesterday. Reaching out with his mind, he touched the flowers and tried to discern if there was any magical effect. At least to him, they appeared to be normal, everyday items. Albeit, gigantic versions of the flowers he was used to seeing in the area.

He glanced up and down the stream for more signs of monstrous flowers that looked out of place, but none existed. In fact, no flowers were along the stream banks as far as he could see at all. He was certain any person would notice this area and thought it would stand out to even the most non-observant person. Yet, he wasn't sure what it meant, if it meant anything at all.

It occurred to him suddenly Deith had been out in the fields. "Wait, were you following me? You were out in the fields."

Deith didn't look over at Ossian, he just kept a watchful eye on scanning the trees, bushes and the stream. "Boa was dispatched when you walked into that damned treeline."

Ossian wasn't sure what else to do at the moment, so he stowed the needle in his pouch. Cut a few of the large flowers and placed them in the bowl, and walked back to Deith.

"I'm going to continue to explore the stream and eventually the Night Forest. You won't be able to always be there for me."

"If you say so." Deith was hiding something from Ossian. Maybe he was just being overly protective.

Ossian walked back to the village. He could never hope to hide from Deith in the woods. How would he keep Deith from following him so he could do some proper research, though?

CHAPTER 36

Ossian spent the rest of the day trying to think of ways to get to the stream without Deith coming after him.

He couldn't just leave early. Deith could follow his bumbling steps through the brush. Late at night wasn't wise. Ossian wasn't sure what creatures existed around. Since the Greenmen were real, there were likely other things they weren't aware of.

Cara and Boa apparently monitored him. He could probably distract them.

Then Ossian realized he didn't have to hide at all. He could announce to the village that he was going to research the stream and the surrounding woods. As the emissary of the King he could command New Meadows to not follow him into the woods. Although that seemed like a poor way to treat Deith. He was just trying to protect Ossian.

Ossian decided that maybe the next day he would just tell Deith he needed to go into the woods alone to research. He could lie to him about how another person being there would interfere with the magical energies or some such nonsense. He didn't feel comfortable lying, though. Deith had done nothing that really deserved to be lied to. Then again, Ossian was here under dubious intentions. Sent to seek information about the Night Forest and keep it hidden from the King, possibly.

He'd decided and was about to head out to tell Deith, him needing to do research without someone else present. Lying if he needed to, but not liking it, when he spotted the weasel. He most certainly felt like a weasel.

Recalling that he had a binding ceremony to perform, he broke out the broom and swept the dirt floor of his tent clean. Laying out the spell circle in a fine white powder known as oyster shell, it was a common ingredient from the port cities. He then put six small jasper rocks on the points of a hexagon inside the circle. Finally, finishing with the symbol of the moon on the north, a knife to the east, to the west a small ball and finally a chunk of charcoal to the south.

Ossian thought he knew what all the symbols meant. What he didn't know was much about weasels. He sat with the red jasper weasel in the middle of the circle he had, slowly forming the spell circle that Mage Mahler had sent him, adding in a symbol for himself where the familiar's bonding element belonged.

It took him far longer than he would have expected to alter the spell circle. This one felt different to him. He'd never really experienced anything quite so old. He knew the symbols were all mostly older representations of things he was used to working with. It caused his brain to think hard about the substitutions and how he could best incorporate the symbols and the meaning they would make to the entire spell.

When he had finished the alterations to the spell, he was already tired from all the mental work. Years ago, back at the Academy, he would have done all this alteration on paper before trying to hold it in his mind. Several years ago, Mage Mahler had made him spend over a year without paper. He could still hear him saying, "A mage must be able to improvise, and that can only happen quickly in the mind. You must practice now, while paper still isn't a crutch."

Ever since then, Ossian had written little down, most of the students had ten or twenty or more grimoires. Ossian himself only had three. One cause they were expensive, very expensive, but also cause he did most of it in his head anymore.

Bracing himself, he wasn't sure how long the bonding ceremony would last, Ossian focused the energy into the first symbol. The energy started at the top of the first symbol and Ossian had to push the energy hard into the symbol. It resisted him the entire time. Slower and slower, the energy flowed out of the symbol into the ones surrounding it. Sweat was beading up on Ossian's skin.

The energy was streaming into Ossian's body. He could feel he had more than enough magical power to make the circle fill-up. Yet, the symbols continued to resist him. They were lighting up, but not even the first quarter of the circle was glowing yet. He hadn't experienced a spell circle fight with him so much since his first year in the Academy.

Ossian heard the first drops of sweat hit the ground with a splat that brought him out of the spell. Quickly, using concentration honed from years of failed experiments in the Academy, he contained the power in the first circle, passed it into the second circle and grounded it into the third circle. The burning smell caused Ossian to open his eyes, hoping he hadn't destroyed Mage Mahler's family heirloom.

Instead, what he saw was the oddest thing. The moon symbol was burnt into the ground. Burning dirt itched the inside of his nose. The charcoal was also glowing red.

In the Academy, Ossian would have assumed he'd researched a spell wrong, put in the wrong ingredients or used the wrong symbols. So much could go wrong with a spell. This spell, though, came from Mage Mahler. Why hadn't Mage Mahler bonded with the statuette?

At first thought, Ossian wondered if Mage Mahler had gotten the bonding spell wrong, or maybe he didn't know what it was.

Either way, Ossian was exhausted. Scooping up the burning charcoal with a clay cup, he walked it outside. He was greeted by the darkness that had enveloped his tent in the hours he'd spent failing to bond with the weasel. He walked to the embers still glowing near the bake oven and tossed the coal into it.

Stumbling back to his tent, Ossian glanced up towards the woods. He could swear he saw a figure standing near the stream, close to the treeline. He couldn't make out if they were facing him or into the woods from here.

The possibility of interacting with a Greenman invigorated Ossian. As he trudged towards the figure, his stumbling became less and less, his steps taking on more purpose as his curiosity overrode the exhaustion that had so recently overwhelmed his body.

He was about just about to leave the village proper when a noise to his right drew his attention. The night guard had come around the corner of the last house and was staring directly at Ossian.

Turning his head back around to the stream, whoever had been standing there was gone.

"Mage Ossian, I'm sorry I startled you."

The voice identified the night guard immediately. "No worries Kamien. They have you pulling watch?"

"They said I could, s'long as I paired with one of the soldiers. Yough's been hounding me all night."

His voice told Ossian he was annoyed at the implication that he couldn't pull the night guard alone. Ossian also knew this was always how it was. You didn't trust your life with the untrained. "I remember my first year, Jorn wouldn't let me do anything."

"A year." His voice was incredulous. Ossian smiled at the memories of that feeling.

"It passes before you even know it. Don't worry, you'll be pinning for the days of someone to talk to before you know it."

"Mage Ossian, how did you become a mage?"

The memory of his first time using magic coursed through him. His hands sparked in the darkness before he could stop them. "I blew up a tree when I was younger. Villagers frown on boys who can throw lightning bolts from their fingers."

"Oh. So, it's not something you just learn?"

"As far as I know, it's something you can or can't do. There are some people I'm aware of who have learned simple spells through extreme practice. Or the use of objects that are imbued with power, but most people can't."

"Then why do you spend so long on training?"

Smiling, Ossian had wondered that exact thing when he had been taken from his life on the farm at age eight. "They teach us control. Do you remember the tree on the way here?"

"Oh yes."

Ossian could hear the awe in his voice. "Well, that was a lack of control. It was dangerous. Uncontrolled magic can do a lot of things. Some of those things have consequences. They teach us to minimize those consequences."

"What are you doing Kamien?" Yough's rough voice came from around the other side of the house. When he walked into view and finally saw Ossian, "Mage Ossian." He nodded formally. "Talking is well and good, but keep it short. I'll continue this way. You turn around and go the other."

They both walked away, one looking sullen like he shouldn't have to be telling someone such obvious points about guarding, and the other sullen cause he didn't need to be told. Ossian wondered if he ever was that green with Jorn, or if Jorn had ever been that upset with him.

CHAPTER 37

Ossian spent the next couple of days trying to figure out how to alter the binding spell. Obviously, the moon symbol and the charcoal were incorrect components for the solitary nature of a weasel and the night into which the weasel could disappear into.

The second thing he did was wait up long into the night, when everyone went to sleep, so that he could watch the woods for a sign of the figure. The figure didn't show again, and Ossian considered just wandering into the woods to look for the Greenman.

Finally, after a week of being mostly isolated, Ossian visited with the villagers again. They were mostly nervous around him and he realized that he'd been neglecting his relationship with them in favor of his own personal tasks. He would need to work harder to balance these things.

Espeth, Piaa and Boa seemed to not even notice that Ossian hadn't been around, as they sped around him as he walked amongst the houses and talked with the families. Many of them had short and curt responses, but just as many had at least a casual conversation, if not polite, with the resident mage.

Exasperated with the three children running around him playing some game that only they understood, Ossian asked them what they should do today.

Boa started with a whisper, "We could go into the stream and find them."

Espeth and Piaa shrieked when Boa said it and all three of them streaked off away from Ossian, disappearing into the village. Ossian made sure they were headed away from the stream before turning and walking towards the stream himself.

He walked up to the same point in the stream he stood at nearly every night, looking towards the treeline that was visible further down. From here, he could smell the small green and brown grasses that led to the scraggly scrub brush that eventually gave way to the thinner trees surrounding the stream. The stream was covered in trees for a very long time before the Night Forest took up the entire view of the horizon. A green-black line that cut off the sky from touching the ground.

He was turning around when a flash of green under a rock surprised him. Kicking at the rock, he saw a green furry leaf there, which blew away as the wind swirled around him and fell into the burbling thin stream next to the village. Racing up the stream, he got ahead of it and stretching out, he plucked the leaf from the stream as it tried to race past him.

Flicking the water off the leaf, he looked around. No one was around, and no one had seen him. He tried to walk casually back to his tent as his mind told him to run.

Inside the tent he open up the chest and pulled the small wooden box that used to hold red jasper but now held five furry leaves. This leaf was larger, and darker than the other five, which hadn't lost even a little of their bright green color since Ossian had plucked them from the body.

He tried to recall the look of the face that had been in front of him. The Greenman who had taken the rag from his hands and dropped it in the water. His mind wouldn't focus on a specific color, so he couldn't be certain.

Maybe this was a random leaf, stuck under a rock by one kid for some unknown purpose. Yet, it had that same furry texture, and the leaf itself felt more tough than leather. He'd tried to rip one leaf some time ago, but it refused to tear despite its soft and supply texture.

His supplies limited his research into the creatures. All of his tests so far had been non-destructive and he'd learned very little. Soon he would need to delve into destructive tests and those would deplete his limited supply quickly.

Leaving the tent, he went to the post in the middle of the square and looked at the list of names on the watch list. He would need to find one with a trainee and maybe one of the more lackadaisical soldiers. Not that he liked to think of them as less, but none of them were Jorn and Ossian wouldn't stand a chance of making it to the treeline on a night with Deith.

Kay and Bakker were the watch in two days' time. Ossian would need to make a plan. As he walked back to his tent, he tried to think of all the things he would need to do to escape towards the treeline while hiding.

CHAPTER 38

The night was near full dark. A small crescent moon provided just enough light to see the two men as they walked around the village. The cool air was still, no breeze was disturbing the wind this night. The village homes he was between provided just enough cover for him to hide from the guards. His heart beat so fast, he was sure they could hear it.

Both guards stopped for a quick chat, whispering about something. Ossian knew they had spotted him. Stealth was not his expertise. Yet, the guards separated and moved back around each side of the nearest houses. Off to walk their rounds for the night.

Ossian counted to fifty. He'd timed both guards on their rounds. Thirty took them past the point of seeing where Ossian would be heading. Fifty gave him plenty of buffer.

He tried to breathe and calm down like Jorn had taught him to. Yet the hammering in his chest got louder and louder as he neared the count of fifty. He dropped the tarp he'd been peering out of, having placed it near the house yesterday.

His first step felt so loud, he could feel and hear the crunch of every piece of dirt and rock under his foot. Glancing around, he kept an eye out for Kay or Bakker. Bakker was the village potter and Ossian was certain his guard duties did not extend beyond the perfunctory. Kay was young and eager. Ossian hoped that his newness would buy Ossian the time to get to the treeline and disappear.

Coming back, Ossian wasn't as worried. No one in the village could really yell at him. Although he knew at least Dieth might have a word with him. That and his food rations might suffer from some of the more judgemental families.

He counted to three between each step. Knowing his tendency would be to dash into the brush towards the trees, making a horrible racket. Each step felt like an eternity, but the darkness quickly enveloped him as he moved farther and farther away from the village. He smelled rather than saw the grass as he neared the space between the dirt field and the scrub brush ahead. Shuffling his feet was easier here rather than taking full steps and stomping on the ankle-high grass.

He'd debated asking Deith to educate him on stealth, but he didn't want to trick Deith. Actually, he wasn't sure he could trick Deith. That man, much like Jorn, had a preternatural sixth sense about things. Maybe that's what war did to you. You learned to survive at all costs. Or maybe Ossian's imagination had just been hyper-fired up the last two days as he planned his excursion into the woods.

As the smell of the dirt and the grass mixed, he was worried about the guards suddenly coming around, but he knew he had at least enough time to get to the scrub brush before they would show. Slowly and steadily, he shuffled his feet through the grass, bumping into the occasional stick or rock. At least he hoped it was a stick or a rock. He had no ability to see very far with the lack of moonlight. Only general shapes appeared to him.

As he was walking, something brushed up against his leg. Ossian nearly let out a yelp as he realized it was just the first piece of scrub brush. His heart was hammering again in his chest and he was certain the entire village could hear it.

Three more steps and his pants were catching on several of the scrub brush branches. Lowering himself down, he lay on the ground, waiting for the guards to pass the village again. He'd positioned one of the mage light torches perfectly for him to be able to see their outline.

Taking deep, calming breaths, he willed himself to be quiet. He knew deep down it was unlikely either guard could see or hear him. Yet still, every single breath felt like it was a squeaking wagon with a braying mule screaming out to the village.

He waited.

He waited so long that he was sure he misjudged the two guards' timing. Just as he was about to stand back up and move closer to the trees, the silhouette of the guards came into view. They stopped and chatted. Ossian continued waiting. The ground was cold and had seeped through his clothes. The damp of the ground was giving him a chill, yet still the guards chatted.

Ossian wanted to scream at them to hurry up and move along. They should guard the village, not be conversing about random things. If he had been in the village, he would have given them such a tongue lashing. Then he smiled. Oh right, he was trying to sneak out of the village with no one the wiser. Guards who were paying less attention were the reason he'd chosen tonight. That's when he felt the flicking of a tongue on his back.

Ossian froze.

A small slick thing was slithering along his back under his shirt. It slid its way towards his head. Ossian tried to keep his body rigid and unmoving, but inside his head, it was a gigantic snake capable of swallowing the entire village in one bite. He couldn't even shake his head to clear that thought as the snake came up out of the neck in his shirt and moved forward into the scrub brush, slithering silently away.

Not wanting to even breathe, Ossian looked again towards the village and saw no sign of the guards. Pushing up, he crouched and looked his way towards the treeline. He didn't dare shake out the heebie-jeebies of being violated by the snake here. The scrub brush would merely telegraph his position to the entire village, or maybe that was just his imagination, again.

Still in a crouch, he felt forward with his hands and counted. He had roughly till the count of three hundred before the guards would circle again. He wasn't sure if he could make the trees by the first time, but was certain the second three hundred would be easy. His hands felt for the easiest path through the brush and he took a single step, reaching his hands out again, feeling for the least pointy path forwards.

He was within ten feet of the treeline when he got to two-hundred and ninety. Lowering himself to the ground again, he was mad. He hadn't made it to the treeline. Yet, determined not to mess it up and have the guards look his way and wake the entire village. He thought back to how fluidly Deith had moved through the brush and wondered if Deith could have just sprinted through the brush quietly.

The guards came, the guards talked again for a long time. Then they walked away and Ossian finished the last ten feet to the treeline.

CHAPTER 39

The dark of the treeline was all-encompassing. Ossian was sure that moving around here would be difficult until he was far enough into the treeline to use a small mage flame to illuminate his surroundings. Sneaking behind a tree, he brushed himself off with both hands. His clothes were now damp from the earth and brushing them off only smeared the slightly damp dirt around. It would be obvious when he returned, unless he could change his clothes before anyone saw him.

His eyes still cast down, he tried to see anything at his feet, when he felt something change in the woods. The noises of the night were still there, but Ossian could feel something in the air. It felt very similar to being in the Academy rooms when people were practicing magic. A tingling on the outside of his awareness.

Glancing up, he spotted the Greenman looking at him. He was forty feet away, across the stream and in complete darkness. Still, Ossian could see him clearly, as if he could make himself visible at will. There was no light source that Ossian could tell, still the Greenman was present and obvious.

Raising his hands to show his palms, Ossian nodded towards the creature. He wasn't sure if the creature spoke or could talk. As the creature sat, the surrounding earth changed. The trees moved, the stream diverted itself and a small patch of grass grew where he sat. The creature motioned with his hand for Ossian to join him. As another small patch of grass grew where the trees had moved for the creature. Each time nature moved itself for this creature, Ossian felt the tingling.

Slowly, Ossian put his foot forward. He didn't want to scare the creature or threaten it. When his foot touched down on the ground, the tingling was immense. Suddenly, he was standing next to the spot where the creature sat. He knew it was magic, but it wasn't magic he understood that had transported him forty feet in a single step.

Sitting down, Ossian had thought about this conversation for the last couple of weeks. Nothing good had come to mind then, and nothing good came to mind now.

Blurting it out. "Do you speak?" Ossian couldn't tell if it was bad or good.

The creature cocked his head to the side, pondered for a bit and pointed to his face. There was a nose and eyes, but no mouth.

"Guess that answers that question."

The creature touched the ground and a line of itty-bitty trees grew up. It was hard to tell, but the distinct line was clearly the Night Forest. Ossian said as much out loud.

The creature pointed to himself and to the Night Forest.

"You come from the Night Forest."

The creature shook his head no, but continued. A small outgrowth of the Night Forest spread forward like a tentacle, tiny plants growing out of the ground to then turn brown and grow a crown of leaves all within seconds. The tentacle wound its way forward and Ossian recognized it.

"The stream."

Then small blockish squares popped up and Ossian recognized the village.

"And that is our village, New Meadows."

The creature stopped for a moment and looked at the village. Running his hand along the buildings, Ossian could see the transformation immediately. The village took on an almost hyper realistic look to it. He could see tiny mage flame torches scattered around the village. Then he saw two tiny shapes wandering around the village. He knew they were Bakker and Kay, or at least tiny versions of them.

"How is it you can do this? Do you know what magic is?"

The creature looked up at Ossian and his eyes showed something bright. An understanding of a word.

"Magic."

The eyes flashed and Ossian knew this was magic. Just not the magic he'd ever been taught. Some new magic he'd never heard of.

The creature passed his hands over the farming fields and small crops grew and it looked closer to harvest time, which was still months away.

Then the fields withered, and the crops regrew. This cycle repeated several times. Ossian was too busy being fascinated by the magic to count the number of seasons. He tried to sense something in the air, anything that might give me a sense of how this creature was using magic.

Then the creature stared into Ossian. He could tell the creature was trying to tell him something, but he could not grasp what it was, or how these creatures communicated.

Finally, something sad passed across his eyes and he looked down. Out in a field to the left, a long metal object jutted out of the ground. A spindly leg broke out of the ground and pulled a bulbous body out of the ground. As it pulled, the surrounding ground erupted in a dirt cloud that quickly settled, revealing more legs.

Eventually, a thing stood out in the field. Ossian guessed its body was the size of a village house if the small diorama was correct. The creature had six legs, but from here it looked like a small squat sphere with legs. He recognized the rock-creature immediately.

Then it moved.

It shuffled towards New Meadows, legs skittering around in an unnatural gait that sent shivers up and down Ossian's spine. He knew whatever this was, it wasn't natural. A bad feeling settled over Ossian as he was pulled into a dreamscape that made the creature full sized.

The clank and creak of the creature filled the air. The tingling that Ossian associated with magic was everywhere, overloading his awareness. He watched as the creature moved towards New Meadows when someone came towards it. It was Deith. He'd appeared out of nowhere.

Ossian watched in horror as Deith was speared through the chest by a leg. Deith didn't even have time to react to anything. Then he was lying dead on the ground, bleeding out over the fields. That's when the screaming started. Men and women came from everywhere. Several of the guards had swords and bows and were hacking and shooting at the creature as its metal body shunted off the blows like there were flies.

A noise came from the woods behind him and Ossian saw several of the Greenmen appear. Ossian at first didn't recognize what they were doing, but then vines sprouted around the creature, as if by magic, enveloping the creature and trying to pull it down. A tree sprouted underneath the creature and shot up like a spear, a spear too big to be real. The tree was easily a hundred feet tall and the body of the creature was pierced thru its top.

Then the legs convulsed and started to move again.

The legs moved around the tree, feeling for where it was. Suddenly, all the legs spread up and out, then came crashing down hard on the tree's trunk. Huge chunks of bark and wood flew everywhere.

One of the Greenmen was knocked down by a chunk of wood. As his body disintegrated on the ground, Ossian saw the earth around him sprout enormous flowers and tall grasses.

The creature's legs extended and slammed into the tree trunk again. Vines sprung from a branch of the tree and wrenched a leg free. The leg fell free, ripped from its body. The Greenmen were looking haggard. Ossian could see the signs of over casting.

A third and fourth maelstrom of legs into the tree trunk and it split, sending the creature and the tree sprawling to the ground. The thunderous collapse of the tree was deafening as wood and creature hit the ground.

Ossian watched as the creature continued to hack at the tree pierced through its torso, sending smaller and smaller chunks flying off into the distance. Eventually, the wood was pulled up and out of its torso, and Ossian watched as the torso's hole closed up. Like it had never been injured at all. The creature's five legs skittered about as it raced towards the village. Spearing people along the way and throwing them high into the sky towards the farmed fields.

When the village was finally empty of living creatures, the spider thing returned to the fields. It hooked onto certain bodies and was moving them with no obvious pattern to the work. Eventually, it grew satisfied with its work, and sat back on the ground and slowly yet surely, its spindly legs worked to bury it in the ground.

Ossian looked towards the stream's trees where seven patches of tall grass and flowers now stood. Not a single Greenman lived, yet the creature had still walked through the village with apparent ease.

A teardrop fell onto the miniature battlefield. The real Greenman in front of Ossian was watching him with eyes full of tears that were falling onto the ground.

CHAPTER 40

Ossian wasn't sure what to do.

"Is this a vision?"

The Greenman sat with Ossian, slowly blinking his tears away.

"Should I lead them away?"

The village disappeared.

"Why did you help them?"

The tentacle of trees ungrew back into the earth. All that was left was the tiny dark line that was the Night Forest.

"Is there anyway to stop this?"

The Greenman's eyes brightened.

"What, what must I do?"

The Greenman reached out a single leafy finger. As it reached out. Something crackled in the air. Ossian could feel a rift of static in the surrounding air. Suddenly, he found himself sitting in darkness. A brief flicker of symbols escaped his conscious mind. Then just as suddenly he was back in the grove with the Greenman.

Something was wrong.

The Greenman stood. Taking a single step forward, he melted

into the trees. The static in the air that had formed as a rift in the air dissipated.

Just as quickly as the rift had appeared, it had vanished. Still, Ossian was left with the feeling of terror. New Meadows would be attacked and everyone in it would die. He knew this to not be a vision or a hallucination. Merely a fact that the Greenmen had shared with him for some unknown reason.

Well, maybe not unknown, seven of them had died trying to stop the thing that came out of the ground. Maybe they needed his help. Maybe he needed their help.

Then again, maybe they were trying to trick him.

He'd seen such strange magics today, he hadn't seen or felt any circles. If there had been any circles, he would have felt them. They would have formed partially in his mind and he would have been able to sense them. He could have memorized at least pieces and parts of them so he could try to replicate them later.

So this magic was something structurally different from the magics the Mages used. Also, there was something hidden. The Greenman had left so quickly, Ossian was certain it feared whatever had happened. The Greenman's magic had faltered at the staticky rift that had formed. Nothing had been visible, but he could feel it.

Standing up, it took Ossian a moment to orient himself in the woods where he was. He was closer to the scrub brush than he initially thought, and the lightness of the fields told him the day was close to starting. It would be hard to sneak back to the village, depending on the guards.

As he walked towards New Meadows, he saw that at least Deith was looking towards him from the outskirts of the village. Deith didn't even have to guess where he was. He just looked over at him, dipped his head and walked away.

Ossian didn't even try to move through the scrub brush quietly or easily. He moved in a direct line towards the village, every stick and branch grasped at his robes. Several of the branches tore holes in his pants, and at least one pierced his skin. His thoughts were preoccupied with a gigantic rock-creature spider that was going to slaughter all the people he was responsible for. Scatter them over the fields they were currently trying to cultivate and then disappear back into those same fields.

During this time, half a dozen Greenmen would try to save them, and die in the trying.

What had the Greenman hoped would happen when he'd showed Ossian this vision? Was it a warning? A message?

Was Ossian supposed to research giant rock bugs that slaughter villages?

He had so many more questions than answers. Which in and of itself wasn't all that strange. He was used to that feeling at the Academy. This time, though, he didn't know where to start looking. He didn't have the Great Library as a resource to spend hours, days, weeks or months researching.

He had a message to prepare. And some seeking to perform.

CHAPTER 41

The air in the tent was humid this late in the evening. On his bed sat Kay and Kamien, looking like the forlorn young men that they were. Ossian wasn't sure they understood what was being asked of them. Still, Ossian wasn't sure he had many other choices. The message seal he had made for Mage Mahler told him about the Greenmen and the giant rock bug. He had stumbled over the words many times while trying to explain to Mahler about the static rift.

He'd cornered Deith later that day, asking him who could be trusted to deliver a message to Mage Mahler. Deith had suggested he could go. He was certain he could be back before the third night. Ossian believed him. Kay and Kamien were the other two people that Deith trusted, and Ossian had decided to trust in Deith.

"I will conduct some experiments in the northern fields. I will need people to understand that I can't be interrupted during these experiments or there are potential issues."

Kay and Kamien both shook their heads. Kamien spoke up, "People won't interrupt you."

"Actually, I really need the kids to be kept away more than the adults. The adults fear magic. The kids, and it's my fault, they think magic is fun."

Kay chuckled at that. "You have built quite the audience."

"Deith will leave before dawn in the morning, and will be missing for two days. He tells me he'll be back before the third day ends."

"I will."

Ossian nodded. He wanted to believe Deith in this. "People are going to ask. I need someone to have overheard Deith being sent for reinforcements. We don't have the people to pull guard duty and farm that we need."

"I mean, no one's going to say no to less guard duty." Kay smiled.

Kamien got a look of concern on his face. "Are you going to tell us why he's really being sent?"

Deith shook his head no. "Not yet."

Ossian had to hand it to the two young men. They took that news better than he thought he would.

"So spread a rumor, keep the kids away from your experiments." Kay repeated back in a very monotone voice.

"The experiments are dangerous, interruption would be catastrophic. I will explain this to everyone in the village." Ossian smiled when he thought of the kids, "Yet some of the younger folks will still be too close. I would like to prevent that."

Kamien chimed in, "Sound like the south fields need some rock picking."

Kay nodded back at this.

"Thank you two." Ossian then followed them to the mouth of the tent and watched as they left. Making sure that they had disappeared into the village back to their houses, before stepping back into the tent.

"How dangerous?" Deith's face was nearly unreadable.

"I don't know. The magic I was telling you about it felt—wrong. I need to investigate."

"Is the village in danger?"

"I don't know Deith. If I think it is, I will evacuate. But where will these people go?"

"Dead people can't do anything."

"I know."

"I'll be back before the sun sets on the third day. If I'm late, you can assume I'm dead."

"Okay, that last sentence was way too morbid. This isn't the army. Or a war."

"I'm not so sure, Mage Ossian."

"Well, I'll keep the people safe."

Deith shrugged like it was what he would say. "We do what we must." The side of his mouth twitched and he let himself out of the tent.

Ossian sat in the tent mulling over his options. He needed research from some place better stocked with magical knowledge. He had so many questions and almost no answers. Hopefully Mage Mahler could provide something.

Anything.

New Meadows was depending on him, and he was close to out of ideas.

CHAPTER 42

The next morning, bright and early, he took his breakfast to go and headed out towards the northern fields. He'd briefly explained to the adults in the area that he was going to go do some experimental research in the fields and he needed quiet and solitude. He hinted that the experiments, if interrupted, would be dangerous to outsiders. Which he guessed could be true, even if he wasn't sure.

Heading towards the northern forest, he poured some water in the silver rimmed seeking bowl and placed the tin needle on the surface. Concentrating on the entity that he saw rising from the fields, with the Greenman, he mumbled the incantation over and over. The surrounding air sparked and drew around him as he focused the energy of the circle around the bowl. The needle angled straight ahead of where he was pointing.

Wanting to make sure the spell was working correctly, he focused on Deith. The needle flipped around to point off towards the direction that Deith would have had to take in order to get back to Mage Mahler. Focusing on the Greenman, he was surprised to see the needle swish back and forth along the frontage that was the Night Forest. Finally, he focused his mind back on the giant rock-spider and the needle led him farther away from New Meadows and closer to the Night Forest.

As he moved closer towards the Northern fields, the needle stayed on course. He knew the needle would stay on course. He'd been taught it in class and used it many, many times to find things he'd misplaced. Still, he would occasionally rotate the bowl just to make sure that the needle would move. He wondered if other people did that as well. When the spell didn't give feedback, would they do things to induce feedback from the spell?

Finally, after trudging into the middle of the one field that was already planted. The tin needle dipped towards his feet. Just to make sure, he walked forty paces in five or six different directions and marked out the dimensions of where the needle dipped. Glancing back over the area, he was sure no one would believe him if he told them that underneath this area was a creature that big. It was nearly thirty paces across.

He'd seen it with his own eyes in the forest, and he wasn't sure he believed it. He was sure someone would yell at him as he cleared a thirty pace circle area of an already plowed and planted field.

It took him almost an hour to make a big enough area to lay out a circle. He wasn't sure what kind of circle to use. There were several kinds of spells he thought he might use. He could try to alter a seeking spell, maybe find the depth of the creature. There was a material spell he could try to find out what the creature was made of. He wasn't fully sure knowing the material would matter, but he had to do something.

Then there was a disembodiment spell. Taking out a stick, he scratched out the runes for the disembodiment circle. He wasn't sure what would trigger a creature like that to awaken, and the reality was he wasn't sure he wanted to find out.

Sitting down, he concentrated on the disembodiment spell and dug deep inside himself. Forcing his consciousness deep underground, he searched for something that wasn't dirt or rocks. Then suddenly his attention was drawn to a void in the earth. It was larger than the village houses. He couldn't see the thing specifically. He was guessing its size based on what wasn't there. Six tentacles of nothing stretched out into the dirt.

He floated around the entity, looking for any kind of clue, something that could help him get any kind of information. Something about the void bothered him. He wasn't aware of anything that could hide from circles like this. It was like the thing just didn't exist, or didn't want to be found.

Curiosity got the better of him and he reached out a hand to touch it. When a spell circle he'd never seen before flared into life in the void and suddenly he was being pulled into it. He wasn't sure what would happen if he got sucked into the void, and he was certain he didn't want to know. Wrestling with the pull was mentally taxing. He pulled and pulled at his own consciousness as the void tried to tug him closer. After what felt like forever, he finally was able to pull himself far enough away from the void that he could no longer feel it trying to suck him into it.

He moved around the creature, being careful not to touch any part of the void with his consciousness. Circling further and further away from the creature, looking for anything unusual or abnormal. Something that could have been a clue.

Moving east out towards the Night Forest, he moved his consciousness up towards the surface and roughly to what he thought the depth of the creature was. He could feel the sweat forming on his actual body. He was nearing his limit for the day.

All he'd discovered was that there was indeed some gigantic murder creature buried deep underground. The spell circle he'd seen was half buried in his subconscious, but he didn't want to focus on it yet, in case it reactivated. He was guessing it was at least a hundred paces down. There was no way they could dig it out. Even if he could convince the village to help him dig. He also wondered if digging it out would activate it.

Racing back towards his body, he reached it barely in time for his gasping body to shake and shiver and fall over into the dirt.

CHAPTER 43

The dry, dusty taste of the dirt filled his mouth. The idea that his body was buried deep down with the creature was his only thought. Pushing himself up off the ground, he leapt to his feet. A small puff of dirt followed him up as the blood rushed to his brain and he swayed where he was. He was facing towards the Night Forest.

"What have you shown me?" He muttered as the headache pounded inside his skull.

A whisper wafted on the wind. "Mage Ossian?"

Could he have awakened the creature so easily? He glanced around him in the dusk of the coming night. Frantically looking for the telltale sign of a leg poking up out of the ground, when he spotted Kamien and Kay standing a good hundred feet away.

"Damn you two, I thought I was hearing things."

Kay smiled, a huge grin visible even in the coming darkness, "Well, you did, Mage Ossian. Are you okay? Mom sent us to check up on you."

"No worries, let me gather my things and I'll come back with you." Ossian tried to steady himself as he bent over to collect his spell ingredients. Suddenly his mouth was full of bone dry dirt again. He heard both boys off in the distance, shuffling around.

"Are you okay?" they shouted.

"Why are you so far away?" It dawned on Ossian that it was weird for him to be collapsed, laying on the ground again. Yet he couldn't for the life of him think of why.

"You said the experiments were dangerous and we shouldn't interrupt." Their voices were still so very far away. Obviously shouting over the distance.

As Ossian's lips went to form a smile, they dragged the dirt across his teeth, making him gag and choke. As he tried to spit, he discovered he had no saliva left. His dry mouth caused him to cough, yet he couldn't raise himself up off of the dirt enough to bring his body off of the ground.

He laid there coughing for what seemed like an eternity before two sturdy pairs of hands raised him up into the sitting position and placed a waterskin near his lips. He tried to drink, but all he did was dribble water all over himself.

"Is he gonna die?" Kay's voice held a concern that made Ossian's heart feel light.

Finally, after coughing for what felt like years, Ossian got some water into his mouth as he swished and spit out onto the dirt. Taking another brief pull on the waterskin, he got a little water down. Not halting, but at least slowing the coughing.

"Okay." His voice was hoarse and ragged, like he had had nothing to drink in ages.

A couple of shorter coughs later and more water, he stood up. Or, more appropriately, the boys held him up as he tried to stand.

He managed to shake his arm towards the village. "Home."

As the boys helped him limp home, they were silent the entire way. Ossian was still slightly coughing by the time they made it into the village and it was full darkness by then.

What surprised him the most was that it looked like the entire village was up and waiting for him to return. There were whispers and mutterings.

"Fetch a chair Espeth." Cara's voice cut across the crowd.

Something small streak away in the fading light. Several of the villagers brought their mage flame torches into the square and formed an area.

"Were you attacked?" Yough asked, who then motioned for several of the ex-soldiers to take up positions around the village. They quickly and silently disappeared from Ossian's view. Ossian's thoughts lingered on how well trained they were.

"No, no. This was all me. Magic has a cost. Too much casting—now I'm weak."

A chair was thrust behind him and his knees gave way as the boys guided him into the chair.

Yough spoke first. "He can't be left alone tonight."

Cara piped up, "Kay, move his cot into the house. He can sleep there tonight. We'll take turns watching him."

On one hand, Ossian loved that the entire village appeared to be out and about, worried about him. On the other hand, he would be fine. He made to stand up, trying to say something about how he would be fine in his tent. Judging by the looks he was getting, he was pretty sure he wasn't making any sense. His last memory was of Yough stepping in and grabbing him as he fell.

Then the blackness enveloped him.

CHAPTER 44

Ossian was sitting in a field as the legs sprouted up around him everywhere. Gigantic shoots of some unknown substance shot out of the ground. Massive clouds of dust and dirt spewing up everywhere. Dozens of legs kept shooting up out of the ground. Ossian finally saw them. Dozens of massive spider like creatures with bodies speared all along their legs.

The blood ran down their legs and formed the stream that led off into the Night Forest. As the stream of blood moved towards the Night Forest, it turned into water and the Greenman stood along the bank, waving and shouting something that Ossian couldn't hear.

The Greenman continued to wave his hands and shout from such a long way away. Ossian still couldn't make out what he was trying to communicate. The Greenman completely captivated his attention. The spider creatures were moving all around him, each leg pounding into the ground with plumes of dirt and debris scattering with every step they took.

Yet, the Greenman held his attention completely. He was trying to tell Ossian something, and Ossian knew it was important.

The blood was dripping on his face. Drip.

He didn't want to look up. Drip.

Unwilling to face the horror of who was dead. Drip.

That Ossian had failed. Drip.

Slowly, he tilted his head upwards, scared of the eyes that would stare back into his soul.

~

THE FIRELIGHT FLICKERED in a covered room. His eyes were heavy. His body felt like he'd just gone ten rounds with Jorn.

"LeAnne, his eyes are opening."

Ossian heard someone mumbling and realized it was him. He tried to form words, but the only thing that came out sounded like the ravings of a mad-man. Spiders and dirt, blood and magic.

Deciding he needed a better grasp of his surroundings, he tried to sit up, before four hands pushed him back down.

"Mage Ossian, please stay down." Yet, the words just made little sense in his head.

More mumblings and he tried to get up again.

"LAY DOWN." The voice was commanding. Ossian did what she said.

The commanding voice continued, slightly less of an I'll-kill-you-edge to it. "If you stand up again, I will have you strapped to the cot."

The fire was too hot, the light was too bright, and the scent of rosemary and sage filled the room. His senses were becoming less and less cloudy with each passing moment. Then his stomach started acting up on him. Rolling to his side, he glimpsed a bucket was already there as he heaved repeatedly into it.

Someone's voice, not far off, he wasn't sure who, sighed loudly. "We just got that into him."

~

HE AWOKE LATER. How much later he couldn't be certain. Hours, weeks, years. His body still felt abused. The knot in his stomach was now a pulsing pain of feed-me-now. A cool rag was on his head and as his eyes fluttered open, he saw LeAnne.

"Hello." He croaked out of a throat that felt like it had been beaten from the inside. Every inch felt raw. Even trying to swallow hurt him.

"Fetch them, now." LeAnne shouted off at someone.

She glowered down at Ossian as she held up his head slightly and tried to place a cup next to his lips. He tried to take a sip, but just as much water fell around him as went into his throat. Still swallowing hurt so much, he winced from the pain.

"How long?" Even that simple phrase felt like he was pulling deep from within himself to not pass out from the pain.

"Less than a day." LeAnne tried to tip some more water into his mouth, but Ossian shook her off.

"If you don't drink, you will die." The look she gave him told him she was on the verge of allowing him to die. Then her eyes softened.

She added, "Please don't die."

Ossian drank half the cup. It felt like all he could do. His throat seared with pain on each swallow, his stomach complained that it wanted something more than cold water. When Cara and Yough burst into the room, he smiled at them, then the blackness swallowed him again.

CHAPTER 45

The whispers filled the room, Ossian could hear them. He was certain he recognized Cara and LeAnne, Yough and Bakker, for certain.

"Deith will be back in another day. He can't make another run so fast." Cara said.

"He's had very little water in the last two days. There is only so much I can do for him." Ossian thought it sounded like LeAnne.

"I'm okay."

All four of them startled at his voice.

"Really, I just need to eat."

Bakker spoke up first, "You've been passed out for two days, Mage Ossian. Eating isn't wise."

"Sorry, should have explained casting sickness to someone." Ossian knew this was a massive oversight on his part. He was surprised that none of the soldiers knew about it. Then again, he didn't fully understand the organization of the King's armies. He understood the King's personal guard and the Castle's garrison. They obviously had mages in them and knew how to handle a stupid mage who cast too much magic.

LeAnne spoke again. "Maybe some bread."

"Please." Ossian remembered throwing up, but the sickly sweet smell of vomit wasn't present. Someone must have taken care of that for him.

Ossian heard the tearing of a loaf as something soft was placed into his hands. Slowly at first, he nibbled on the bread. The outer crust was hard and crisp with the sharp edges of bread baked yesterday. The inside, though, was squishy and soft, just enough air to make the bread pliable and chewy. The taste was bread. He never knew how to describe it. Bland yet there.

As he nibbled, a cup was placed in his other hand. He nibbled and sipped till the bread was all gone. Then he laid there. He could feel the four pairs of eyes staring at him.

"Really, I'll be okay."

"You look like you've risen from the dead." Yough's rough manner never hid his feeling.

"Could I have some more bread, please?" He croaked out. Ossian would not try to sit up yet. He still felt weak, but the bread was settling in nicely. His stomach wasn't rolling, his head was a kind of clear, but he was thirsty enough to not trust himself with a bucket of water.

Opening his eyes, the daylight streamed in from the doorway that hadn't been closed. Between the sunlight and the smoke in the house, he gathered it was mid-day.

Cara tore off another chunk of bread and placed it in his hands as Yough refilled his cup from a barrel outside and brought it back, placing it in Ossian's hand.

"Two days, huh?" Ossian choked out. Even to him, his voice sounded more like an old man on his deathbed. Now that he had time to think about it, he wondered it if was the sucking of the void object that did this to him. The disembodiment spell certainly had lasted longer than he'd meant it to, but that spell was minimally taxing at best, even when sustained for hours.

When he noticed no one was answering him, he wondered if he'd even said it out loud. He was just about to speak up when Kamien rushed into the room.

Kamien looked over Ossian, "Oh, good, he's still alive. Deith just came over the hill." Then his face brightened and he broke into a grin.

As everyone was distracted looking at Kamien, Ossian swung his legs off the cot and tried to sit up slowly. As one, they all swiveled. LeAnne's frown came back to her face.

"It's okay, LeAnne, I just need to eat. Thank you all for taking care of me."

"Cara insisted we keep you alive." LeAnne's word sounded on the edge of hard-bitten truth, but her small upturned mouth told Ossian she was trying to go for levity. He was pretty sure that was the first time that he'd heard her joke.

"Well, I'm still grateful for the efforts, even if they were forced upon you." Ossian stared longer at the door than he should have. Slowly taking bites out of the bread, chewing and then, with a healthy swig of water, he'd swallow it all. He wasn't sure how to politely ask for something more substantial.

That's when Deith appeared silent as a ghost. Ossian knew he'd been staring at the door, when suddenly, Deith was there. One minute sunlight, the next Deith.

His frown was abundantly apparent as he scanned the room and probably put the pieces together before anyone spoke. Cara took two quick steps and threw her arms around him. Ossian was pretty sure she was trying to squeeze the life out of him. As Deith kissed her on the head.

He looked over at Yough and raised an eyebrow.

Yough sighed, "Mage Ossian passed out."

Deith's expression didn't change a bit. He just glanced over at Ossian, "When?"

Ossian took a last swallow of water and bread, then spoke, "The day you left, at dusk."

"Is that the first food you've given him?" Deith was obviously experienced with casting sickness. If the mage was up and able to, you fed them.

As far as Ossian knew, that was the only cure, if that word could even be used for casting sickness. Time and food.

"We tried to get him to eat and drink, but he kept throwing it up." LeAnne's voice was defensive.

"I didn't explain casting sickness to anyone. That's on me Deith."

Deith just nodded his head. Then finally, over the oppressive silence added, "Still hungry?"

"Starving." Ossian couldn't help from saying it. It sounded so mean, but it was also true.

"It's close to mid-day. Bakker, Yough, can you go tell everyone they'll need to make more?"

Bakker's face was confused. "Everyone?"

Deith's face broke into a massive grin. "Casting sickness. He's going to blow your mind, Bakker."

It took nearly an hour for everyone in the village to prepare their mid-day meals. Normally, the mid-day meal would be sent by children out to the surrounding people working. As Ossian slowly walked outside with Deith, he noticed that everyone had brought out blankets. Some villagers had chairs.

"Seriously, you gathered everyone?" Ossian wasn't sure how much of a spectacle he wanted to be for the village.

"They just spent two days scared you were going to die. They need to understand." Deith's grip was firm on Ossian's arm, firm but not demanding. "No one believes us when we try to explain casting sickness, not until they see it for themselves."

Deith's voice got suddenly very serious, "Assuming they don't die from it."

"Deith, I wasn't casting a dangerous spell. I'll have to explain later."

Deith didn't seem mollified, but he also wasn't openly challenging Ossian in front of the entire village.

That's when Ossian noticed the table of food. It was piled high with breads, at least a couple of slices of meat, a couple of bowls of porridge and what looked like half a meat pie.

Deith sat Ossian down at the table, smiled weakly and spoke out loud to everyone but him, "The casting of magic has a cost. Over-casting has a cost some of us have seen more than once. It usually results in the mage's death. Sometimes, if the mage is very, very lucky, they survive."

Ossian could already feel the eyes on him. Deith wasn't informing the village. He was admonishing Mage Ossian.

Deith continued, "The caring of a mage that has casting sickness is food. I know it sounds strange. Since we have a mage in our village, we all need to understand this."

He glanced at Ossian, as the edges of his mouth turned up, then back at the village. "I thought it would be nice for us to all share this meal together."

CHAPTER 46

Later, as Ossian lay in his cot, his mind wandered back to the table laden with food. He'd wanted so much to have carefully eaten a handful of food and proven Deith wrong in front of everyone. After the first couple of bites though, he almost couldn't stop himself. It was like every time he'd overextended himself at the Academy.

Even he wasn't sure where all the food went.

Everyone was at least polite enough to not gawk at him. As he shoveled handful after handful of food continuously for over an hour.

"Are you going to be okay?" Deith had followed him to his tent, apparently to make sure he was okay. Ossian had assumed he'd already left the tent in Deith's silent way.

"Yeah, I'll be fine."

"Normally, I'm not one to chide a mage, but what were you thinking?"

"I was exploring the Northern fields for the creature. I found it Deith, it's real." Ossian thought about that for a second. "Well, something is down there."

"Something?"

Ossian explained the void and how it had tried to suck him in. How he was pretty confident the pulling of the void was what had drained him so much. Deith, to his credit, stayed silent as Ossian tried to explain it.

"When I touched it, there was a spell circle that activated."

"So it's magical?"

"If not magical, it's unmagical. If that's even a thing."

Ossian moved to his desk, cracking open his grimoire. Then he tried to sketch out the circle that had flared to life when he'd touched the creature.

"The Greenman was trying to warn us. Something is dangerous here."

"Or he was trying to bait you into a trap?"

Ossian glanced up at that. Deith's face was serious. Ossian spoke more to himself than to Deith, "I don't think so. The Greenman felt... right. I don't know how else to say it, Deith."

"Will you at least consider taking someone with you next time?"

"Into the fields? Yes. Into the forest, No."

"You are the boss, Mage Ossian." Deith clearly disagreed with his choice, but he also knew Ossian was the person in charge of the village.

"Deith, the void, it's wrong. Everything I understand about magic says it shouldn't exist."

"Yet, there it is." Deith held out a message seal for him. "Mage Mahler made me wait while he made this. He said it wouldn't help much. But he'd start looking in the archives for information."

"Night, Deith."

"Get some sleep, Mage Ossian."

"I will. No more excursions without telling someone. I promise."

Deith's eyes told Ossian he didn't believe him, but Ossian knew his words were true. He realized today how dangerous he'd been. How much he'd placed the village in danger, and how little he'd learned.

After Deith left, Ossian got up and broke open Mage Mahler's message seal. The purple seal dissolved into a glittering miniature image of Mage Mahler bent over his desk. Ossian was certain he could see the haggard look of Mage Mahler, who was trying to be useful, but had nothing yet. Or maybe Ossian was just projecting his own fears.

The message wished Ossian well. That Mage Mahler had only heard rumors of creatures living in the Night Forest and to be careful with the Greenmen. He asked if Ossian had tried to bind the weasel, admitting that he himself had never gotten the spell to work. That surprised Ossian. Mage Mahler had always known everything, always had an answer for Ossian. Yet here he was, sending him a family heirloom that he'd never managed to successfully bond to.

The real world was surprising Ossian at every turn. Creatures only rumored to exist in the Night Forest. He now knew them as the Greenmen. Strange murder creatures in the fields around New Meadows that were magically protected. He'd need to warn Mage Mahler about that, even if it wasn't tonight. And now an admission of magic that Mage Mahler himself hadn't been able to get working.

It was a strange new world for Ossian. One in which he thought he had understood the rules. Around every corner was a new rule that seemed to defy the rules he knew. His stomach was bulging from all the food he ate. His body was exhausted from the spells and his mind was just winding up with all the possibilities.

Pulling out the secret grimoire from Mage Mahler, he opened to the first blank page and copied over the spell circle from his early sketch in the grimoire. It was a complex circle, and it took Ossian late into the night to fully draw out the circle. He didn't want to wait longer in case his memory failed him. When he'd finished drawing out the circle, in two halves, to his satisfaction, he collapsed on the cot Kay had been kind enough to bring back to his tent.

His mind quickly collapsed into sleep.

CHAPTER 47

Ossian was back in the field. Floating above his own body. He dove into the ground down to the level of the spider creature. Glancing at the creature, he felt the spell circle flare and suck him inside of the spider creature.

Sucked into the void.

He sat up, gasping hard. Daylight streamed in through the tent's cloth. His body was soaked in sweat, the tent was hot and overwhelming. Looking around, he realized he was still in his cot. He was safe. Well, as safe as one could be from nightmares that were true.

Ossian wasn't sure what he should do. He could concentrate on the weasel, but that didn't seem to be a priority at the moment. The mystery of the Greenman was prominent, still the only actual way to discover anything about that was to disappear into the forest. Then again, he had the spare leaves and a bit of the substance that they turned into. He could experiment with those. He knew he should experiment with them, understand them. What was their link to the spider creature?

Still, what he wanted to do was research into the spider creature.

The spell circle he had copied was dangerous, though. He wasn't fully sure what the consequences of using the circle would be. Could it suck him into nowhere just by using it? Not having access to the Academy Library was a limiting factor to any of the things that he wanted to do.

He was debating using the circle on one of the houses. Maybe it would just suck him inside the house. The symbols in the circle were archaic though. Altering them was harder than the spell circles he was familiar with.

There was also the factor of how tired he still felt. From his previous experience at the Academy, he was guessing he had a day or two before he should try any magic. However, being out for two days was most certainly the longest and closest he had ever come to full-blown casting sickness. Reality was he shouldn't cast another spell for four days, minimum.

Satisfied that waiting for magic limited his choices in what he could do. Ossian decided he could at least research something to replace the moon symbol in the binding spell. He also avoided the Greenman. He wasn't sure if even other people casting spells on him could drain him. Another thing to ask Mage Mahler in his next missive. He knew other spell circles cast on him wouldn't drain him, but the Greenman didn't use circles. Their magic was different.

Ossian searched through the tomes that Mage Mahler had given him and saw *Symbols of Transmutional Power*. Ossian wondered if Mage Mahler sent it up on purpose. Although he also knew it was one of the more comprehensive tomes of symbolic magic that existed. It was a foundational tome for the aspiring mage. Still, he felt obligated to Mage Mahler. This tome alone was expensive, and he'd been set up with seven tomes.

Grabbing a stool, he walked outside. Sitting outside his tent, looking into the village. The village was already past the fast break, but it was before mid-day meal. The children were absent from what Ossian could see. Occasionally, a villager wandered out of their home, smiled while waving, then wandered back to whatever chore they had been doing before noticing him. No one the wiser that a deadly spider creature was lurking just on the edge of the fields.

Ossian thumbed through the tome, he knew most of the book. He just needed something to trigger his brain into searching down a path of some change to the binding spell for the moon symbol. He was guessing it represented the nocturnal nature of the weasel. However, the moon could also symbolize that the weasel was female, or maybe that the idol wasn't active in the daylight.

Then it came to Ossian like a bolt. Ossian groaned out loud at his lack of understanding. He'd tried the binding spell in the daytime. If it was a nocturnal animal, he needed to do it during the night. Since it was the symbol of the moon, it would be the most powerful in the full moon. He'd need to ask a farmer when the next full moon would be. His father, the farmer, always knew the moon cycle, why he wasn't sure.

Ossian had a feeling as he put the binding spell together in his head that this was the right path. It just felt right. He would still need to wait till the next full moon. Hopefully, the next one wasn't in the three or four days he needed to wait for his body to gain back its strength.

He closed the tome of Symbols and sat back, happy with himself for discovering the binding spells secret. The air smelled cleaner. He knew it wasn't actually cleaner. It was probably just a trick of his mind, but there you had it. The sky was bluer. The village was looking brighter.

The last couple of days had been a blur, or more appropriately, a nightmare for him. Yet with the villages help he'd pulled through, if barely. He smiled and leaned back on his stool, placing the tome in his lap. He had to admit, he had it pretty good. Sure there were things looming in the distance. Things he would work hard to stop. New Meadows was under his protection, and hopefully he could garner a peace with the Greenmen, or maybe even a truce.

He briefly entertained the idea of opening diplomacies with the Greenmen. Then he decided they probably didn't want diplomacy with the Kingdom. It wasn't like they didn't know the Kingdom existed. They hadn't been surprised at the sight of a new village. They had contacted Ossian, or at least one of them had established contact with him. Was that a good thing?

Deith had been wrong. Ossian could feel the Greenmen's sincerity in wanting to help.

For some unknown reason, he knew, deep down, that the Greenmen could have already wiped out the village. They choose not to.

That's when the pitter-patter of small footsteps first came to Ossian ears. A set of small footsteps off to his left. He was certain, as he was of anything, they belonged to one of the smaller children. Espeth, Boa or Piaa. He tried to not move, so they would think they had snuck up on him. The footsteps grew closer as Ossian continued to look off into the village.

They were close enough Ossian could hear their breathing when he finally said, "Sneaking up on a man with a sword is a risky business."

"Ah, Mage Ossian, you spoil everything." Piaa said.

Ossian tilted his head towards Piaa and smiled, "Hey Piaa, how are you doing today?"

That's when he felt the *Symbols of Transmutional Power* being lifted off of his lap. Piaa had doublecrossed him. He wondered if she'd convinced Boa to do it. Most likely it was Espeth. She was the boldest of the three, despite being the youngest.

"That tome is worth hundreds of crowns, Espeth."

"What does it say, Mage Ossian?"

"It's one of the most comprehensive collections of symbols that mages use to build spell circles."

"So it's a magic book?" Espeth's voice leaked with wonder and awe. "Can I read it?"

"You can look through it, yes. Reading it takes years. Even I still have to use it occasionally to solve some problem I'm having."

Ossian was still looking at Piaa as he talked. He could hear the parchment leaves shuffling as the pages were turned. Piaa dashed around him towards Espeth, so she could look at their ill-gotten gains.

"It's just those squiggles you do."

Ossian laughed as he stood up. Carefully taking the book from the girl's hands, he placed it on the stool he had been sitting on. "Yes, squiggles. But those squiggles have power."

He leaned down near the tent and drew the four symbols needed to make a mage flame circle.

"Those four symbols, when powered, are what create the mage flame spell. And they have to be in the right order and be perfectly balanced in order for the power to flow through them properly."

"How hard is magic?" Espeth, as usual, was the one speaking.

"Well, it can kill you. As you no doubt saw these last few days. But if you are careful, and listen to the Mages who teach at the Academy," Ossian thought back to all the yellings and screaming most of the Mages did to the apprentices, "well then you stand a decent chance of not killing yourself."

"Did you almost die?" Piaa's voice was barely above a whisper as she said it. Her eyes were downcast and she wouldn't look up.

"Yes, I think I came as close as I have ever been. Luckily—"

Piaa rushed forward and threw her arms around Ossian's leg, locking him into place. "Please don't die Mage Ossian." Then, just as quickly, she dashed off to her house with Espeth screaming after her.

A wind whistled in between the houses of the village as Ossian collected his tome and stool. The legs of the stool left a triangle of imprints on the ground. The smell of the mid-day meal was wafting on the air and Ossian could already feel his stomach grumbling. He was wondering who he would eat with as he turned around, when Cara waved him over.

"You're with us today. You can take Deith his meal out in the fields." Cara's smile was infectious and almost made Ossian forget the last few days of his ordeal.

"I'll be right over, just need to put these things away." Carrying them into the tent, he secured his copy of *Symbols of Transmutional Power* into his chest. Spying the red jasper weasel, he stroked it as he told it they would try again soon. Then walked off to hopefully not eat Cara out of house or home.

CHAPTER 48

The grasses around the stream were a bright green, standing upright and tall in the mid-day sun. He couldn't even see the scrub brush where, just four days ago, he'd come crashing out of the treeline to surprise Deith with his revelations. Crossing the stream, he wandered south along the dirt paths that threaded between the fields.

Plowed fields, the smell of turned dirt left to dry, reminded him of his childhood. The familiar smell anchoring him to his family so far away in physical location, but also in time. He'd spent more time at the Academy than he had on his family's farm.

Rock picking and harvesting were what he had primarily been involved in. As of age eight, he'd still been too young to drive a horse strong enough to plow a field. He could barely remember the actual farming much, it being mostly a blur in his memory.

Except for that fateful day. The entire day had felt auspicious. He'd woken up with the air feeling staticky all around him. Everything metal he'd touched sparked against his hand. By the third time he'd touched the metal pot near the fire, his mom had commented about dragging his feet too much. Little did she know.

Rock picking that day was harder than most. His brain flashed between symbols and lightning bolts. The symbols he now recognized. Back then, they were just squiggles, like Espeth had said.

He could feel something inside of him building all day. Every rock seemed to be a monumental effort and when his brother had finally smacked his head, he'd nearly lost it at him. He thanked the gods he hadn't.

Ossian yelled at his brother Alois, but his head felt like it was practically splitting open at that point. Something was coming to a crescendo inside his body and he did not know what it was. When suddenly Ossian had turned and thrown a rock, across the field, aiming for a tree that had sat between the fields his entire life, screaming as the lightning built up inside him and as the rock left his hand, the lightning arc'd up and out his arms, through his forearms and over both his hands, crossing the field and obliterating the tree.

He could still feel the heat from the lightning, the charred burning of the tree that he could smell from a field away. The look on Alois's face, that he would remember till the day he died. Absolute terror.

The pounding in his head quickly subsided, but his arms and hands hurt. The lightning scars from the wild magic, as the mages called it, never went away. Dad had sent one of his brothers into town on their fastest horse to fetch a King's man to come see. It had been a surprisingly fast transition from son of a farmer, to appentice at the Academy.

Ossian now knew it wasn't unusual for magic to manifest in non-magic families, but at the time he'd just been a scared little boy who had thrown a lightning bolt and was scared to touch any of his family, lest they be obliterated like the tree.

Mage Mahler had been on a trip for the King when he'd been accosted by the King's men to see about a little boy throwing lightning bolts. That had been so long ago.

The sight of Deith out with a plow nag, turning over the dirt brought Ossian back out of his maudlin mood. He waved and pointed at the sack he was carrying, food for Deith and his son Boa. Boa was apparently helping in the fields, most likely for some punishment. Cara had been cagey as to what. Ossian had learned not to pry when families got quiet about things.

As Deith unhooked the horse and set it to eating a bag of oats. He snatched the food out of Ossian's hand and laughed out loud.

"Ah, so you are alive?" Deith said as he threw a roll over to Boa.

"And you seem no worse for having run to the castle and back."

Deith shrug his shoulders, and bent at the waist, "Well, maybe a little, but it was a good run. Going back into the forest tonight?" Deith said it like it was just a casual conversation. Not like Ossian had nearly died this week.

"No, gonna play it calm for a couple of days. They teach us we need a cooling-off period."

Boa finally spoke up, "Did you really almost die?"

Ossian raised his hand up and shook it side to side. "Yeah, kind of. With magic, it's hard to tell. Without your mom and LeAnne, yes, you probably would have found my corpse out in the north field."

Boa didn't continue speaking. He just looked at the ground as he ate his roll.

Ossian changed the conversation then, "How long before the next full moon?"

Deith didn't even look up. "Twelve days. Why?"

"I just lost track of time, what with being unconscious and near death and all." Ossian knew Deith would hear the lie. He also knew Deith would let it go. Ossian didn't want to scare Boa, though. "Finally, learning how to farm, huh?"

Boa's response was quiet enough. It took Ossian a moment for it to register. "I don't want to be a farmer."

"He wants to be a mage." Deith said it with just enough condemnation. Ossian wondered if perhaps he was to blame.

"Oh." Ossian looked over at Boa. "I'm sorry, that's not something you get to choose. How old are you now?"

"Nine and a half." Boa's voice told Ossian that his family had had this conversation more than once now.

"Ah, well. My understanding is that most children manifest early. Some as early as six, eight is the norm. That's when it happened to me. Ten is abnormal but has happened. After ten, I've never heard of magical power manifesting after ten, though."

"So I still have time."

Ossian didn't want to give him any false hope, mages in non-magical families, while not extremely rare, still did not happen often.

"You know what I find the most interesting, Boa. Is that whoever you are, it seems like someone else's life is always more interesting?"

"That's what dad said." His voice leaked derision.

Ossian sat down in the dirt. "I wanted to be a bard. I wanted to sing and play an instrument and tell stories. Travel to far-off lands. But you know what?"

Ossian let it hang there in the air. He waited till Boa glanced up at him. "You don't want to hear me sing. It's like cats mewling."

Boa smiled at that. "It can't be that bad."

"No really, I debated using it when the bear attacked your dad and me. It's that bad. Then when I got these scars," Ossian put out his hands, to make sure Boa could clearly see the lighting patterns in his skin that always lurked just below the surface. "I was dragged to the Academy and told I would be a mage. I hated it."

Ossian let that hang in the air between them for a bit.

"For a while, I got fed and learned magic and could cast spells. You know the one thing I wanted? To be a farmer. Farming is simple. Then Mage Mahler made me train with the soldiers. I didn't hate it, in fact I grew to love it. But it took a very long time to grow into it. To really love it."

"Jorn would beat me till I was bruised and sore. Then I would return to the Academy where they would stuff my head with knowledge, till I felt like I couldn't think. Then I would go to bed and do it all again the next day."

"I don't want to be a soldier." Boa was back to pouty.

Deith finally spoke up, "Ah, that you get little choice in either. Up, we have a field to plow."

CHAPTER 49

His lunch delivery duties taken care of, Ossian needed to find something to occupy his mind for several days until he could cast spells again. He could research the spider, but he knew that would tempt him into magical research, which led to casting spells. He knew from his time at the Academy his ability to stop himself from unwise things was low.

So each morning he volunteered with someone to help be their hands for the day. Bakker didn't object when he volunteered to do whatever random labor he asked of him. Piaa was also glad for the help as it meant Ossian split a lot of firewood for the next kiln firing. Followed up by mixing random containers of dirt and water, or decanting water off from a settled bucket.

Bakker explained, as they decanted, how the slurry mixture was the clay slurry without the rocks and gunk, or the excess water he would have to wait to evaporate off, anyway. Ossian had always loved to learn about new topics. One of the few things about magic he truly loved was the breadth of knowledge he could learn.

He ended that first day covered in clay and physically exhausted.

Mentally, his mind was still on the giant lurking spider, but sleep came quickly and the nightmare did not return.

Day two was much the same, but with the blacksmith, Ossian spent most of the day breaking up large chunks of coal into smaller chunks for the forge, as the blacksmith made various necessary items.

Mostly the day was taken up with pounding out horseshoes, the speed with which the smith could turn a small length of metal into a flat rod, then a horseshoe, followed finally by piercing the nail holes through the metal, was astounding. Ossian felt like it was its own kind of magic.

The blacksmith preferred to call it skill. The smooth progression and ease with which he performed those simple steps, Ossian was certain it required months if not years of skills to do so easily. Each step a learned progression from the next, almost like the circle formation for a spell.

As he stepped out of the blacksmith's shop, the sun shone so brightly he wasn't sure how the blacksmith could stand it. Working in the dark so much, staring at his own small fire, looking for colors that Ossian wasn't sure were there. The blacksmith, his arms bulging from the hammering, had tried to point the colors out to him.

On the third day, Ossian was feeling back to his old self. He'd still slept amazingly from the physical exhaustion, but he was hoping today would be the last day and he could get back to doing what he did best.

Magic.

He missed it, the energy flowing through him, coursing out his hands into some form of useful result. Still, he had another day of rest before he should try even a simple spell again.

CHAPTER 50

The next day, Ossian found Anton, the woodsman, and asked if they could do with a laborer for the day.

Anton looked at him for a long time, before finally asking, "You gonna bring another bear?"

Ossian waited for the smile, or the laugh, that small polite gesture of just joking, but it never came. Finally, after too long of a silence, Ossian said, "No."

Anton nodded at this and hitched up his horse to the cart. When he was done, he turned to Ossian and said, "Sure, you can help me."

The day was the strangest one he'd experienced. So far, the village had been polite, if not outright glad of his contributions. Anton though, maybe he was just surly, maybe Anton was not used to being helped. Ossian got the impression he was not wanted.

Ossian tried to help Anton prepare and hitch up the horses, but the woodsman continued with his morning ritual of preparation. Ignoring Ossian, he continued tacking up the horses in the same order, regardless of Ossian having just finished doing that part.

Eventually, Anton swung up into the wagon and mumbled, "You can sit in the back or walk. Your choice." Then he snapped the reins, made a clicking sound and the horses ambled off to the north-east towards the Bear woods. The village had renamed the woods after the first week's defining incident. Ossian had tried to discourage it, but like today, he'd had no better luck back then, either.

Watching the village receding from the back of the wagon, Ossian was rocked back and forth in the wagon as it traveled along on the uneven path that the wheels had etched into the landscape these last couple of months. The village houses slowly got smaller and smaller. The ruts in the prairie were just deep enough to catch the wheel, but not deep enough to keep the wheels in them yet.

It took almost half the morning before the wagon pulled up in front of the Bear woods and Ossian was certain he could have walked it faster.

Anton climbed down off the wagon and unhitched the horses, hobbling them to nibble at the prairie grass around them.

Ossian stood around, feeling useless. He wasn't even sure which of the tools in the back of the wagon he should drag out. "Can I get any of the tools ready?"

"You'll be tired enough soon." Was all Anton replied.

Reaching into the wagon, he grabbed a large rope and handed it to Ossian, then he himself grabbed an axe and a stone.

As they walked into the woods, Ossian did not feel the oppression he associated with the trees. Maybe that was a unique feature of the Night Forest on the other side of the valley. Or maybe he was just getting used to it.

Ossian noticed these woods were almost airy, the morning light filtering in from the canopy of green leaves overhead. Dead leaves littered the ground as they walked, obscuring any path that Anton was deliberately taking. Ossian knew enough to recognize ash, oak and maple trees. As well as enough to know that some of these trees were none of those.

They walked for what seemed like forever, passing trees and the occasional game trail that even Ossian could see. Anton ignored them all as they trudged deeper into the woods. He had to admit he didn't understand the job of the woodsman. He just assumed he would go up to the nearest tree, cut it down, and haul them out. Yet, he clearly had some goal in mind.

"Sorry. I'm not questioning your methods. Why we are headed so far into the woods?"

The sigh that came out of the woodsman was so loud, you would have thought he'd asked him for his first-born child. They trudged along in silence for several more minutes and Ossian had given up on an answer when Anton started to talk.

"Most people don't understand my job. You think I go to the woods, chop down a tree and bring it back to the village to be used to build things or to burn."

"Yes, I'll admit my ignorance in such matters." Ossian tried to keep his voice neutral. It was hard not to be sarcastic, when yes, that's exactly what he thought Anton did.

"They never think of next year, or the year after. Do you know how long it takes a tree to grow Mage Ossian?"

"Years."

"That depends on the tree. And the purpose of the wood. Some take years, some take scores of years."

Anton was looking at Ossian, staring through him. Ossian thought he was trying to beam the thoughts straight into his head. Then he realized, this man normally wandered off into the woods alone with only the horses for company, he was trying to think of the words to use and that took so much effort on his part, he couldn't do other things while doing it. It was completely outside of his normal effort.

Ossian would need to remember to talk with him and the couple of other loners more. Keep them used to being part of the village.

"What do you mean, purpose?"

Again the far off look, then after a minute, "Take a bow, for instance. A bow stave from an ash tree can grow in two or three years. But it's not as powerful as a slower growing wood. Sometimes speed is more important than power, though."

"That makes sense." Ossian nodded his head as he thought about it. It was like the difference between spell circles. Some were easy for him to cast, like mage flame. Others were so difficult, he avoided them.

"So, my job is to think ahead. Usually farther ahead than most people even consider. We're gonna chop down this tree here." He pointed at a tree that looked straight as an arrow to Ossian. "Cause the blacksmith wants a beam to lift heavy objects. That means straight and one piece. Those over there." Again, he waved towards a collection of smaller trees. "Those might be ready to cut down in five, maybe seven years, if something doesn't happen to them."

Ossian was shocked at the time frames he was talking about. He was looking at trees and ascertaining their purpose, possibly after Ossian was assigned to a new post. He wasn't even sure that Anton would still be in New Meadows. Reassignment wasn't unheard of, but you served at the whim of the King.

"So when the village needs firewood?"

"We take thinning trees." He glanced around the area and spied a tree. Pointing with his hand, "That one there, the crooked one, if we remove it, the surrounding ones will grow better. And since it's crooked, it's not much use for anything else."

"So you have to think not about trees, but about the forest."

Ossian was finally rewarded with a slight smile from Anton. "Yes, I have to think of how best to use the forest without turning it into a field."

"Thank you for that explanation. I had never thought of the woods in those terms before."

A slight head nod was all he got in return.

"Find yer way back and grab one of the horses. Leave the rope." With that, he placed himself to the side of the tree, raised his axe high and with a swing that was well practiced, the bit sunk into the tree. Pulling the axe out, he threw another swing into it, removing a much larger wedge than Ossian had expected.

"Hurry, or we'll be here all day." Followed by another thunk from the axe.

As Ossian wound his way back to the wagon and the horse, he heard the thunk of the axe slowly receding off behind him. Before he got to the wagon, he heard the telltale crash of a tree falling in the woods.

The horses were where Anton had hobbled them. Ossian looked at them, "Which one of you wants to work first?"

Neither horse even glanced his way, so he took the dark brown one on the right. When he grabbed the fetlock of the hobbled hoove, he noticed the brown lightened at the bottom. He'd never looked that closely at a horses hoove before and he inspected it for the horseshoe, seeing the blacksmith's work from yesterday in place. Till the horse grew tired of standing with his hoove in Ossian's hand and stepped away to rip up some more grass from the prairie.

He was sure they would end up using them both throughout the day. Ossian wound his way back by following the rhythmic thumping of the axe deeper in the woods.

Hauling the logs was more difficult than Ossian thought it would have been. The blacksmith wanted a beam so he could lift heavy objects. Which meant the beam had to cross both walls. Anton chopped the tree into two enormous pieces, each twice the height of Ossian. Then Anton attempted to show Ossian how to tie up the log to the horse and have the horse haul the log back to the wagon.

Ossian could tell by their pace it would be dark by the time they reached the village. He wondered how many days Anton spent alone, working for the village, leaving before light, and coming back after it. Anton assured him it was the size of the logs that took such a long time this day.

Ossian fell asleep exhausted yet again that night. Another physically exhausting day. Tomorrow, he'd try something simple, like a mage flame spell and see how his body took it. He still had nine days till the full moon.

CHAPTER 51

The next morning, Ossian awoke refreshed. He hadn't felt so good in quite a while. Forgetting he spent so much time with the soldiers back at the Academy. He'd need to be more mindful of his physical health.

All the houses were almost done, except for his. His house was to begin soon. The tent he'd been staying in was excellent though and he was considering staying in it full time. He knew the villagers would protest and rightly so, he guessed, the tent would not do during the winter months. Plus, maybe he could convince the villagers to let him help build the house. That would at least make the house partially his.

Thinking his worries for the day were over, Ossian swung out of his cot. Reaching over to his desk, he touched the quill laying on its surface. Forming the spell circle in his mind, he felt for the power and shoved it into the circle quickly. The quill took on the brilliant blue flame with ease. Ossian, standing quickly, searched himself for any sign of weakness from the casting, but his head felt fine. He wasn't woozy at all.

He would not press his luck with the north field today, but he'd see if some kids wouldn't mind target practice with him. Plus, he could charge up the sword outside the village. One day, he would need to charge the sword in the village, maybe when he had a house of his own to destroy first. Despite charging it several times, he was still wary of the spell getting loose and not going into the sword.

Maria and Ivy agreed to join him at the field today. Most of the other children were helping an adult with sowing or other tasks to finish up the fall planting. After several castings of lightning spells at sticks thrown by the girls, Ossian still felt great. No longer worried about casting spells, Ossian thanked the girls and said they could do what they wanted for the rest of the day. They wandered off towards the village, most likely to join their parents and get back to normal, everyday tasks.

That night at dinner with Yough and LeAnne, Deith dropped by.

"Heard you were casting again today?"

LeAnne's dinners had gotten less bland than when Ossian had first joined them. Supper was still mostly some root vegetables boiled over the fire, then mashed, with a slice of salted pork. Still, it was not porridge for dinner.

"Yes, I took it easy today, and tested the waters with some simple spells. I give myself a clean bill of magical health." Ossian chuckled at his own joke. The physician at the Academy would always give you a clean bill of health when you healed up from a cut, scrape or broken bone. He also noticed that no one else was laughing. Yough was smiling politely, but everyone else was just staring at him.

Victor, the middle child, finally said, "Sorry?"

"When the physician declares you fit to go back to duty at the Academy after a mishap, or wound. He always used to say you had a clean bill of health." Ossian realized he was displaying his privilege having grown up in the Academy, "Sorry, I thought it was a funny way to say I'm all good."

Deith shook his head ever so slightly. "What are you going to do till the full moon?"

Piaa pounced on that piece of information. "What happens at the full moon?"

Deith must have realized his mistake, as Piaa spoke up. He just shrugged and walked out of the Yough household to leave Ossian to fend for himself against one of the trio. His eyes narrowed as he thought about it. He was sure that Deith had done that on purpose.

LeAnne piped up then, "So, would anyone like more mashed vegetables?" Overriding Piaa's obvious insistence on knowing what was going down at the full moon.

Ossian could already see from the look in her eye that the trio would be around.

Helping himself to a spoonful of seconds, the mashed vegetables had just a hint of butter, a dash of salt and were delicious. Thanking LeAnne for a lovely meal, he excused himself with Yough clearly holding his daughter's arm, as she could barely contain herself to chase after Ossian and demand to know what was happening on the full moon.

CHAPTER 52

Ossian sat in his tent. He'd prepared a pot of tea and set out three extra cups. He was certain the trio would be by as soon as they could escape from their families and collect each other. Actually, he wasn't sure they would even need to collect each other. They seemed to have an ability to know when they needed to gather.

The steam from the teapot had finished swirling. The aroma of the dry earth filled the tent. Ossian was worried that maybe he'd prepared the tea too soon. When he heard the whispers outside his tent.

The trio was trying to decide who was going to knock first.

"You know I can hear you whispering, right?" Ossian wondered if he should just remove the tent flap. No one seemed to actually notice it existed, anyway.

Boa flipping the tent flap open and walked in like he owned the place. Espeth came in second, followed by Piaa, who at least had a small smirk, knowing she'd been asked to leave him alone for the night.

"So what's happening at the full moon?" Boa just dove straight in, like always. Piaa snapped her fist out and punched him in the arm. "Ow, hey."

Ossian shook his head. "Would you like some tea? It's just about the perfect temperature." Pouring three cups for the children first, he finished by making sure his cup was also full. Taking the cup in both hands, he held it up to the kids, in a kind of salute with the cup.

"It is polite to be invited to sit and drink before one talks about things." Ossian smiled at the words coming out of his mouth. They were exactly what Mage Golon would have said, "Or so says the man who taught me how to drink tea."

He waited till the kids had sat down and taken their cups. Then Ossian sipped the liquid. It was still warm and just the right side of brewed properly. The earthy texture of the leaves mixed with a subtle yet taste-able smoke that had been used to dry out the leaves. The subtle art of brewing tea, as Mage Golon had called it. Despite the man's insistence that everything be divination related, he understood the true intricacies of the combination of tea and hot water. Too bad he mainly used it as a source of Tasseomancy, for which most of the students endlessly mocked him.

"Although we won't be following all of Mage Golon's instructions, he always insisted that additives be made to the tea before drinking, depending on the situation." Ossian paused, wondering if the kids would be curious. When they weren't, he continued, "I never liked the additives. The tea itself, I thought, was always delicious by itself."

Each of the kids blew across their cups and took tentative sips. Piaa's face was neutral. Ossian could tell she wanted to get to the secrets. Espeth's mouth formed a big smile and she took several more tentative sips. Boa frowned at the mixture and placed the cup back on the tray.

"Why would you drink that?" Boa's sour face hid nothing.

"It's not for everyone I guess, but you drink it cause it was offered as a sign of hospitality, Boa. In a more proper house or manor, your actions would be taken as a great offense." Ossian really didn't care about the etiquette, he was just avoiding telling the trio about what he was going to do.

Ossian wasn't certain why he didn't want to tell the children. They already knew the jasper weasel existed. He'd even told them he was trying to bind it to him. Although he hadn't told them what that meant, cause he wasn't fully sure himself.

Mages that were far older than him could make homunculi, small humanoid or creature-ish like beings that had a semblance of life and would carry out minor tasks in the laboratory for them. These homunculi always died when the mage themselves died. Ossian was certain it would be something like that, or at least he hoped that was so. Mage Mahler himself admitted he didn't completely know the power that laid dorment in the weasel.

The trio was staring at him, Boa having abandoned his tea. Piaa politely taking small sips, or Ossian thought more likely making the sipping noises. Espeth had finished her cup completely and placed the cup back down.

"Would you like some more tea, Espeth?" Ossian was taking any excuse to delay.

Boa reached over and swapped cups with her. "She can have my leaf juice."

Espeth picked it up quickly and continued to drink it.

Finally, Piaa sighed loudly, then spoke, "Would you like us to leave you alone?"

Both Espeth and Boa stared at her. They wanted to gossip and this was the first time one of them had been even mildly aware that maybe someone else didn't want to tell them something.

"No, I can't explain it. Not fully."

"Explain what?" Boa's hand flew through the air as he said it.

"I think that the binding of the statue needs to take place on a full moon. I think the symbology of the spell circle wasn't about the nocturnal nature, well it was about the nocturnal nature of the creature, but it means something different." It all tumbled out of Ossian so fast, he wasn't sure he was making any sense.

Given the looks on the children's faces, he wasn't.

"The red jasper statue of the weasel I have." He pointed over towards the statue, still standing guard near his bed.

The children's head swiveled to look where he was pointing at.

Espeth took the cup away from her lips and asked, "What's a weasel?"

"Well, Mage Mahler's notes mention that it's nocturnal, meaning it's active during the nighttime."

The children all nodded their heads at that.

"It's a stealthy creature, that's why the charcoal, as a symbol of the night. The weasel is like a stoat or ferret. They are carnivores, meaning they eat primarily meat. Small rodents like mice, rats and probably anything it can catch."

The nodding continued.

"And the full moon?" Piaa offered.

"Well, the spell I originally cast was in the daytime. Since the creature is a nocturnal animal, I think the moon in the spell has a double meaning. Night activity for the weasel, but also a time that the spell must be cast."

Saying it out loud made Ossian doubt himself. He wasn't sure that was true; it was just his current most accurate guess. "Well, at least that's what I think right now."

The head nodding continued with the children for a little as Espeth finished her second cup of tea. As she placed the cup down, Piaa swapped their cups as well.

Ossian picked his own cup and guessed you couldn't make people like something. He sipped the now lukewarm tea.

"Is it dangerous to bind the weasel?" Boa asked.

Swishing the tea around in his mouth, Ossian thought for quite a bit before answering. "Well, truth be told, I don't know." Ossian doubted that Mage Mahler would send something he thought was dangerous. "I don't think so. No."

Then the smiles came up on all three children at once. Ossian found it disconcerting how they did that. It was as if they shared one mind, or the same thought popped into their head simultaneously.

"Can we watch?" Espeth was the first to speak.

"No, this is a private ceremony." He'd said it far more abruptly than he had meant to. Ossian was pretty sure there wasn't any harm in the children watching. Still, some things were meant to be done in private. He wanted to be alone to explore this magic. Plus, some niggling self doubt existed deep in him that kept chipping at his self-confidence. What if it was like the spider?

All three children said it in tandem, "Aaahhhh!"

It reminded Ossian that these three, even though they had grown so much in the last couple of months, were still little kids. They showed amazing intelligence and cunning subterfuge when they needed to. Yet, when it came down to it, they were still little children at heart.

Ossian also knew they would ignore any and all rules if they needed to. "Do I need to ask your parents to lock you away during the full moon?"

All three hung their heads and refused to look at him. "No." came the response in unison.

As each child stood, he could tell they were hurt by being excluded.

Ossian let the children go. He didn't know what to say to them.

As they left, the scent of the earthy tea changed from a welcome reminder of Mage Golon to a headache that reminded him of his failure to explain why he didn't want the children present. Then he remembered that in the next couple of days, he would likely have to fight the children off on multiple occasions. They were tenacious.

CHAPTER 53

While waiting for the full moon, Ossian need to spend some time researching the hidden death out in the field. Flipping through *Symbols of Transmutational Power*, he'd identified nearly all the symbols. They made little sense, though. Some symbols even contradicted each other. The symbol for pulling was present, but also the symbol for locking in place. Those two symbols were direct opposites and shouldn't be in any spell together. Isolation was present, but so was collection. They weren't direct opposites, but they represented slightly different ways of doing the same thing to not the target of the spell, but the result of the spell.

There were two symbols he couldn't identify yet. He knew them from somewhere. They were sitting in his brain, teasing him just on the edge of his knowledge.

It was a frustrating exercise that found Ossian in his tent with too much pent up energy wondering how he was going to research this creature with so little information about it.

When Boa strode into his tent unannounced, Ossian snapped at him. "Boa, you have to at least pretend to knock."

Boa stood stock still. Ossian could clearly see on his face, try to play it off like Ossian was joking, or back out quickly and leave.

Then Espeth and Piaa's faces appeared behind Boa, less certain of entering.

"Sorry, sorry. Come in. I'm just researching a spell, and it's not going well."

Espeth and Piaa moved around Boa, who was still frozen in place wondering if he should bolt from the situation.

"Get in here Boa, it's not you."

Piaa asked, "So, uh, what's the problem?" She said it so casually, like magical research was her normal everyday task. Not like she was a ten-year-old girl whose only reading and writing education had come from Ossian himself. Even that had only been going on for a couple of weeks.

Ossian had to be extremely careful. He didn't want to scare the children with the concept of a killer spider thingy hidden deep below in the dirt. Plus, how much could the kids really help him? Shrugging his shoulders, he guessed he could at least describe the problem he was having. Their ideas came from ignorance, but at least they wouldn't be hampered by their own magical knowledge.

"I have a spell I'm trying to research. But some symbols make no sense. The symbols for pulling and staying in place are present. Several of the other symbols also seem to contradict each other. So I can't figure out how the spell works?"

Boa had finally moved into the tent and was poking around Ossian's things. By now, Boa had to know everything in the tent except for what was locked away in the chest. "Can't you just draw out the circle and use it?"

"I'm afraid of what the circle will do. I'm even afraid to draw it in a complete circle. It activated when I touched it."

Piaa's eyebrows raised up at hearing that and Ossian knew he needed to be more careful with his words.

"Why not have someone else touch it?" Espeth said as she practiced her writing on the wax tablet she kept on her. Her writing was small and neat and Ossian was already jealous of how precise her letters were.

"I'm afraid they might get hurt. I couldn't ask someone else to do that."

Piaa was sitting on Ossian's cot, staring off at the tent's patch. "What if the circle is around something, but you can't touch inside of it?"

Boa then chimed in as he petted the red jasper statue, as of late it was his most favorite. "Why can't you pull someone in, then try to hold them in place? Like when we go fishing?"

"Well, that would..." Ossian had to stop. He'd never heard of a spell circle without a middle. He wasn't fully sure what it would do.

Piaa's hand was moving like it was tracing something in the air. "Like a ring with a hole in it."

"Uh, I have no idea. But as usual, you three have given me more avenues to explore. Thank you."

Boa spoke up, "We do what we must." Then, cocking his head, he heard something no one else did. "Mom's calling us." At that moment, Boa looked amazingly like Deith, hearing things that no one else did.

Piaa and Espeth both looked over at him. The trio slowly got up and headed to the tent entrance.

As the three of them headed off. Espeth added, "Good luck Mage Ossian."

Ossian noted they headed off towards the stream that headed into the woods, not towards where Cara was likely to be. Maybe Boa had just grown tired of the conversation and wanted to leave.

Ossian sat there for what felt like forever. How could he form a ring with nothing on the inside?

The ring also had to be something he could replicate the patterns on, so not too small. The blacksmith could probably make a ring, but he would need something too big to waste so much metal. Maybe Anton could make it out of wood, although they didn't have anyone skilled enough at carving to replicate the symbols properly.

Walking over to Bakker, he queried how difficult it would be to make a flat ring out of pottery. Bakker asked Ossian a bunch of questions and said he could try, but with a ring, the difficulty would be in the ring's shrinkage. It was most likely to crack. Especially with a ring as wide as his shoulders. Which is what Ossian thought he would need.

Back to frustrated, Ossian wandered the village looking for things that could be made into a ring with nothing on the inside. There were log houses. He was pretty sure that wouldn't work. The shingles on the houses were a possibility, but none of them were larger than his foot in width and he was sure he'd need a bigger ring because of the complexity of the patterns in the symbols he was less familiar with.

The shingles led his mind to a coopers top for a barrel. That would work, but they didn't have a cooper in the village. So yet another dead end and Ossian reminded himself yet again it would be made of wood and need to be carved.

Seeing the village oven in the center of town, he thought about making each symbol on a rock and forming that into a circle. Mortar could make the ring a whole. Thinking hard about it, though, Ossian had never created a circle out of multiple pieces to create a complete whole. He wasn't sure he wanted to add in more unknowns.

Ending back up at his tent, he reached his hand out to the tent flap when he looked at the tent. Backing up, Ossian stared. The tent wall was a large piece of flat oiled canvas. He chuckled to himself. Like an artist's canvas used to make paintings, but without the wooden support. There was the answer. Cut a hole in his tent and make the circle on the outside. Simple, elegant, easy. Well, maybe not so easy, but doable.

Walking into the tent, he gathered the items he would need and prepared to work on the circle's outer drawing.

CHAPTER 54

Preparing what he would need to draw out the circle, Ossian decided it would be best if he prepared a missive for Mage Mahler. In case something unspeakable happened, he would at least leave a trail to what Ossian had already discovered.

Grabbing several sheaves of parchment and a quill, he decided he should probably use the phoenix feather and encase this message. Secrecy and all that. After four pages of messages, notes and spell circles, including the symbology he could not bring his mind to remember. Ossian broke out his secret tome with the spell using the phoenix feather.

The spell was pretty simple and within a couple of seconds, the parchment flared into flames. The acrid stench of burning animal hide quickly disappeared up into the phoenix feather's quill nib and a single drop of ink looked ready to write. It would stay there, ready to be used as a component in the modified individual message seal Mahler had also noted in his last message.

Flipping the page to the next spell circle, Ossian dropped the feather. Staring at him in the face was the solution to his real problem. None of the symbols in the creature's defensive spell made sense, cause it wasn't a single spell. Staring back at him from the page was the individual message seal, intermixed with the secret message spell. Each symbol in the circle alternated between the two spells.

Leaving the feather on the ground, Ossian grabbed another sheaf of parchment and the two pages of the half circle spider spell and tried at first to copy each alternating symbol into a new circle. What he ended up with was a bunch of nonsense symbols placed in two separate circles. Neither of them clicked in his head and he was certain they did not form any kind of spell.

Still, he had to power them up to truly test them out. Could he do that here, in this tent? He was certain it was not safe, yet who could he trust with the potential knowledge he was about to unleash?

Running out of the tent with the two circles in his hands, he ran straight into Deith. "Uh...sorry Deith. Uh—," should he tell him?

"The tent on fire, Mage Ossian?" Deith looked past him towards the tent.

"No, No. Deith, I need to try this spell. I need you to watch, and should anything bad happen..."

"Bad as in."

"I don't know. I just need to do this. Please make sure no one interrupts."

Deith gave his non-committal shrug. "So if you fall onto the ground unconscious, just leave you?"

Ossian had to actually think about that, "Hrm—No, I think if I'm unconscious there will be no danger."

Deith's face registered surprise. "I was joking."

"I am not."

"Should I get some more soldiers?"

"I need someone I can trust and, right now, that's you. If something bad happens, there is a feather in my tent on the ground. Hide it and give it to Mage Mahler only." Then Ossian grabbed Deith by the shoulders with the parchment still clutched in one of his hands. "Promise me."

The stare that Deith gave Ossian felt like Ossian was being measured. "Okay, just make sure nothing bad happens."

Ossian wasn't sure if Deith found him lacking when he measured him, but he needed to do this.

Walking out into the practice range, Ossian assembled the spell circle in his mind. It still felt so wrong. There was no logic to the symbols assembled. Yet Ossian dug deep, grasping at the power inside him and tried to force it into the circle. The first symbol lit up, but the symbols next to it wouldn't even accept the power.

Ossian wasn't sure how long he tried, but he was sweating by the time he stopped. Deep, ragged breaths were moving in and out of his open mouth as his chest heaved with the exertion of a poorly made spell.

Ignoring the familiar feeling from his first few years as an apprentice, Ossian assembled the second circle in his mind. Again the circle felt wrong, still he felt obligated to try it. Powering up the spell, yet again he was gasping and wheezing and the symbols just wouldn't take the power.

Defeated, Ossian walked back to where Deith was standing with the surrounding trio.

"Mage Ossian, you okay?" Boa never seemed to shy away from asking the obvious questions.

"No, not really. I was hoping I had a breakthrough."

"Well, you broke out in a sweat." Deith said it. Ossian thought he was trying to lighten the mood given the children were there.

Ossian tried to smile, but it felt forced. "Sorry, I need to get back to the research."

As he walked past them, he didn't trust himself to speak. He wanted to reveal everything to them. They deserved to know the danger they were in, and he himself was failing at being their protector. Still, how would knowing how much danger they were in help them?

Back in his tent, Ossian tossed the parchment onto his cot. Frustrated with himself, he snatched up the phoenix feather and the wax components and went to work preparing a message seal with the ink trapped inside of it.

As the wax melted, the gentle scent of pine tar and beeswax mixed into the air. His mind was taken back to when they first learned to cast message seals in the Academy. He'd been the last of his class to cast it successfully. The rest of his class had managed it within the first or second try. Still, Ossian had taken seven tries to get it to work properly.

Ossian knew this was the same. He would continue trying until he died trying, or he found the solution. As he formed the spell in his mind, he gently touched the phoenix quill's nib to the wax and watched as the ink mixed with the ink and quickly disappeared.

Then, pouring the mixture over the brass plate, he watched as it cooled into a circular red wax seal with the symbol of a plow sowing a field in a book.

As it was cooling, a thought tickled his mind. If there could be two spells in a circle, why not more than two?

CHAPTER 55

As Ossian raced through the village, he spied what looked like the last house that needed to be built being laid out by Anton. It was going to be his. That made what he had to do next all that more important. Ossian had to make sure this village had a future and one without a horrible ending.

Reaching Deith's house, he knocked on the door.

Boa answered the door. Looking up at Ossian, he left the door open as he walked away into the house. "Hey Mage Ossian, Dad's out wrapping up the last of the plowing. He should be back soon."

"You can wait inside." Cara yelled from somewhere on the inside of their home.

Ossian wanted to get back to his research. He was on a roll with the tertiary spell within a spell within a spell and he wanted to prove he was right. Deciding, he spoke, "Cara, can I see you outside for a minute?"

Cara appeared at the door, wiping her hands on her apron, smiling up at Ossian. "Wanna stay for dinner?"

"I'm sorry Cara, I have loads of research to continue with. I'm on a promising lead right now."

Cara shrugged just like her husband, like it wasn't any skin off her back if he stayed and ate or if he chose not to. She finished wiping her hands on her apron and locked eyes with Ossian, giving him her full attention.

Holding out the message seal, he said very low, "If something happens to me, this must be delivered to Mage Mahler. No one else." Ossian willed the seriousness of the situation into every syllable of the message. He needed Cara to understand the importance of what he was asking.

Cara's entire body language changed instantly from carefree to serious. "Of course, Mage Ossian. Deith knows what he looks like, right?"

"Yes, thank you Cara, this is important. I promise."

As Ossian turned around to leave, Cara's hand grabbed his shoulder. "We won't let anything happen to you, Mage Ossian. We're here if you need us. The entire village is here for you."

Ossian had to leave quickly before the information burst out of his mouth. Barely making it back to his tent before his heart was beating too fast in his chest, he sat down on the cot. Was he being irresponsible in not telling anyone? Deith mostly knew what was happening. Yet, he had told no one else yet.

Then his attention snapped back to the tent. Looking around, something was off. He'd left the brass plate on top of his secret tome as he'd prepared the message spell. Yet now the brass plate was on the desk next to the tome. Had someone been in his tent?

Ossian hurriedly flipped open his chest and started sorting through his ingredients. Nothing was missing. The phoenix feather was still sitting nearby. The tome he'd closed and it was sealed.

Maybe he'd moved the plate and forgotten it in his haste to give someone the seal. That must be it. He was just so distracted from what he did he was imaging things.

He placed everything in the chest, just in case. Then withdrew only the secret tome, ink, quill and a piece of parchment. Methodically, he copied out every third symbol into three circles and even as he completed them; he knew there was nothing to them. Just another mess of incomprehensible symbols with no meaning in their congregation.

Throwing the parchment onto his cot, he grabbed another piece and started segmenting out every fourth symbol. Even before he got halfway done, all four circles felt powerful. The symbols felt like they belonged together.

As he put the last symbol in each spell circle, he was certain of the first one's purpose. It was very similar to his pushing spell, except it pulled forwards. Much like a fishing lure pulling you in to its source, just this time the source was the spell circle.

The second circle was at first confusing cause it was so similar to the first spell. Just the two symbols were different, stillness and isolation. As Ossian formed the spell in his mind, it clicked without even having to power it on. It held whatever had been pulled in. Held it in place.

The third circle was a modification of the pulling spell, but a complex one. Ossian didn't want to form the spell in his mind. It felt dangerous. He was confused about what it pulled on, though. The source of the spell was the thing held in the second spell's grasp. That much was clear. Yet it wasn't pulling the being anymore, it was pulling its essence.

Ossian put the parchment down. His mind was racing with the implications. Did this machine suck people in and then kill them?

What a horrible way to die. Having one's essence pulled forcefully from your body. Ossian wasn't even sure that was possible. Yet the circle felt correct when Ossian viewed it, and there was no way he could activate it to tell. Would that leave a living husk to roam the world? Or would that cause someone to disappear, or would their bodies be nothing? Mere muscle, blood and bone to feed the fields.

Ossian's heart stopped for a beat.

The Greenman had shown him the creature, killing everyone and then sowing the fields with their bodies. Ossian knew that farmers often sowed the fields with dead fish. It helped to make the plants grow. Could that be done with any body of flesh and blood?

Not wanting to look, Ossian shivered as he picked back up the parchment and looked at the fourth spell. Both symbols he couldn't recall were in it.

Placing the parchment back down, he needed to jog his memory. Mage Mahler had always said the best way to do that was to do something totally and utterly different. Forget about what it was you were thinking on and bam, your mind would bring the memories you wanted front and center at the most inconvenient time.

Luckily for him, tomorrow would be taken up with building him a house. He would need to inject himself into the house building process and do the most labor intensive things he could handle. Dragging his mind as far from the spell circles and symbols of magic as he could.

Tonight, though, he knew that sleep was going to elude him.

Deciding that he was unlikely to get any decent sleep, he walked out to the wax tablet posted in the town center and looked down the list. Bakker was on first watch and the watch started soon. The darkness was almost complete as the sun set.

After a brief conversation with Bakker, Ossian sent him back to get a full night's sleep, as he was going to take first watch. If he couldn't sleep, he could at least let someone else get some.

CHAPTER 56

First watch crept along at a snail's pace. Darkness enfolded the village as Ossian walked around and refreshed mage flame torches that were getting dim. Looking up at the moon, Ossian was certain the moon had slowed down in its arc across the night sky.

Walking the village, Ossian could feel his eyes getting tired and he had to splash water on his face more than once. The village settled on three watches in the night, so Ossian had to wait till the moon was near the star Ther before he woke up second watch. Yet, every time he looked up at the moon and stars, he was certain they were no closer together than the last time he'd looked.

Afraid to stop for fear he would fall asleep standing up. Ossian continued his walking route around the village. With only his house left to complete, the village was substantial in its size now. Walking the outskirts of the village took far longer and in his watch shift, he would only traverse the outside maybe three times tonight. Although the more he walked, the slower he seemed to get.

～

AFTER SECOND WATCH took all too long to come, the morning came all too early. Ossian was up and walking around the lines drawn in the dirt around his house before the last watch even finished. Wandering around the lines, he sat down on some of the peeled wooden logs destined for his house. The smell of the dirt and the fresh peeled scent of the logs reminded him of spring on the farm so long ago. These poles were massive and looking over the lines in the dirt, the house was going to be nearly twice the size of the surrounding houses.

Finally, Anton showed up.

"Why is the layout so much larger than the rest of the houses?"

Anton's eyes looked around, then focused back on Ossian. "We have decided that certain modifications were necessary."

"We?"

"Everyone, except you."

He was about to protest loudly when Anton raised his hand up.

"Mage Mahler sent suggestions with Deith. We have incorporated all of them. Deith told me they were to be a surprise."

Ossian was trying to not be grumpy, yet again other people were influencing his life without any of his involvement. "What suggestions?"

"How much table space you would need for experiments, space to layout your books. He was pretty specific that you would need lots of flat open tables."

Ossian had to admit it was hard to do his research on top of his chest right now. A large open table would be a welcome respite.

"If you want, we can still change back to a normal house, Mage Ossian." Anton looked nervous. He was offering a course of action that Ossian could tell Anton didn't want to follow.

"Who all agreed to this plan?"

Ossian jumped when Deith's voice was right next to him. "Everyone in the village."

"You got every single person to agree to make modifications to my house?"

Anton chirped in, "Why do you think it took us so long to get all these things together? Every other house took us a week or less. We've been piling just the logs together for the last two weeks now. Have you not noticed?"

Ossian didn't know what to say. He hadn't noticed, not in the slightest. Would that be rude to tell Anton? Should he be grateful that the village had decided to build him a different house? His mouth opened, then he closed it again, unsure of what to say.

"He's had lots on his mind, Anton."

Anton didn't look mollified, but others had showed up.

Anton came to some conclusion, keeping it to himself he said, "Mage Ossian, would you like to lay the first log?" Anton pointed at a massive peeled log that Ossian could never get his arms around, it was nearly twice as tall as he was.

"We'll save the really long ones for the roof line. You said you wanted a single room, right?" As Anton continued to look around at the log supply and point to specific areas, mumbling words like lintel, windows and roofline.

Ossian wasn't sure if Anton was making fun of him, but he decided since it was the first move of the day. "Alright, everyone, back up. Show me where it goes."

Anton glanced over at Deith. "Mage Ossian, I'm sorry, it was a joke. We have the entire village to move the logs, that's—"

"I need to take my mind off my research right now Anton, this isn't me being mad at you. Where does it go?"

Anton pointed at what looked like the back wall of the structure. Making a point of showing Ossian where the end of the log needed to be.

"Okay, I'm not sure how many of these I can do, but I can at least do the first one."

Ossian stepped behind the log, it only need to move slightly more than his height, and shifted to the left an arm's length.

In his mind, he drew the levitation circle. Ossian substituted the log for the target. Powering up the spell, the log lifted itself up barely.

Sweat was already beading on his forehead. He was trying to control the spell extremely precisely. The effort was immense. Control was always so much harder. He stepped forward and pushed gently with his mind. The log floated along slowly.

Ossian was trying not to will the log along faster. Speed would get someone hurt or killed. When the log was finally in place, he willed it to stop. It took more power than he thought it should. Finally, he flipped the power to the circle off, and the log crashed the hand span to the ground, throwing up a cloud of dust to envelop everyone.

Coughing and choking could be heard from everyone around the house. So amazing magical effect kind of ruined. The inside of his mouth was gritty from the dirt as he sucked in great lungfuls of air. "Okay, that was a bit much. Next time I listen to you all."

Several of the men hocked saliva onto the ground, clearing the gritty, dirty taste from their mouths. Swirling spit from his own mouth, he tried to think of a more dignified way. When he decided around these people, it didn't matter. Hocking it onto the ground, it puffed up another tiny dust cloud that didn't envelop everyone this time.

Ossian could see everyone smile awkwardly. He'd just doused them in enough dirt to make the rest of the day uncomfortable. "I'd offer to blow the dust away, but I don't think everyone downwind would appreciate that."

Several of the villagers smiled at that, when Anton said, "Well, at least the first log is done, lets get to it." Clapping his hands together, he startled everyone into moving.

Ropes, cant hooks and horses were brought out. By mid-day meal, Ossian was more sweaty than he had been in weeks and was gritty and grimy from all the dust he'd sprayed over everyone. He was certain the rest of them could feel the grit, yet no one complained.

The house was mostly up, with holes for the windows and door still to be axed out. Anton assigned the more skilled axemen to that task when lunch showed up.

The chit chat was mild, general talk about the seasons, plowing, when fall harvest would be. Someone asked Anton about any harvestable fruit or nut trees in the forest. Anton shrugged and said there were a couple, but nothing big enough for the entire village. Looking over at Ossian, he loudly said that someone would have to decide who was to harvest them and how they were to be distributed, but also added that wouldn't be for some weeks still.

Then Anton must have decided lunch was over, cause he added work tasks for everyone while shooing the axemen off to create holes in the beautifully assembled box without a roof.

As the door and windows were cut out, there was one massive log left to place on top to form the lintel in the building's front. Ossian had to admit he was amazed at the jigsaw of logs forming up around him that looked like a well thought out plan.

Several large logs were stacked against the front wall and ropes were strapped from the lintel log over the house to where the horses were. Given the weight of the log, it was going to take four horses to pull it up the improvised ramp and several men to position it. Ossian stood back to watch. These men had built most of these houses and were accomplished.

The stretching of the rope could be heard as the horses pulled the lines taunt. The log bobbled up the improvised ramp as Anton shouted for the left or right team to slow down or speed up. It was a carefully choreographed dance that reminded Ossian of a well put together spell.

He'd spent the entire day trying hard to forget his research, but everything he did this day just reminded him of his inability to remember several symbols. No matter how much manual labor he did, he was the least skilled and capable man here. Not that he couldn't help, but everyone else spent their day doing manual labor. Ossian's labor was in the magical world, where he was currently not even feeling the best at that right now.

A sharp snap brought him back to the moment. A second snap showed part of the roped flying off over the house. The immense log rolled sideways and the two men on the right side would not get out of the way in time. Ossian could feel the entire moment slow as he formed the levitation spell in his head. The log was weighty. Hoping to fling the log off out of the village, he could save two men from being crushed. All he had to do was overpower the spell.

As he placed his hand on the hilt, the storage symbol came to his mind. The missing piece had been with him the entire time. The two missing symbols were the storage symbols used on his sword.

Drawing the sword, he altered the levitation spell to draw from both sources, him and the sword. He overpowered the spell as much as he dared and with a flick of mental power, he grabbed the log and threw it sideways out over the village.

Suddenly, he was in the black void again. There was absolutely nothing around him. This was the same place he'd felt when the Greenman had showed him the buried spider creature.

Then, just as quickly, he was brought back to the moment.

The sword was completely drained. Ossian had managed not to flow everything from himself into it. Falling to his knees as he watched the log sail over the house off to the north field. It didn't just clear the village. Ossian was worried for a minute that it might have made it to the Night Forest.

Everyone was gathering around him. Several voices were calling his name. Realizing that he was on his knees, with the sword tip held in the dirt, he stood up.

Staring off into the northern field, he knew what the last spell circle was on the creature. It was a storage spell, very similar to his sword. It wasn't for magic though, it was for storing life.

Several families rushed towards the house. Apparently, the sight of a flying log was a good reason to investigate.

Someone slapped him, "Mage Ossian, are you alright?"

Deith was standing in front of him. "Deith, I know what it's for."

CHAPTER 57

There was no time to explain it to Deith. He guessed a giant flying log was reason enough to question what was happening, as the entire village gathered near Ossian's almost assembled house. Several of the men went out to retrieve the large log, but to no one's surprise, it was firewood.

Anton told everyone he would need a couple of days to find a new one big enough when Cara started whispering to the families. Several of them disappeared and food was ready to eat quickly. How they prepared so much food with no warning, Ossian had no idea.

Chatter around the village was one-minded, everyone kept talking about how Ossian had saved Yough and Gideon's life. No matter how much Ossian tried to play it down, no one would let him. Eventually, he relented and grudgingly accepted the thanks from everyone, adding how glad he was to help.

The trio found him and grilled him on how it felt to use the sword to throw a log clear across the valley. When LeAnne saw them, she quickly corralled the trio and sent them on several errands to run them off. Ossian had to smile. LeAnne saving him was not something he would have expected even just weeks ago.

It was several hours later and darkness had fallen before Ossian found himself in his tent with Deith.

"So, what is it?" Deith asked.

"It's a giant life battery."

"That doesn't sound so horrible."

"Deith, it sucks the life out of people and stores it."

"Oh...Why?"

"I don't know."

"Do the bodies also get sucked up? Is that why the village is always gone?"

"No, I think it plants the bodies in the fields."

Deith stopped at this. He rubbed his hands together nervously. Ossian had never seen Deith nervous before. Looking over at Ossian, Deith continued, "How does the village disappear, then?"

"Deith, it kills them all. Who cares how the buildings disappear?"

Nodding his head at that, Deith continued. "How do we stop it?"

"I don't know. I'm not even sure how to or when it activates."

"So it just activates, kills everyone, sucks them dry and then goes back to hiding?"

Ossian admitted he didn't have all the answers, but he knew how the spell circles worked, or at least what they did. "Deith, this is four spell circles in one. This is complex, hard magic. I think it's old. The symbols in the spells, they are archaic forms. I recognize them, but only just. Primarily cause they appear similar to ones still in use today."

"Does that change anything for us?"

Ossian was silent for a long time. He wasn't sure what value there was in knowing what horrible death awaited them. "I'm not sure. Something else Deith, when I used the sword, I went...somewhere, it's happened every time I've used the sword. Well, every time I've used it here. I just thought it was a symptom of the sword's effects. But what if it's the creature?"

"The suck-everyone-dry creature is trying to talk with you?"

"No, it's not like that, but also when the Greenman tried to warn me about the creature, the same thing happened. I was pulled into a black void, where nothing was, then poof back here."

"So you have no idea when it will activate?"

"No." Ossian then remembered the creature tried to suck him in when he'd touched it in his disembodied form. Would that actually pull him in? Was his disembodied form the essence or life of Ossian. Mage Mahler had never discussed that before. He knew from previous sessions with other disembodied spells that the spell being disrupted was disorienting to the mage, but not fatal.

"I think I have a plan to find out more about the creature. I think we need to inform the village, though, so they can be ready should an issue occur."

"You're gonna wake it up on purpose?" Deith had returned to looking nervous.

"Well, I think in case I wake it up. We need to have a plan. I wonder if I can convince the Greenmen to help?"

"Help with what?"

"They know magic Deith, I wonder if they can help get me out of the creature if necessary, if I end up trapped inside it. I think we need to have a counsel with the Greenmen. Which means we need to inform the village of the intent of what we are going to try. I can't force anyone blindly into my experiment. Not if it will kill them."

"So many bad ideas." Still, Deith stood, the nervousness on his face disappeared and a hard resolved took its place. "I'll inform the villagers of tomorrow's meeting."

THE NEXT MORNING went better than Ossian thought. No one seemed really surprised that Ossian was going to be counseling with the Greenmen. Most of them took the giant death creature better than Ossian could have imagined. None of them wanted to battle the creature, but they were willing to help with whatever plan Ossian made with the Greenmen.

Deith, Yough and Ossian went off into the forest, hoping to find the Greenmen. Ossian had brought parchment symbols and charcoal powder to get his request across to them.

They took a single step into the treeline near the stream when Deith said, "They're already here."

Looking around, Ossian could not spot them. The trees looked normal. The leaves were not in the shapes of bodies.

Then Ossian heard it. There was no noise what-so-ever and it was deafening.

The stream ahead of them parted as an island grew out of nothing. Soon the island was overflowing with grass and flowers, which continued to grow till a bridge of thick grasses and flowers crossed the stream to Ossian's party.

Ossian crossed the bridge, with Deith and Yough following behind him.

"Is this wise, Mage Ossian?" The fear in Yough's voice was understandable. Ossian was a mage who'd spent the last decade interaction with magic daily and even he was scared of what they were seeing.

"I need their help. You are free to leave if you must."

Neither man behind him left.

First, what appeared to be a leaf fell into the grass...followed slowly by another, then faster and faster, more and more leaves fell onto the island, slowly yet surely assembling the body of the Greenman that Ossian had dealt with last time.

Ossian knelt down and placed the box he'd prepared ahead of time on the ground in front of him. Inside it were all the leaves he'd collected from the dead Greenman's body when Honey had killed him, and the cup of liquid he'd never experimented with. As he opened the lid, the Greenman peered inside, then glanced at Ossian.

Removing the cup, the Greenman walked to the stream, where he poured the liquid out into the stream, then washed the cup in the water several times. Returning the cup to the box, he lifted the leaves out in his fist and threw them high into the air, where they disappeared in the wind.

The Greenman's eyes settled on Ossian, waiting for something.

"I need your help to deal with it." Ossian wasn't even sure they understood language. Although last time he seemed to hear him, if not able to speak to him.

Ossian took the parchment and showed the Greenman the spell circles. The Greenman's eyes grew sad as it shook his head.

Ossian flipped the parchment over and showed him the disembodiment spell. "I can leave my body and visit the creature underground. Can you protect me from the creature?"

The Greenman shook his head no.

Then he sat down and waving his hands, the north field appeared again. Ossian's spell circle was still mostly visible out in the dirt. A miniature Ossian sat in the circle, with several of the Greenmen standing over him. Suddenly, the legs of the creature burst out of the ground as Ossian and the Greenmen scattered. Then the dirt melded back into lush green grasses.

"If I touch it, the creature will activate?"

His eyes leaked a tear as he nodded his head yes.

"Good."

The creature's sad face changed to one of confusion.

"We're not going to sit around waiting for it to one day activate and kill us all. We're going to prepare. Then we are going to destroy it."

Ossian wasn't sure how to ask the next piece, or if the Greenman would even understand what he was asking. "Will you help us?"

A wind blew through the Night Forest, whipping up the stream and blowing into Ossian's face, nearly shoving him over. The Greenman stood, offering his hand to help Ossian stand up. The sadness in his eyes changed to what Ossian recognized as Deith's hard resolve.

The Greenman handed Ossian a stick. Waving his hands, yet

again over the grasses, Ossian saw miniature him throw the stick into the forest as a dozen Greenmen emerged from the trees.

Then, just as quickly, the real Greenman disappeared into the grass at their feet. The island collapsed in upon itself, with water flowing quickly to cover their legs and soaking them. Deith, Yough and Ossian found themselves standing in the middle of the stream.

Deith's voice was cool and sarcastic. "He could have at least put us on the bank." As he trudged towards the stream bank, now soaking wet.

Ossian was less certain of the next piece, convincing the village that preparing to attack a giant killing machine was the easiest way to deal with it. Deith and Yough had suggested trying to trap the legs with ropes and using the horses to pull the legs out from under it.

Feeling that the most important piece was getting close enough to disrupt the spell circles. Ossian had to be close, given the reaction of the small rock spider to his sword. He hoped the creature reacted poorly to lightning, or that the sword could penetrate the creature's side.

It had been a surprisingly quick conversation, Ossian explaining how there was a death-killer magical rock-spider creature hidden under the north field. Deith and Yough took turns explaining how they were going to attack the creature's legs while Ossian disabled the body. They sounded much more confident than Ossian felt.

Ossian wasn't convinced it was a very good plan, but no one seemed to question it. The village would mostly be up near the hill in case everything went poorly. Ready to head to the nearest settlement, which was a long seven day walk. The village prepped by disassembling all the rope they had and winding long, long ropes as thick as they could make them. Three teams of four horses would try to pull the legs out from under the spider.

Later, when they were alone, Ossian asked Deith, "What if this doesn't work? What if everyone dies cause of me?"

"We will have died following you. Even Jorn couldn't ask for more."

CHAPTER 58

The dark brown bark of the treeline stared back at Ossian. The green leafy canopy revealed nothing about the creatures inside. Knee high barley covered the north field and would be a horrible waste. Still, waiting for the entire village to be killed just wasn't an option to Ossian.

Turning around, he held the stick casually in his hand. The Greenman had showed they would help. Once he threw the stick into the forest, there was no going back.

Looking out over the nearby seventeen men and women, Ossian was touched that so many of them had volunteered with no sign of hesitation. The rest of the village was away back on the hill with instructions to flee should the creature reach the village. They had several missives with them, all of them imploring for aid for the plighted village, should the worst happen.

Kamien finally spoke up, "Let's get this over with."

LeAnne had been furious with Yough when he'd allowed the boy to volunteer. Ossian was absolutely sure he was back on LeAnne's permanent bad side when he hadn't stepped in to stop him.

The ropes had been laid out in large swooping circles and the horse teams were being minded by a single individual each right now, which brought their rag-tag bunch up to twenty humans and twelve horses in number. Keeping them calm now was the simple part. Once the spider emerged, he imagined it would be all they could do to keep the horses steady till the trap was sprung.

Ossian gripped the stick and threw it high into the treeline.

At first, nothing happened, then a rumble sounded from the inside of the forest. Birds flew from the canopy, something none of them had seen in the weeks and months they had been here. Then they were there.

Nine Greenmen stood before them. Each of them with a wooden staff, several of those ended in sharp points, some of them ended in brightly colored rocks, but one of them ended in a log, forming what clearly looked like a maul.

The Greenman with the maul looked broad and thick and reminded Ossian of the blacksmith from the village who was with one of the horse teams, right now.

The Greenmen walked towards the villagers, each of them covered from head to toe in a variety of leafy green colors. As they reached Ossian, the Greenman he knew held his hand out when Ossian grasped it and shook.

"Thank you." Then Ossian turned and walked back towards the spell circle he had in the middle of the field. He wasn't sure if he started a full-blown conversation if he would lose his nerve here.

The charcoal powder was finely ground and he'd made sure none of the ropes touched the circle. Only a dozen of the men with him had swords. The rest had quickly made spears, thanks to the blacksmith. As Ossian sat down in the spell circle, several of the Greenmen surrounded but did not touch the circle. One Greenman was also near each set of horses.

Ossian knew what was left to do. He just didn't want to do it.

"Keep them calm till the body emerges. I can't do anything without the main body."

Deith was in charge of the right and signalled ready. They were to engage the teams of horses and catch the ropes on the legs of the spider. Hopefully tripping it.

Yough, in charge of the left, also signalled readiness. They were to harass the spider, hopefully drawing its attention away from the people trying to trap its legs. Ossian wasn't sure it was even distractible, but the plan was sound, or as sound as a plan could get with an unknown enemy.

It was now up to Ossian to poke the bear. The stench of heated air and meat filled his head from the first time he'd poked a real bear, although he had to admit at least they'd survived it.

Sitting down in the dirt, Ossian had carefully plucked every green sprouting plant in the circle. Clearing his mind, he then slowly placed each symbol in its place for the disembodiment circle. The circle left him cold even as he powered it up. His body slumped over onto the ground as he saw the Greenmen's auras growing brightly. Each of them had a large tendril of essence that stretched back to the Night Forest, like a rope tethering them to this world.

Sinking his incorporeal form into the ground, Ossian headed for the creature that he knew existed. When suddenly he felt the presence of someone else, the Greenman was next to him, traveling with him. Not a disembodied form like Ossian, but the physical body was traveling through the earth like it was water.

When they reached the void that was the creature, Ossian stood there for a moment. He wasn't sure what was going to happen when he touched it. He might have led all these people and Greenmen to their deaths. In his hesitation, Ossian saw the Greenman reach out and touch the creature.

The black glossy rocks blinked into existence, filling the void.

A collection of spell symbols etched into the side of the creature illuminated by some unknown light set deeper in the void, the light pouring from the creature as every fourth symbol was activated, pulling the Greenman in.

The lighted symbols rotated to another set which, when activated, moved themselves along the surface of the creature to form an inner circle. The inward moving symbols locking into place, holding the Greenman in place.

Ossian shouted, but to no avail. His disembodied form could make no sounds. The Greenman was sacrificing himself. Had this been the Greenman's plan all along?

The inner circle stayed lit as the third set activated. Ossian could feel the magic ripping at the Greenman's essence, pulling it from his corporeal form. The essence link that extended out to the forest dwindled but did not sever. A ball of white light, tinged with flecks of green and brown, floated in the middle of the spell circle as the lighted symbols finally shifted to the final set.

A hole in the creature's side opened up and a large red crystal was visible. Ossian could feel from here the pulling of the crystal on the Greenman's essence. The ball of light was slowly being pulled towards the crystal.

Ossian tried to think of what he could do, but the disembodiment spell didn't allow interaction with anything. Well, except for the void where the creature had been originally. Could Ossian pull the Greenman's essence from the creature before the crystal could collect it?

Before Ossian could think himself forward, the tether to the forest grew thick as the ball of light was pulled away towards the surface. The tether itself ripped the ball up and away from the creature, disappearing before Ossian's very eyes.

The creature's legs hinged, as through some unknown means it dug its way up towards the surface. Ossian, scared out of his mind, shot his way to the surface. Colliding with his body, he sat bolt upright, screaming the entire time.

The truth of what had just almost happened made Ossian wonder why he'd ever wanted to have become a mage. He wasn't sure if the Greenman was alive or dead, or could even be killed. Had the Night forest refused to allow him to be absorbed? Was that why the Night Forest stopped here?

CHAPTER 59

The villagers, greenmen and horses all jumped as Ossian lept up from his slumped over body. His voice echoed off the dirt field. The villagers and greenmen kept the horses under control as Ossian fought to stop himself from screaming.

"It's coming." Ossian voice was far too loud, like he was shouting into a high wind that wasn't present.

A silent moment went by and Ossian started to doubt what he had seen below the surface when the first leg burst out of the ground. A dust cloud filled the surrounding area. Coughing, inside the cloud, could be heard as loud thudding resounded around them. The dust was making it nearly impossible to see anything.

Ossian focused his mind on a pushing spell and cleared the dust cloud from the area. Hoping, in clearing the dust, it would allow people to see what they were doing. At the same time, he was worried they might become frightened and run.

The black glossy rock looked just like the smaller spider creature they'd encountered so long ago. Metal struts attached to dark wooden legs, except these were the size of tree trunks. Somehow, the horses hadn't already bolted from the monstrosity before them.

Ossian himself fought the urge to run. Something deep down told him to run far away and never return.

That's when Jorn popped into Ossian's head. Jorn would already have attacked the creature. Standing around thinking was for the dead.

"Yough, GO." Ossian hoped they wouldn't be charging in to their deaths.

Yough and his contingent ran at the creature as a spear bounced off the body. A leg of the creature rose up and tried to crush Kamien, when a sudden sprouting of vines moved him two feet to the left and the thudding of the leg just hit dirt. Ossian could feel the magic flowing from one of the Greenmen's staff like water through the forest. The magic felt so different from his own abrupt resolution of power.

"Deith, bring it down." Ossian was hoping they could finish this early, before anyone was hurt.

The ropes around one leg tightened as the horses, having been slapped in the rear, ran forward. Straining with all their might, they pulled the leg taunt, forcing the spider to extend one of its legs.

The second set of ropes wasn't around any of the legs, but one of the Greenmen raised its staff and vines shot out of it, wrapping itself around another leg. The staff merged with the Greenmen's body as he reached out for the ropes attached to the horses. Then the blacksmith got the horses moving as a second leg was pulled out from under the spider.

The third set of horses was getting ready to pull when one leg swept over them and killed three of the horses with one gigantic thud. Honey, the only horse left in that group, didn't even startle. It just sat there staring at the leg that was now next to it.

The Greenman with the maul stalked over to Honey. With each step, his bark grew thicker, and his height increased till he was taller and bigger than even Honey. He grasped the ropes in his hand and pulled away from the spider, swinging his hand, trying to get Honey to follow him.

Deith was busy with the first group of horses, so Ossian clicked the plowman's signal to get Honey moving. That huge, beautiful horse plodded forward, the rope stretched taut. As the rope strained, it did nothing to stop Honey from moving forward as the third leg was pulled out from under the spider.

Ossian watched as the body of the spider tried to pull its legs back, but the straining teams of horses and Greenmen's magic were too much for it as it fell to the ground, sending up another smaller dust cloud.

Ossian ran towards the creature, pulling his sword. He was hoping he could pry open the creature's portal before it could activate.

Inside the dust cloud, the first set of symbols lit up. Ossian could feel himself pulled towards the creature's body. Ossian's mind screamed at him to fight, but he needed to be closer. He was certain he could deface the second spell circle and not be trapped standing next to the creature as it sucked the essence of Ossian out of him to be stored inside the creature.

Mentally, Ossian was prepared for the moment, he would be pulled into the creature, and he would have just a split second to strike at one of the spell circle symbols for the holding spell. Defacing the symbol with his sword to deactivate the holding spell.

As the spell pulled him in, he raised the sword above his head, preparing to strike. The floating feeling of his body was unnatural to him. He imagined this is what the spider's legs currently felt like as they were pulled outside of its control.

Then, before he knew it, he was in front of the spider. The lights of the second spell powered up as Ossian swung his sword down in an arc. He watched as the sword struck the symbol perfectly, neatly bisecting the symbol with his strike. As the symbols continued to power up, Ossian was shocked to see the black gleaming carcass of the spider-creature was unharmed from his sword's blow.

Suddenly, he was motionless as the spell symbols moved towards the inside of the spell circle. The symbols locking in place.

Ossian was frozen as the second set of symbols stayed lit up and the third set shone. The tugging started inside of him, pulling something from deep inside the core of his being.

Ossian also saw the portal of the creature snap open as he felt it tugging at his essence. With only his mind left, Ossian forced his thoughts to his natural inclination.

A lightning spell.

The source symbol was split between the sword and himself. Powering up everything he had, he allowed the sword to pull everything inside of him and more, as the pulling of his essence from the spider stopped briefly.

As if powering the spell had always been Ossian's essence. In using it, he denied the creature's spell a source for its own spell circle.

Ossian focused the lightning at the opening of the creature and released it. A bright sudden light blinded him. The smell of electrified air filled his mouth and he could feel every muscle in his body contract as the electricity flowed through and around him towards the portal. The shockwave that followed made his ears ring.

The creature lit up from inside, not just the spell circle symbols, but the entire black glossy surface looked as if a light shone through parchment. As small arcs of lightning flashed from round surface to round surface, it continued to bounce around inside the creature as parts of the black glossy surface turned first red, then white. Finally, bits and pieces started to melt and drip down first into the dirt of the field, but then eventually even inside the creature itself.

The legs of the spider gave way and collapsed completely as the lightning continued to reverberate inside the creature's body. More and more of the spherical body continued to heat to white and then start to melt till the sphere looked more like a melon that worms had gotten to.

～

OSSIAN WASN'T sure how long he stood there watching the lightning play over the sphere of the creature. Never once did the lightning try to exit the now pock-marked surface of black glossy rock. It continued to sizzle and melt inside itself.

The spell circle inside Ossian's head had been powered down for a while, yet the lightning inside the spider continued.

Walking up, Deith said, "Uh, I think you can stop now."

"It's not me Deith, I think it's self-destructing?"

Yough limped over with Kamien shouldering his dad, "Minimal injuries, surprisingly no one is dead Mage Ossian."

Ossian turned to face Yough to tell him excellent, when Yough and Kamien face's paled. Ossian spun around quickly to make sure the spider was not getting up.

The sudden spinning causing a streak of red blood to splash off his face and fall upon the dirt at his feet. Raising his hand to wipe his face, Ossian's hand came back, covered in blood.

"Mage Ossian." The sound was so far away, Ossian wasn't even sure who was calling his name.

He felt himself falling when a soft, leafy green hand reached out and grabbed him. Then another soft, leafy hand grabbed his other shoulder. A third and fourth hand touched his chest as a sudden warmth filled Ossian. The sensation was like taking a hot bath back at the Academy, but he could feel the warmth down deep in his bones.

The warm wet feeling covering his face slowly went away as if it was moved back inside his body. The spot that had been first touched by the spider creature's spell was filled up with the warmth and Ossian knew somehow the Greenmen were healing whatever damage he'd sustained from the spider trying to suck his essence from him.

Then, just as fast as they had emerged from the forest, the eight remaining Greenmen walked back into the forest.

Deith shouted at the forest, "Thank you!"

Followed up by everyone in the group also screaming a thank

you, across the field, at the Greenmen that had risked their lives to help them.

"So, I guess that's it?" Ossian was no longer sure what they should be doing.

"Can we just leave it here?"

"I don't think it's going to do anymore harm to us, Deith. We can keep a watch on if you want, though."

Yough replied then, "Oh, I suspect not a soul will sleep tonight."

"We'll need to send someone to the Academy and the King. They'll want to send someone to see this. I guess. There isn't all the much left to see. Why don't you all recover the villagers? I'll stay here while you get the village settled. Then someone can take watch."

Everyone left, leaving Ossian to inspect the creature and its remains.

CHAPTER 60

atching the villagers, nay soldiers, who'd just fought with him walk off, Ossian realized how much danger they had just been in. The carnage of the battle was everywhere. The spider was enormous, far larger than Ossian had expected at first. Vines and ropes, blood and horses and strange melted rocks littered the ground around him.

Somehow, no one had died. Well, actually, he guessed the Greenman that had been with him initially might be dead. Something deep inside him told him the forest didn't allow him to die.

Walking around the spider, he inspected the ropes and vines that laced up the one side of the creature. The legs were still massive tree trunks connected with metal links to each other. Reaching out a hand, he tried to detect if they were enchanted. Ossian could feel a slight magic that seemed to fade as the lightning kept sparking inside the creature's sphere. Casually and carefully, Ossian would glance up and see how far the group of people were.

He needed them to be far enough away that they didn't see what he was about to do next.

WALKING up to the central sphere, or at least what was remaining of it, Ossian looked inside the sphere from several vantage points. The red crystal was still present inside the sphere, held securely, deep in the center of its body, by three long black posts that tapered to a point. As if the crystal wasn't quite touching them. Even from here, Ossian could tell he was going to have to crawl into the spider's body just to reach the crystal.

While he looked, another spark shot out of the body and arc'd along to impact the other side of the creature. The lightning air burnt his nostrils this close to where so much electricity had been discharged repeatedly. Not knowing if his lightning spell had done all the damage or somehow triggered something on the inside of the creature, Ossian wasn't fully sure what to do.

Standing there would not help him decide, though.

He settled on grounding the spider and trying to release the lightning that was clearly still inside of the body. Grounding both his feet firmly into the dirt, he slapped his hand onto the inside surface of the spider as he formed the basic lightning spell, forging the source to be the spider, he forced the power through the circle of a spell and out his feet into the dirt around him.

The lightning danced around the ground, leaving small bits of fused glass pockmarked around the area.

That dealt with, Ossian leaned into the creature, knees resting on the open portal that the creature had tried to use to suck him in. Reaching his hands out, he could feel the power stored in the crystal from here. It vibrated as Ossian's hands got close.

Finally, with his hands resting on its surface, it felt just like his sword. Power was stored in the crystal, and Ossian was certain if he tried, he could cast spells using the power in the crystal. His only qualm was that power came from killing people. It also felt like much, much more power.

Tugging on the crystal, it came free easily as the three shafts that connected it to the outside sphere of the body dissolved. As if it had been built to be removed.

Hurrying before the villagers could return from the hills, Ossian ran to his tent and using an earth spell, he buried the crystal in a three-foot deep hole. After placing the dirt back, he shifted his chest to be over it. Hoping that would clearly hide the freshly dug ground of the hole.

CHAPTER 61

To his surprise, the village returned to life as normal, except for the guard rotation they established to watch the spider day and night. The children were warned to stay away and even Ossian made a point of not going near the spider. He wasn't sure, but he could faintly feel the pull of the red crystal's power still.

Kamien and Bakker were dispatched on horse to alert the King and the Academy. Ossian warned them that telling anyone else was extremely dangerous. They were only to contact Mage Mahler directly and give him a specific message seal. Ossian had prepared the message seal and explained about the giant spider creature they had fought off with the help of the Greenmen from the Night Forest.

He left out the part about the red crystal inside the creature for fear it would be discovered. Feeling this was something that could shake the foundations of the magical world. He decided he could communicate this to Mage Mahler when he was present, hopefully without someone else overhearing.

~

THE VILLAGE INSISTED on finishing Mage Ossian's house. Ossian was certain most of them just wanted to return to life as normal, and their normal was finishing the village.

On the first night, deep in the darkness, Ossian moved the red crystal from its hiding spot to under his house. As he used the earth spell to reveal it, the crystal called to him. It showed him the power it wielded, or more precisely, the power he could wield with it.

This time, Ossian buried it twenty feet down, trying to make sure that even he would have to stretch his limits to uncover it. The power it suggested he could have scared him, primarily from it being dead people's live, but also cause deep, deep inside of him he craved to use it.

A WEEK PASSED WITHOUT INCIDENT. Then Ossian was alerted by the day guard that someone was racing down the hill. As Ossian emerged from the house, it was still new to him and it did not feel like his yet. He could clearly see the cloud being thrown up by a horse racing towards them.

Eventually, the cloud of dust resolved into a single rider, that slowly and surely became Jorn. Jorn's horse Swift came skidding into the village as Jorn lept off him.

Jorn eyed him up and down, finally saying, "Well, you might regret this one. The King is coming."

Ossian had not expected that, Jorn wasn't a surprising sight as the King frequently sent him on the most important tasks. Ossian just stood there with his mouth open. He wasn't really sure what to say to that. Deciding at some point he needed to say something, "Good to see you, Jorn."

"Bakker says you melted a giant rock spider. Seriously, the man was making no sense."

"Well, the village and I defeated it, yes." Turning towards the northern fields, Ossian pointed out where the spider could just be made out.

Jorn walked up beside him, staring out into the field. "Oh, humble..." Jorn's smile was extra large at that. "Shall we go see it?"

"We haven't been near it since the battle."

"I'm not about to let the King near a giant battle thingy. Yet, once he gets here, you know he won't wait for us to inspect it and make sure it's safe. He'll be here before the day is done. Where's Deith?"

"Here." Came a voice from behind them.

Both Jorn and Ossian spun around at the sound of Deith. He was within an arm's distance of them. Ossian used to Deith and the steathy Greenmen didn't even register shock anymore at sudden appearances. Jorn, on the other hand, was taken completely by surprise.

"Wow, did you not hear Deith sneaking up on us?" Ossian had to rib him. How often did someone get the better of Jorn? He was pretty sure it was never.

Jorn's side-eyed look told Ossian that he wasn't fooled, that Ossian was surprised to see Deith.

"The King and a very large contingent of soldiers, plus the standard extras," Jorn waved his hand dismissively at the word extras, "will be here before the end of the day. Find somewhere for them to camp. If we're not back by the time they show up, meet them. I'd suggest the entire village be prepared to greet him. He's in a great mood, so let's not spoil it."

A single nod from Deith was all they got as he turned and walked away into the village.

"Greenmen?"

"Yep, they helped us. I'm certain without them we would not be talking."

"The King is most interested in meeting them."

Ossian looked over at Jorn. "We haven't seen them since the battle."

"Well, one problem at a time. Let's see this battlefield."

Sunset was just starting when the King and his entourage showed up. Jorn had been wrong. The King had brought hundreds of people. Soldiers, cooks, porters, horses and even a couple of mages. Ossian was surprised by how few mages were brought, though. Magus Senoraske, Mage Mahler and three apprentices.

Ossian himself recognized only a single apprentice, a younger girl by the name of Sondra. She'd been behind Ossian at the Academy by a year, but everyone whispered she was responsible for weeks of rain that had racked the Kingdom some years back.

The arrival was formal. The King was surprisingly gracious and praised the village repeatedly, several wagons of live chickens and pigs, plus enough supplies to last them for several months. Later, Ossian would learn the supplies included arms for the entire village.

Jorn had also been correct. The King wasted no time in wanting to see the creature, even as the sun set. The King, upon seeing the spider creature, did not register the surprise that everyone else did at its size, or that a creature such as this existed at all. Ossian wasn't sure if anyone else noticed the King's reaction but him.

Nothing new revealed itself about the spider under the guise of Mage Mahler or Magus Senoraske. Neither of them recognized the strangely archaic, yet vaguely recognizable symbols of the spells, or at least neither of them talked about it openly. The construction of the creature was a mystery. The King mentioned they would, of course, be taking it back with them and left it to the Magus to figure out how that was going to happen.

Then they all retired for the night.

Ossian stayed up late that night, waiting for Mage Mahler to contact him. He wasn't sure how, but he hoped that Mage Mahler knew how to sneak into his house. They needed to talk and alone.

Before long, Ossian heard a knocking sound. Ossian bolted for the door and opened it. Fully expecting Mage Mahler to walk through the door. Instead, the knocking came from behind him in the fireplace. Walking carefully over, Ossian wasn't sure what to do.

Inside the fireplace were several logs, but Ossian hadn't even started a single fire in them. It was too warm still for a fire. Also, since he didn't cook for himself, he hadn't bothered.

"Move the logs already," came Mage Mahler's voice from inside the base of Ossian's fireplace.

Grabbing the logs, he pulled them out of the round fireplace he had in the center of the room. When Mage Mahler materialized in front of him like the hourglass trick they'd done through the red door back in that alley.

Eventually, Mage Mahler was sitting on the side of the fireplace, sweat visibly covering his face. "Phew, that is a lot harder than it looks." Mage Mahler was still taking deep, ragged breaths as Ossian just stared at him.

"You can just cast that?" Ossian didn't even know what the spell was called.

"Well, obviously." Mage Mahler smiled up at Ossian, "The distance is the real trick. Shorter is easier. And my tent isn't that far away. I wouldn't suggest you learn it anytime soon."

Mage Mahler explained he thought it would be easier to talk if no one knew he was here. It being less likely that some spy followed him, also that he would walk back to his tent. He hadn't expected the spell to be that draining.

Ossian filled him in on everything, the spider, the crystal and the Greenmen. When Ossian mentioned his suspicions about the King not being surprised about the spider, Mahler told him to be careful with suspicions.

When Ossian mentioned what he thought the red crystal was, Mahler grew very serious. Mahler mentioned they already had a plan of how to move the crystal out. Unelma was traveling as a serving girl and could take possession of the crystal, then disappear in Barrosuk and take it to nowhere.

The troublesome part worked out. Mahler and Ossian talked long into the night. Ossian pulling out his secret tome and showing Mahler all his notes on the spider and the quaternary spell circle and how he'd decoded it.

When he saw the spell circle, Mage Mahler frowned. "I've seen this already, on a parchment in Senoraske's office. Now that I think about it, it was in your hand. But it was in two circles that made little sense."

"No, no, all my notes are here." Ossian pulled out his parchments from earlier and sorted through them. "I'd been scared to draw the entire spell circle as one, just in case it wasn't safe."

"Spell circles are always safe, Ossian."

"The rock-spider activated at touch Mahler. Not by me powering it up."

Finally, Ossian placed his notes on the desk. "See here, two separate halves of the circle. Then I had the idea of an interwoven circle. Well, really, the trio did. But I drew it—" Ossian laid out the parchment with the three circles and the final one with the four spells laid out. Yet, he was missing the parchment with the two spell circles that made little sense.

Then it clicked for him, "So Bakker is a spy. Where did you see the circles?"

"Be careful how you say that out loud. His freedom might not be as simple as yours." Mage Mahler was staring at the papers.

"I'm going to transcribe these into the tome and then destroy the originals."

"I'm not sure we can contain the spell. But the way the spider powers up on its own—you kept at least half of it secret. Good job, Ossian, not what I was hoping for. Yet you saved all these people."

CHAPTER 62

The next morning the King insisted on a retinue, dozens of soldiers led by Jorn. Gleaming arms and armor with dozens of colorful banners surrounding the King as he walked up to the treeline of the stream. Magus Senoraske, Mage Mahler and Ossian were instructed to be following the King but at a respectful distance. They flattened most of the scrub brush leading up to the stream as they trampled up to the treeline. Doing what Ossian thought was probably more damage than the battle with the rock-spider had done.

As they stood outside the treeline, Ossian noticed that every single man and women was a soldier wielding a weapon, except for the Magus and Mahler who were living weapons. Then again, even Ossian had a sword on him at all times now. Since the battle, he'd slept with the sword. Ossian understood Jorn's paranoia more and more.

The King, ever the patient type, finally waved his hand. "So where are they?"

At his words, the treeline grew upwards in height and outwards in size. The stream became a walkway of silver bricks leading into a canopy of two absolutely massive trees whose branches formed an archway into a space, no that word wasn't big enough, it was a field that had not been there mere moments before.

The Greenman who had saved Ossian's life was standing in the center of the silver road and bowed, waving them along the road as he stepped to the side.

Ossian noticed Deith was whispering something to Jorn, who turned around and looked around at the trees. Ossian looking around, seeing nothing unusual, except for the sudden appearance of a massive grassy field where earlier there had been none. Trees lined the field so tightly packed together they formed a living set of walls.

As Jorn made to step forward ahead of the King, the massively broad Greenman with the maul for a staff stepped out of the nearest tree. One moment not there, the next moment holding up his hand, he motioned for Jorn to stop.

Something passed between the broad chested Greenman and the one who had saved Ossian. When the first one waved his hand and butterflies formed into the images of the King, Jorn, Ossian and Deith.

Jorn clearly did not like this scenario. He wasn't about to be led into a space he wasn't certain of with the King. He turned away from the Greenmen and was about to have a quick talk with the King. When the King silenced him with his hand and shooed him to go into the field.

A giant throne in the middle of the forested chambers formed. Inside the throne, a being formed. As branches grew and leaves formed over the being, Ossian knew it was the Night Forest itself. He could sense that the forest itself was alive.

Finally, Jorn turned around and bowed, walking forward into the green prairie chamber. The broad-chested Greenman fell in line with Jorn. The King signalled for Deith and Ossian to follow him in.

As Deith crossed the threshold, a wisp of a tree stepped out, something so thin and light that Ossian wasn't even sure it was a creature. Then he noticed that the ends of its hand ended in elongated fingers that looked wicked sharp. Ossian had never seen wood that leaked with such malice.

As he was watching, the sharp fingers shortened and formed into normal hands. Yet still, this creature had no leaves. It was a solid entity of bark and as they moved through the cavern of grass, Ossian knew that in the forest, no one would ever see it.

The original Greenman that had been with Ossian since the beginning matched steps with him as he crossed the threshold. While Ossian wasn't sure if there were escorts or merely being cautious, he got the impression that the Greenman that had just save his life not a week ago, would swiftly and easily end him. Ossian hoped the King understood the predicament they were in.

The King was not paired with a Greenman, as he walked far too casually into the green field of grass surrounded by woods.

As they came up to the giant on his throne, the giant stepped down off his chair. With each step, his gigantic form shrunk down, first the foot, then the leg reduced in size, followed by the body, arms, and finally the head of the creature. When the creature was only slightly taller than the King, it sprouted an eruption of leaves in every color of green that Ossian had ever seen, and some that he was sure weren't natural.

His head sprouted antlers that seemed too big to be real, spreading and forking in a rack that was larger than the creature itself was. Yet his head did not move with the weight of those antlers.

Then two stools grew out of the ground, sticks at first that sprouted, grew, interwove into a formation and solidified into bark in the span of a second. Ossian could feel the magic just on the outskirts of his senses. The creature with the antlers sat on one stool and waved his hand for the King to sit.

The King, at least imitating that this was a normal situation, spoke, "I'm told you helped to save my village, for that I am thankful."

No expression formed on the Forest's face but the slightest incline of its head showed that it had heard and acknowledged.

Ossian hoped the King noticed the complete lack of a mouth, when the King continued speaking, "I mean you no harm and wonder if we might share an alliance."

Fire flared in the Forest's eyes and a shock wave of yellow, orange and finally red started in the leaves in its head and traveled down its body like a wave. Extending his arm, the grass grew into a village being built, then slowly yet surely the spider walking through the village, pulling everyone upwards and a bright light being evicted from their body to disappear into the spider.

Then dozens of tiny spiders, which Ossian recognized from the tiny rock spider he'd found so long ago, moved the bodies into the fields and buried them. As the giant spider dug itself back into the ground. Faster and faster it went, as a new village was built, the people killed and the bodies scattered to the fields.

Every time the spider emerged, Greenmen exited the forest and fought the spider. Only to be stomped or sucked up into the spider or forced to retreat into the forest.

Seeing it for the first time, it dawned on Ossian how many people had died to this creature. He was glad the Greenman hadn't shown him that rendition of the spider. Ossian was certain he would never have recommended they attack it.

"Might we trade resources?"

The antlers shook one time. A clear and obvious no.

"Why are we here, then?"

The Forest waved his hands again and a new grass picture started. It showed the King's caravan going around the Night Forest. When suddenly a path opened up through the Night Forest and the antlered form of the forest, guiding them with his hand, moved the caravan through the forest. Ossian knew it would cut weeks from the trip it took to get from Barrosuk to Lachut.

"You wish to offer us a path through the Night Forest."

The antlers shook yes this time.

"And in exchange?"

A picture of Ossian and the Greenman formed, sitting in the clearing, each of them showing the other magic. Ossian recognized the magic he was showing the Greenman and did not recognize the magic the Greenman was showing Ossian.

"An exchange of knowledge for passage through the Night Forest?"

Holding up his hand, the antlered forest pointed back to the picture as it changed to a closeup view of the caravan. In it were generic men and women. They passed through the Night Forest clear through to Lachut with so issues whatsoever.

Then the image reset to the caravan in the middle of the Night Forest. One man moved into the forest with an axe and chopped at a tree. When the forest closed around the caravan like a book slamming shut.

"Passage through, but we may not harm the Night Forest."

The Forest's antlers shook yes. Then also pointed to the picture again, which reset to a wider view as the antler bent down. His hand glowed brightly as the passageway opened up. Moving his hand from east to west. When his hand reached west and the light went out, the passage closed again.

"The passageway will only be open during the daytime."

The Forest nodded yes again. Standing up, the antlered form of the Night Forest held out his hand to shake.

The King, also standing, asked another question before shaking. "How do we get hold of each other?"

The grass suddenly changed to the image of Ossian.

"Mage Ossian, yes, I understand he is the emissary. Should the worst happen? Is there another way?"

Ossian didn't like the King talking about him being dead, but also had to admire his forward thinking.

The antlered form reached up and snapped off a piece of antler, holding it out for the King. The King took the piece of antler, then shook the Night Forest's hand.

Just as suddenly, the field of grass, the wall of trees and the Greenmen themselves were gone. The King and his meager escort were standing just on the inside of the treeline. The stream burbled next to them as it flowed off into the Night Forest.

Deith finally spoke up, "At least we're on the bank this time."

CHAPTER 63

The next few days passed by in a blur. The King sent Jorn and a small contingent of soldiers off, first thing in the morning, through the newly opened Night Forest passage. To explain to Lachut the contingencies of the deal with the Night Forest.

The King decided New Meadows would need to be a much larger stop-over for trade between Barrosuk and Lachut. Three dozen soldiers were stationed there and would build a fort nearer to the new passage. Mage Ossian's duties expanded to include the fort now. He would need to spend time with both.

The King was so ecstatic at the turn of events that he pledged to upgrade New Meadows' monthly supplies. At Mahler's suggestion, a much more appropriate library for Mage Ossian. With an understanding that he expected updates on the teachings from the Greenmen.

The King also suggested that Mage Ossian himself would need to return to Barrosuk for an official ceremony where he would be properly gifted with a larger library and supplies befitting a new mage in charge of an entirely new scholarly learning.

Ossian was unsure if he should be happy or not. It seemed like his lifelong dream to be sheltered in some small village studying laborers and farmers was becoming further and further away with each new piece of news.

EPILOGUE

The red door was in front of him. The smell in the alley is of nothing, no refuse, no flowers, there is no scent at all. The lack of smell puts Ossian on edge as he stands there, brown leather satchel in hand, the red crystal stowed in it. The darkness of the evening hid him from prying eyes as he wandered the streets, looking for anyone following him.

As he's about to raise his hand, that itching in the back of his mind happens. He spins and draws his sword. A small girl, no a woman, is removing a hood from her head. Ossian remembers the young women he met so long ago. She barely looks old enough to be twelve or thirteen. He ponders how rude it is to ask her age.

Beneath the robe's hem, she's wearing plain brown pants and shoes that look warm and comfortable. Then again, all shoes looked warm and comfy to Ossian. He walked around with no shoes in case he needed to ground a spell quickly. Mage Mahler had told him he should don shoes in the city, but he'd been out in the village and the Night Forest for so long they were no longer comfortable.

"All's clear." Unelma said it casually as she kicked a box towards the door. "I'll wait out here."

Ossian put his sword away. She hadn't even blinked at it when he'd drawn it, as if she was used to having weapons pulled on her all the time. "How long have you been following me?"

Her lips turned up at the edges, but just barely, "Since New Meadows. Mahler wanted another set of eyes. Just in case."

"Do you want to give it to the Guardian?"

The tiny smile on her face changed quickly to a frown. "No."

Ossian stood for several moments waiting for an explanation when Unelma finally walked over to the box she'd kicked and sat down, leaning back against the wall.

Passing through the red door, Ossian steadied himself on the other side. Holding in the meager lunch he'd eaten on purpose just in case this happened. The Guardian was reading a book and sitting in a chair at the table.

"It gets easier the more you do it." The Guardian said as he placed the book down. "Or so I'm told."

"I'll trust you on that."

"Rumor is the Night Forest has agreed to teach you its magic."

"Yes, that was one stipulation of the new trade route through the Night Forest."

"Well, you should be honored. I'm not aware of the Night Forest sharing its magic with anyone. Ever."

"Oh. Why would it do it now? Surely it knows I'll report the magic to the Academy."

"Honestly, I don't know why. This place is as much a prison as a vault." The Guardian motioned for Ossian to sit. "However, I can tell you. The Night Forest wouldn't teach you if it didn't think it was important."

"You mentioned last time the Night Forest was older than you?"

"Yes, yes, I did. Since you'll just continue to ask. I discovered the first object stored here in this vault, so very, very long ago."

The silence stretched on for so long, Ossian finally removed the red crystal from the bag. It sang to him, told him of the power he could wield with it.

"Ah, so it wasn't the Night Forest causing all the problems. Does it call to you?"

"How do you know that?"

"It was a flaw in the original design."

"How old is it?"

"Before any written record that you'll find here at the Academy. It was hubris when I first made them. Thinking my peers wouldn't turn them into weapons. It will be safe here."

Picking up the crystal, The Guardian made to stand.

It finally dawned on Ossian, "Is this the only way in here?"

"No, but the other three entrances are lost. Good luck out there Mage Ossian, Mahler choose well." Then the Guardian disappeared into the wall.

Ossian couldn't help himself as he brushed his hand against the stone wall where he'd disappeared. The wall was rough, solid and unmoving.

Shaking his head, he was finally sure there was indeed magic that shouldn't be shared with the world. He hoped he would never again come across another piece of it.

BUT I NEED MORE...

https://isaacrhoward.com
for more stories and monthly updates.

or just
Scan Me

ABOUT THE AUTHOR

Author Photo ©Lyndsey Wright

Isaac R Howard is a collector of hobbies, easily distractible and likes to play games with dice. Having spent the last twenty years destroying computers and software for a living, he now has opted to amuse himself by creating fiction via the written word.

After starting to write short stories as a random hobby, he hasn't been able to stop his imagination from continuing to invent new people, places and worlds.

His work has appeared on Creepy Pod and in the Anthology of Choice Volume II. You can find more of his characters, worlds and writing on his website isaacrhoward.com.